ALL QUIET ON ARRIVAL

Recent Titles by Graham Ison from Severn House

The Hardcastle Series

HARDCASTLE'S SPY
HARDCASTLE'S ARMISTICE
HARDCASTLE'S CONSPIRACY
HARDCASTLE'S AIRMEN
HARDCASTLE'S ACTRESS
HARDCASTLE'S BURGLAR
HARDCASTLE'S MANDARIN
HARDCASTLE'S SOLDIERS

*Contemporary Police Procedurals
including the Brock and Poole mysteries*

ALL QUIET ON ARRIVAL
BREACH OF PRIVILEGE
DIVISION
DRUMFIRE
JACK IN THE BOX
KICKING THE AIR
LIGHT FANTASTIC
LOST OR FOUND
WHIPLASH
WHISPERING GRASS
WORKING GIRL

ALL QUIET ON ARRIVAL

Graham Ison

This first world edition published 2010
in Great Britain and in the USA by
SEVERN HOUSE PUBLISHERS LTD of
9–15 High Street, Sutton, Surrey, England, SM1 1DF.
Trade paperback edition first published
in Great Britain and the USA 2011 by
SEVERN HOUSE PUBLISHERS LTD.

British Library Cataloguing in Publication Data

Ison, Graham.
    All quiet on arrival. – (A Brock and Poole mystery)
    1. Brock, Harry (Fictitious character : Ison)–Fiction.
    2. Poole, Dave (Fictitious character)–Fiction.
    3. Police–England–London–Fiction. 4. Detective and
    mystery stories.
    I. Title II. Series
    823.9'14-dc22

ISBN-13: 978-0-7278-6920-3   (cased)
ISBN-13: 978-1-84751-269-7   (trade paper)

All Severn House titles are printed on acid-free paper.

Severn House Publishers support The Forest Stewardship Council [FSC],
the leading international forest certification organisation. All our titles that
are printed on Greenpeace-approved FSC-certified paper carry the FSC logo.

Mixed Sources
Product group from well-managed
forests and other controlled sources
www.fsc.org Cert no. SA-COC-1565
© 1996 Forest Stewardship Council

Typeset by Palimpsest Book Production Ltd.,
Falkirk, Stirlingshire, Scotland.
Printed and bound in Great Britain by
MPG Books Ltd., Bodmin, Cornwall.

ONE

It was a hot and humid night at the end of July. The police immediate response car, its windows wound down, drew silently into the kerb outside 27 Tavona Street, Chelsea. The crew had seen no reason to activate the vehicle's siren, or to switch on the blue lights. After all, a call to a domestic disturbance on a Saturday night in this part of London was a frequent occurrence, even though the property in this particular street was probably more upmarket than most. And that, for Chelsea, was saying something.

When police arrived to deal with this type of incident they usually found it to be a riotous party, fuelled by alcohol and a little heroin or, at the very least, a few joints of cannabis. And in most cases the disturbance that was the cause of the call had ceased by the time the police arrived. Provided the police didn't get there too quickly, that is.

The man who answered the door of number 25 – the house whence the call had originated – looked to be in his seventies. For a moment or two he stared at the constable on his doorstep.

The PC referred to his incident report book. 'Mr Porter is it?'

'Yes, that's right. Ah, the police. I called you.'

'Yes, sir. I understand you reported a disturbance at the house next door. Number twenty-seven.'

'Yes, I did. It sounded as though someone was being murdered.' Porter laughed apologetically, thinking that he was being a little dramatic. 'There were screams and shouts, and my wife and I couldn't get to sleep.'

'Anything else, sir?'

'Yes, loud music. I think it's called reggae or rap or some such thing. I'm not very familiar with this noise that passes for modern music. It could even have been those Rolling Stones, or the Beaters that everyone makes such a fuss about.'

'I think you mean the Beatles, sir,' said the PC, whose name was Wayne Watson. 'Or maybe The Seekers.' It was a group that he recalled his mother enthusing about years ago.

'Ah, The Seekers, yes I remember them,' said Porter. 'No, I don't think it was them.'

'It doesn't really matter whose music it was, does it, sir?' said Watson, tiring of Porter's rambling prevarication.

'No, I suppose not, but as I told you, I'm not familiar with this modern stuff,' Porter said.

'Seems to be quiet now,' said Watson, anxious to finish with the matter in hand.

'Yes, it does.'

'All right, sir. But we'll have a word next door just the same.'

'Thank you, officer. That's very good of you.' Porter closed the door, satisfied that his civic duty had been done. He went upstairs to the bedroom he shared with his wife and told her that the police were going to deal with the noise.

'But it's stopped, Frank.'

'For the moment, dear,' said Porter, 'but they'll make sure it doesn't start again.'

PC Watson returned to the car and leaned in through the window. 'Nothing in it, Charlie,' he said to PC Holmes, the driver. 'I'll just have a word with the people at twenty-seven.' He glanced at his watch: it was twenty minutes past midnight. 'Then it'll be time for a cup of coffee.'

Watson crossed the pavement to number 27 and rang the bell. But it was some time before there was a response.

'Yeah?' A man in his mid-thirties eventually opened the door and stared at the PC. He wore a pair of jeans and was stripped to the waist. His hair hung about his muscular sun-tanned shoulders untidily; he looked to be the sort who would normally wear it in a ponytail. Around his neck he wore a slender gold chain. And in his right hand, he was holding a woman's bra.

'We've had a report of a disturbance here,' said Watson, glancing pointedly at the item of underwear.

'I can't hear anything,' said the man with a confident grin, and cocked his head in an attitude of listening. He too glanced at the bra, and then tossed it aside. 'Who put the bubble in?'

'We've been told that there was loud music, and shouts and screams,' said Watson, declining to answer the man's question. He took a pace back; the man's breath reeked of alcohol.

'So? We were having a party that got a bit out of hand. But it's all over now, mate, and most of the gang's gone home. All right?'

A girl with a gorgeous figure and long black hair appeared beside the man, and smiled at Watson. She showed no sign of embarrassment to be seen wearing nothing but a thong. 'What is it, lover?' she asked, slipping an arm around the man's waist and leaning into him.

'Nothing to worry about, Shell. It's only the Old Bill. Apparently there's been a complaint about the noise. I s'pose it was some envious neighbour who was pissed off he hadn't been invited.'

'Oh, that's all right, then.' The girl winked at the PC, turned, and sashayed provocatively back into the house.

'OK,' said Watson, 'but keep it down in future.'

'Yeah, sorry, Officer, but like I said, it's over now. I guess you guys have got enough to do without dealing with noisy parties.'

'You can say that again. And your name, sir?' Belatedly, Watson realized that he should take a few details.

The man paused before answering. 'Carl Morgan,' he said eventually. 'Why?'

'Just for the record.' Watson afforded the man a crooked grin. 'And you live here?'

'Yeah, of course.'

'Thank you.' Watson scrawled a few lines in his incident report book, and pocketed it. 'I'll not need to trouble you any further.' He crossed the pavement, and got back into the police car. Taking out his pen, he wrote 'All quiet on arrival' against the entry in the logbook regarding the disturbance call. He put his pen back in his pocket, and glanced at the driver. 'I reckon that was some party,' he said. 'Some bird came to the door wearing a thong and nothing else. Some people have all the luck.'

'You could have told me earlier,' muttered Holmes.

'A cup of coffee, then?' said Watson, and yawned.

'Good thinking,' said his partner, and putting the car into 'drive', accelerated away.

But almost immediately, Holmes and Watson received a call to an attempted burglary in Draycott Gardens.

'Suspects on premises,' said the control-room operator. 'Silent approach.'

'There goes our coffee,' muttered Holmes. He turned on the blue lights, but not the siren.

*   *   *

After he had closed the front door of number 27, the man who'd
told the police he was Carl Morgan walked into the front room
of the house. Briefly parting the closed curtains, he glanced out
at the street. He turned to the girl who was reclining in an armchair.

'It's all right, Shell, they've gone,' he said. 'That was a bit
too bloody close for comfort,' he added, letting out a sigh of
relief.

'Well, what do we do now, lover?' asked Shelley.

'There's something I've got to do first, and then we'll get
the hell out of here. And we'll go as far away as possible.
Home, in fact.' The man laughed nervously.

'What about the hotel you booked, lover?' complained the
girl.

'Forget it,' said the man. 'And you'd better put some clothes
on. Otherwise there'll be another complaint.'

'Only from a woman,' said Shelley drily.

Donald Baxter was unable to sleep. The temperature was still
in the seventies despite it being half past twelve in the morning.
He thought about reading for a while, but realized that the
light would disturb his slumbering wife. He slipped out of
bed and walked to the window.

'Christ!' he exclaimed and, reaching for his mobile phone,
called 999.

But his wife woke up. 'What is it?' she asked sleepily.

'The house opposite's on fire.'

'What, the Bartons'?'

'Yes,' said Baxter.

The emergency service operator answered the call. 'Which
service?' she asked in a calm voice.

'Fire brigade.'

Another voice came on the line immediately. 'London Fire
Brigade.'

'The house opposite me is on fire,' said Baxter.

'What is the address, sir?'

'Twenty-seven Tavona Street, Chelsea. The fire's on the
ground floor, but it looks pretty fierce.'

The operator repeated the address. 'And your name and
telephone number?'

Baxter hurriedly furnished those details, irritated that the
fire brigade operator appeared to be wasting time.

'Is there anyone on the premises that you know of, sir?' If there were 'persons trapped', to use the fire brigade's term, it was of prime importance for them to know before they arrived.

'There's a married couple called Barton living there, I think, but I don't know if they're at home.'

'Thank you, sir. Appliances are on their way.'

It was that long, hot summer that peaked at the end of July. Children fretted and cried, and managed to get ice cream all over their clothing. Men walked about looking like under-dressed tramps in dirty vests and the cut-off trousers that my girlfriend told me were called cargoes. Overweight women cast aside any dress sense they might have possessed in the first place. They slopped around in unsuitable tight shorts, crop tops with bra straps showing, bulging bare midriffs and cheap beach sandals. Unfortunately for us men, slender well-shaped girls preferred *not* to wear shorts. Such is life.

Regrettably, and despite the weather, convention dictated that I should wear a suit and a collar and tie. There were two reasons for that: firstly I am a detective chief inspector in the Metropolitan Police, and secondly my commander is a stickler for what he terms 'officer-like comportment'. He labours under the misapprehension that once the rank of inspector is attained, the holder automatically becomes an officer and a gentleman ... or lady. The fact that inspectors and above are not the only officers in the force has somehow escaped him; every policeman and policewoman is an officer.

I was not, however, wearing a suit on that Sunday morning when my mobile rang; I wasn't wearing anything. It was early in the morning. In fact, it was five o'clock. My girlfriend, Gail Sutton, was slumbering peacefully beside me. She and I had been in a relationship for some time now. I'd first met her while investigating the murder of a chorus girl at the Granville Theatre. Gail was also in the chorus at the time, although she was really an actress.

But there's a story behind that. She was once married to a theatrical director called Gerald Andrews, and, having felt a little off colour during the matinee, came home early and unexpectedly one afternoon to find him in bed with a nude dancer. The thing that really annoyed her, Gail said, was that they were making love in the bed she normally shared with her husband, and it was that, more than anything else, that spelled the end of the marriage. And she'd reverted to using her maiden name of Sutton. Andrews, with typical male chauvinism, harboured an unreasonable grudge, and did his best to prevent Gail from getting any acting parts thereafter. Hence her appearance in the chorus line of *Scatterbrain* at the Granville.

That, however, was all in the past. Although our relationship had burgeoned, Gail had declined to move in with me – we neither of us wanted to marry again – but we often spent time in each other's beds. It was a very satisfactory arrangement. Until I was called out. I lived in constant fear that she would finally tire of having the man in her life disappear at the most inopportune moments, like now.

I reached out to stifle the ringing tone of my mobile as quickly as possible, in the hope that Gail would remain asleep. Vain hope. She stirred, cast aside the sheet, turned on her back and stretched sensuously. I wish she wouldn't do that every time my phone rang and we were in bed together.

'Brock.' I said that because my name is Harry Brock, and I am attached to the Homicide and Serious Crime Command West.

Our remit, as the hierarchy is fond of saying, is to investigate murders and serious crime in that third of London that stretches outwards from Charing Cross to the back of beyond, also known as Hillingdon. We operate from a building called Curtis Green, just off Whitehall, that was once a part of New Scotland Yard. Most of the general public, and quite a few police officers, are blissfully unaware of its existence.

Just so that you won't be confused, the original Scotland Yard was much nearer Trafalgar Square. But in 1890 it moved to the other end of Whitehall. The new building was constructed from Dartmoor granite quarried by convicts from the nearby prison of the same name, and was christened *New* Scotland Yard.

However, our illustrious members of parliament eventually wanted that building for themselves, so seventy-seven years later the Metropolitan Police was forced to move to an unattractive glass and concrete pile in Broadway, Westminster. At the time there was a suggestion that it should be called *Brand* New Scotland Yard to avoid confusion, but the idea was vetoed. There again, the Metropolitan Police is all for a bit of confusion from time to time. But just so that you're in no doubt, there is a wondrous revolving sign telling the world that it is, indeed, New Scotland Yard. Rumour has it that it's operated by a police cadet winding a handle in the basement. But don't believe all you hear about the police.

However, back to the present.

'It's Gavin Creasey, sir,' said the voice of the night duty incident room sergeant.

'Don't tell me,' I said wearily. 'Someone's found a body that requires my attention.'

'Yes, sir. To be exact, it was the fire brigade that found it.'

'And where is this drama unfolding, Gavin?'

'Chelsea, sir. Twenty-seven Tavona Street. There was a fire – which must make a change for the fire brigade – and when they arrived on scene, they found the dead body of a woman in the master bedroom.'

'Did she die as a result of the fire?' I asked, vainly hoping that this death might not require my attendance.

'No, sir. She'd been stabbed. And Doctor Mortlock is on his way.'

'Have you alerted Dave Poole?'

'Yes, sir, and Linda Mitchell and her forensic team are also on way.'

Dave Poole is my right hand who thinks of the things that I don't think of. And that happens quite often. A detective sergeant of Caribbean descent, his grandfather arrived from Jamaica in the nineteen-fifties and set up practice as a doctor in Bethnal Green. Dave's father is an accountant, but, declining a career in a profession, Dave became a policeman, which, he often says impishly, makes him the black sheep of the family.

Before that, however, he had graduated in English at London University. It's a degree that's had a lasting effect on his use of English, but more particularly, its misuse by others, including me. Most of the time he's grammatically fastidious, but has been known to resort to criminal argot when the situation calls for it.

Dave is married to a charming white girl who's a principal dancer with the Royal Ballet. Rumour has it that she occasionally assaults Dave, but given that Dave is six foot tall, and Madeleine is only five-two, that story is put down to

canteen scuttlebutt. Mind you, it's well known that ballet
dancers of both sexes are possessed of a strong physique.

Gail stretched again. 'What is it?' she asked in her most
beguiling voice.

'I've got to go out,' I replied, trying not to concentrate on
Gail's body. 'A murder apparently.'

'Oh, another one,' said Gail. 'Dammit!' She's obviously
getting used to my bizarre occupation. She pulled up the sheet,
turned over and went to sleep again.

For some reason best known to themselves, uniformed officers of the Chelsea police had closed Tavona Street completely.
The red and white tapes of the fire brigade, and the blue and
white of the police vied for precedence, and a PC stood guard
at the door of number twenty-seven. Or what remained of it.

'Who's in charge?' I asked, waving my warrant card.

'Our DI's inside, sir,' said the PC, 'talking to your DS Poole.'

But before I could enter, Linda Mitchell, the senior forensic
practitioner – wonderful titles the Job comes up with – stopped
me, and presented me with a set of overalls and shoe covers.

Once suitably attired, and having reported my arrival to the
incident officer, I made my way through an inch of water,
stepping carefully over pieces of debris. I found Dave Poole
in what had been the kitchen, but which was now completely
gutted.

I introduced myself to the local DI who was chatting to
Dave. 'Where's the body?'

'First floor front, guv. Doctor Mortlock's giving it the once
over as we speak.'

'We'd better have a talk with him before we go any further,
Dave,' I said, and made my way towards the staircase. It was
badly charred, but apparently still reasonably secure.

'Watch the staircase, guv,' volunteered Dave. 'It's a bit dodgy
in places.'

I can always rely on Dave to inject an air of pessimism
into any investigation, but we reached the first floor without
mishap.

Dr Henry Mortlock, a Home Office pathologist, was on the
point of leaving. 'Nice of you to drop by, Harry,' he said, as
he finished packing his ghoulish instruments into his bag.

'My pleasure, Henry. What's the SP?' I asked, culling a useful bit of jargon from the racing fraternity. In detective-speak it's another way of asking for a quick summary of the story so far.

'You don't have to be a pathologist to determine cause of death, Harry,' said Mortlock. 'She was stabbed several times in the chest and abdomen, six or seven times, I'd say at a guess, and she bled profusely.' He stepped aside so that I could see the body lying in a pool of blood. 'It's ruined the mattress,' he added drily. Henry Mortlock has a macabre sense of humour that rivals that of any CID officer. But, given the nature of our respective jobs, that's hardly surprising. 'Expensive bed that,' he continued. 'The sheets and pillow cases are black silk. Must've cost a fortune.'

The dead woman was naked and lying on her back. She was, or had been, an attractive woman with a good figure and short blonde hair, and appeared to be in her mid-forties. It looked as though she spent a lot of her time and money at a beauty salon.

'How long has she been dead?' I asked.

'Rough estimate, about five hours, but I'll have a better idea when I get her on the slab. There don't appear to be any defensive wounds. Here, see for yourself.' Mortlock held up one of the woman's hands, and I could see that her well-manicured nails did not seem to have been used to fight off her assailant. He glanced at his watch. 'I was supposed to be playing golf this morning,' he complained.

'After you'd been to church to pray for your soul, I suppose, Doctor,' said Dave.

Having exhausted the customary badinage that takes place between the detectives and the pathologist at a murder scene, Henry Mortlock departed, whistling some obscure aria as he descended the staircase.

Having decided that there was little else to be learned from the corpse, I glanced around the bedroom. It was sumptuously equipped. Carpet, curtains, furniture and bed linen were carefully co-ordinated, and undoubtedly had cost the owner a huge amount of money.

Dave summed it up. 'There's a bit of cash here, guv,' he said.

'Any idea who she is, Dave?'

'The local DI said that the house belongs to a Mr and Mrs Barton: James and Diana. Presumably, that's Diana Barton.' Dave waved a hand at the body. 'If it is, that makes James Barton her husband.'

'Any sign of him?'

'No,' said Dave. 'The fire brigade are satisfied that our dead body was the only one in the house.'

'We'd better let Linda get on with it, then,' I said, and we returned to the ground floor.

Linda Mitchell entered the house followed by her team of fingerprint officers, video-camera recordists, photographers, and all the other technicians of murder. I never quite knew what they all did, but the results were always outstanding.

By now, a few members of my team had arrived, having been called out by Gavin Creasey.

Standing on the pavement outside the house was Kate Ebdon, one of my DIs, and the one with whom I work the closest. Kate is an Australian, and a somewhat fiery character. She came to us on promotion from the Flying Squad where, it is rumoured, she gave pleasure to quite a few of its officers. Male ones, of course. She usually wears a man's white shirt and tight fitting jeans, a mode of dress that looks great, but doesn't please our commander who doesn't have the bottle to tell her about it. When she first arrived, he asked me to 'discuss' her mode of dress with her, but I preferred not to risk it. Kate herself is blissfully unaware that she's making a mockery of the commander's oft-quoted desire for the 'officer-like comportment' I've already mentioned.

'How many have you got, Kate?' I asked.

Kate looked around at the assembled detectives. 'Six, guv.'

'Good. Get them on house-to-house enquiries,' I said, and gave her a brief rundown on what was known so far.

Dave and I stopped for breakfast on the way back to Curtis Green, and arrived at the office at about half past eight. That gave us an hour and a half to get organized before the commander arrived. The commander, a sideways import from the Uniform Branch who thinks that he really is a detective, could be relied upon not to arrive before ten o'clock, and would leave not a minute later than six. There is a theory among the troops that Mrs Commander nags him, but if the photograph of the harridan that adorns the commander's desk were actually of his wife, I'd be inclined to stay out all night.

Dave obviously knew what I was thinking. 'At least the commander won't be in today, guv.'

'Why not, Dave?' I wondered if our boss was on annual leave.

'It's Sunday, guv.'

You see what I mean about Dave thinking of things I don't think of?

Colin Wilberforce, the incident room manager, and an invaluable administrative genius, had already begun the task of documenting our latest murder. So far, he had declined to take the inspectors' promotion examination, even though I keep encouraging him to do so, but only half-heartedly. It will be a sad day for HSCC West if ever he's promoted and posted elsewhere.

'Message from Doctor Mortlock, sir,' said Colin. 'Post-mortem is at twelve noon at Horseferry Road.'

'But I've no doubt he'll have managed to get his eighteen holes in,' said Dave.

'What have you to tell me, Henry?' I asked. We'd arrived at the mortuary at twelve only to find that Mortlock had completed his examination.

'Bloody disaster, Harry,' said Mortlock, peeling off his latex gloves.

'In what way?' I asked innocently. After all these years, I should have known better.

'I sliced into the rough at the very first hole, and it just went downhill from then on.'

'Should play on a level golf course, Doctor,' observed Dave quietly.

'Tough,' I said, 'but what about her?' I pointed at the body of the woman we believed to be Diana Barton.

'As I said at the scene, Harry, death was due to multiple frontal stab wounds, and my original assessment of death having occurred about five hours previously still stands.'

'Anything else?'

'Yes.' Mortlock smiled a lascivious smile. 'She'd recently had unprotected sexual intercourse.'

'How recent?'

'Sometime during the two or three hours preceding her death, I'd say. And before you ask, I've recovered a semen deposit.'

TWO

'Tell me about this suspicious death that you're dealing with, Mr Brock.' On Monday morning the commander appeared in the incident room on the stroke of ten o'clock. He would never call a murder a murder just in case it turned out to be manslaughter or suicide, or was eventually proved to be an accident that did not call for police action. In common with real detectives, I call a murder a topping, but the commander is not only a careful man, he is one who abhors slang. He would never call me Harry either. I suppose he was afraid that I'd address him by *his* first name, and that would probably cause him to have a seizure.

I explained what we knew of Diana Barton's death, which wasn't very much. In fact, we weren't even sure that she *was* Diana Barton. Linda Mitchell had taken fingerprints from the body, but there was no match in the central records. No surprise there; I didn't expect her – assuming it to be Diana – to have any previous convictions.

'Doctor Mortlock has recovered semen from the body, sir,' I told the commander, 'and we're awaiting the result of DNA tests.'

'House-to-house enquiries?' asked the commander loftily, as though he were thoroughly conversant with what we call 'first steps at the scene of a crime'.

'Enquiries are ongoing, sir,' I said. 'The only witnesses, if they could be called witnesses, were a man called Porter who lived next door, and a Donald Baxter who lived opposite. He was the one who called the fire brigade.'

'Good, good. Keep me informed,' said the commander, and turned on his heel, doubtless to take refuge in his piles of paper. He loves paper, does the commander. I doubt that he'd be much good in the field of criminal investigation, but he can write a blistering memorandum when the mood takes him.

What I hadn't told the commander, because he would immediately think of disciplinary sanctions, was that Mr Porter of 25 Tavona Street had earlier called the police to a disturbance at the Bartons' house.

I was now awaiting, with eager anticipation, the arrival of the two officers who had attended. They were off duty today, but murder enquiries take no account of officers' welfare. First thing this morning, Dave Poole had sent a message to Chelsea police station demanding their attendance at Curtis Green at three o'clock.

At five past three, Dave ushered the two PCs into my office.

'PCs Holmes and Watson, sir,' said Dave, a broad grin on his face.

'You wanted to see us, sir?' asked one of the PCs nervously. Both were dressed in what passes for plain clothes among young coppers today.

The PC's apprehension was understandable. There is a constant fear among policemen that whenever a senior officer from another unit sends for them, they immediately think 'complaint'.

'Are you really called Holmes and Watson?' I asked, as I indicated that Dave should remain.

'Yes, sir,' said Watson.

'How come you finish up doing duty on the same instant response car? Coincidence, is it?'

'No, sir,' said Holmes. 'It's the duties sergeant's idea of a joke. Unfortunately, whenever I say I'm PC Holmes, and this is PC Watson, people think we're having them on.'

I laughed, and putting aside the Chelsea duties sergeant's impish sense of humour, got down to the business in hand. 'Which one of you called at twenty-seven Tavona Street on Saturday night? Or did you both call?'

'It was me, sir,' said Watson. 'And it was actually Sunday morning. We got the call at twelve ten and arrived on scene at twelve sixteen.'

'I'm the driver, sir, and I remained in the car,' said Holmes, 'in case there was another call.' He seemed pleased at having made such a decision now that Watson's actions were being questioned.

'Of course,' I said, and turned to Watson. 'So tell me about this disturbance.'

Having heard that a dead body had been found at 27 Tavona Street not long after he had called there, Watson was justifiably anxious. I suppose he could visualize disciplinary proceedings for neglect of duty, and everything else that went with such a charge. He was probably wondering whether he should ask for the attendance of his Police Federation representative. Believe me, once an investigating officer starts digging, you'd be surprised what he can come up with. Like incorrectly completed forms, inaccurate incident report book entries, a disparity between the times in said document and in the car's logbook, and Lord knows what else. I know because I've been on the wrong end of a disciplinary enquiry, and it's not a comfortable experience. And to think that the public is convinced that we whitewash complaints.

Personally, I felt rather sorry for Holmes and Watson – there but for the grace of God et cetera – but their commander would probably take an entirely different view once the facts were laid before him.

'A man called Carl Morgan answered the door, sir,' said Watson, referring to his notes.

'Did you verify that name?' I asked. 'Did you ask for proof of identity, for example?'

'Er, no, sir. I didn't think it was necessary.'

'Go on.'

'The man Morgan was wearing jeans, and was stripped to the waist. Oh, and he was holding a woman's bra, sir.'

'What did he say?'

'He apologized for the disturbance, and told me that it was now quiet, and that most of the guests had left the house. Then a woman appeared, sir. She was dressed in a thong and nothing else. Oh, and she had two butterflies tattooed on her stomach.'

'Did the bra he was holding belong to this woman?' asked Dave as though it were of vital importance.

'I don't know, Skip.' Watson, in common with many others, including me, didn't always appreciate when Dave was exercising his sense of humour. 'Anyway, the man Morgan called her Shell, presumably short for Shelley. She only stayed at the door for a minute or so, and then went back into the house.'

'How old was this woman?' I asked.

Watson thought for a moment or two. 'Middle to late twenties, I should think. She had long black hair, shoulder-length,' he added, as though that might help. 'And she had a bit of meat on her. Good figure, not like some of those anorexic models you see in women's mags.'

'And I suppose you didn't take her full name,' suggested

Dave, with sufficient scepticism in his voice to imply that Watson had not done his job properly.

'No, Skip.' Watson was beginning to look quite miserable by now. Meanwhile, Holmes stood silently aloof, undoubtedly thankful that he'd stayed in the car while Watson was making his enquiries. Even so, he probably wasn't too hopeful that he'd escape any flack that was going. He knew instinctively that once an investigating officer started issuing Forms 163 – notice of complaint – that he'd get one too.

'And you marked the log "All quiet on arrival", did you?' I asked, well knowing the answer.

'Yes, sir,' said Watson unhappily. I imagined that he was thinking how easy it was for blokes like me to be wise after the event. 'It's all right for the bloody guv'nors' is a phrase often heard among 'canteen lawyers'.

'We've not told the press that this is a murder enquiry, so I don't want them to hear about it from you. Understood?' Regrettably, there were coppers who'd happily part with confidential information for the price of a large Scotch, but perversely would be outraged by the offer of a straightforward bribe.

'Yes, sir,' said the two PCs in unison. They were probably hoping that no one else would hear about it either for fear that a finger, most likely mine, would point in their direction.

I turned to Dave. 'Take these two officers into the incident room, and get as full a description as possible of the two people at Tavona Street he spoke to.'

'Yes, sir,' said Dave, and frowned. He always called me 'sir' in the presence of strangers: police and public. If he called me 'sir' in private it usually meant that I'd made a ridiculous comment. As for his frown, I assumed that was because I'd ended a sentence with a preposition.

'And then take Watson to the mortuary. I want to be certain that the woman he spoke to was not the woman whose body was later found in the master bedroom.'

'From Watson's description, sir,' said Dave, 'there would appear to be quite a disparity in the ages of the two women.'

'I know,' I said, 'but from what we know of Watson's action so far, he could have been mistaken about that, too.'

Watson looked decidedly dejected, as well he should.

'Yes, sir,' said Dave.

As Dave and the PCs departed, Colin Wilberforce came into

my office. 'I've just taken a call from Chelsea, sir. A Mr James Barton went into the nick about ten minutes ago, wanting to know why his house was boarded up, and what had happened.'

'Tell Dave Poole to hand over those two PCs to someone else to take descriptions, Colin, and to get hold of a car. Oh, and tell him not to bother about getting someone to take Watson to view the body. At least, not yet. I think we might be about to solve that particular problem.'

Minutes later we were on our way to Chelsea police station.

James Barton was a tall, spare, silver-haired man of advancing years. He stood up when Dave and I entered the lobby of the police station. We escorted him into an interview room.

'I'm Detective Chief Inspector Brock, Mr Barton, and this is Detective Sergeant Poole. Please sit down.'

'What on earth has happened, Chief Inspector?' asked Barton. 'I got home from a trip abroad this morning, and found that my house had caught fire. The police here seemed unwilling to tell me what had happened. Either that or they don't know. And where's my wife?'

This was the difficult part, the part that policemen dislike the most. Over the years I've had occasion to tell many people of the death of their nearest and dearest, and it doesn't get any easier. The worst is having to tell parents that their young daughter has been the victim of some paedophiliac killer.

'After the fire was put out, sir, one of the brigade officers found the dead body of a woman in the main bedroom. We think it might be your wife,' I said quietly.

'It couldn't have been anyone else. We live there alone.'

'So I understand, sir,' I said. 'However, before we can be certain that the body is that of your wife, I'm going to have to ask you to identify it.'

'Was it the fire that killed my wife, Chief Inspector?' Despite not having seen the body, he seemed convinced that the victim *was* his wife.

'No, sir, it wasn't the fire. The brigade put it out before it reached the upper floors.'

'Was it smoke inhalation, then?' Barton asked the question in an absent manner, as though he was having great trouble in taking in this news.

'She had been stabbed several times, Mr Barton.'

'You mean murdered?'

'Yes, I'm afraid so.'

'But who could have done such a thing?'

'That's what I'm trying to discover, sir.'

'It couldn't be anyone else but my wife, surely?' Although Barton looked at me with a piercing, questioning stare, he was really expressing his thoughts aloud.

'As I emphasized just now, Mr Barton, we shan't know until the body's identified. What's more, our enquiries are being hampered to a certain extent because there had been a party at your house,' I said, and went on to tell him about the call to a disturbance that Holmes and Watson had attended.

'A party? But why on earth should there have been a party at my house? We've always lived a sober existence. Perhaps this isn't Diana that was found. I mean she might have gone away for the weekend. Is it possible that someone could have broken in and held a party? You hear all sorts of things these days about people just turning up somewhere, and holding one of these . . . what do they call them, a rave party?'

'Perhaps you're free to go to the mortuary now, sir?' I suggested. I felt sorry for Barton. He was obviously hoping against hope that the dead body was not his wife. But it was time to remove his doubt, and put his mind at rest. Not that learning it *was* Diana would do that.

'Yes, I suppose so. How do I get there?'

'We'll take you, Mr Barton,' said Dave.

'All right, then.' Barton stood up, and glanced at his watch. He now appeared more stooped than when we had entered the interview room, but that was hardly surprising.

'Had you been abroad on business, Mr Barton?' I asked, as we escorted him out to the police station yard where Dave had parked the car.

'Yes. I'm a director of a hotel chain, and I visit our hotels abroad from time to time.'

I was surprised at that. Given Barton's apparent age, and having seen the house in which he had lived, he was obviously not short of money. Had I been in his position, I think I'd've called it a day years ago, and enjoyed myself doing nothing.

The identification at the mortuary took only a few seconds.

The attendant flicked back the sheet – just enough to uncover the victim's head – and stood back.

For a few moments, James Barton stared impassively at the woman's face, and then turned away. 'Yes, that's my wife, Chief Inspector,' he said softly.

'I'm afraid we'll need to ask you some more questions, Mr Barton,' said Dave, as the three of us walked out into the sunshine of Horseferry Road. 'Might I ask where you're staying?'

'Staying?' Barton stopped and stared vacantly at Dave.

'Yes, sir. Your house is obviously uninhabitable. Are you perhaps staying with friends? We'll need your current address, you see.'

'Oh, I see. No, I'm staying at one of the company's hotels in Bayswater.' Barton took a business card from his pocket and scribbled the name of the hotel on the back of it. 'Incidentally, I've arranged to have any calls made to my home to be trans-ferred to my mobile.' He added the phone numbers to the card.

'When would be a convenient time to see you again, sir?' I asked.

Barton glanced at his watch. 'I suppose the sooner the better as far as you're concerned,' he said.

'Yes, that would be helpful,' I said.

'Well, it's five o'clock now. Give me a chance to unpack and have a shower. Shall we say half past seven?'

We found James Barton in the cocktail bar of his Bayswater hotel, a large whisky in front of him. He stood up as we approached.

'May I offer you gentlemen a drink?' he asked.

'No, thank you, Mr Barton.'

'Ah, not when you're on duty, I suppose.'

I didn't bother to reply to that widely held fallacy. Detectives are not averse to drinking on duty; in fact, drinking on duty is often called for. I'd even heard of one detective, a teetotal-ler, who had taken to drink because informants, of whom he had many, wouldn't trust a detective who refused to take a drink with them. But this was not the case here. I made a habit of not drinking with anyone who might turn out to be a suspect, and I was not satisfied that Barton could yet be excluded from that category.

'D'you know of anyone who might have wanted to harm

your wife, sir?' I began. It sounded a stupid question to pose, but it had to be asked, and sometimes – just sometimes – it had given us the answer that had led to an arrest.

'No, nobody. She was a bright, friendly sort of person.'

'Is there anything at all you can tell me that might assist?' I asked, almost in desperation, but held out no great hope that he would know of anything useful. But in that I was surprised.

Barton's chin dropped to his chest, and he appeared to be deep in thought. Eventually, he looked up. 'I'm sorry to have to tell you that my wife was not above having the occasional affair, Chief Inspector.' He went on, quickly. 'She was much younger than me, you see, and I . . . Well, I . . .' He lapsed into silence, but it wasn't necessary for him to complete the sentence for me to understand the problem.

But before I was able to ask another question, Barton went on. 'Diana was forty-five, and I'm seventy-two. It's a second marriage for each of us.'

'You mentioned the occasional affair, sir. Does that mean there was more than one?'

Barton nodded sadly. 'I'm afraid so, Mr Brock. The last occasion was on a cruise in January this year. We went from Southampton, and spent just over a month going around Spain, Italy, Greece, Israel and Egypt. I have preferential rates because my hotel company – I think I told you I'm a director – is associated with the cruise company.'

'And it was on this cruise that the affair took place, was it?' I asked. I wouldn't have thought that Barton had to worry about cut-price cruises, but I've met several millionaires who are very careful with their money. I suppose that's how they became millionaires, and then couldn't get out of the habit.

'Yes, on the last day before we docked at Southampton, although I got the impression that it had been going on for some time.'

'What date was that, Mr Barton?' asked Dave.

'Early February, I think. Yes, it was the sixth if memory serves me correctly. Anyway, I discovered that she'd been consorting with a steward, for God's sake.' Barton picked up his glass, stared into it, and put it down again. 'It wouldn't have been so bad if it had been a first-class passenger.'

That struck me as an odd and rather snobbish comment to make. 'How did you find out?'

'I'd been to a lecture given by some fellow who claimed to be an expert on wine. Between you and me, I don't think he knew much about it, but these chaps wangle themselves a free cruise on the basis that they can talk knowledgeably about something. However, that's neither here nor there. Anyway, I gave up halfway through his banal chat, and returned to our stateroom. As I was almost there, I saw the steward coming out. But stewards were always coming and going, and I didn't think anything of it. I assumed that Diana had ordered tea or something, but when I entered, she was getting dressed. I asked her if she'd ordered tea, and she said no. So I said I'd seen the steward emerging from our stateroom, but she denied that he'd been there. Said I must've made a mistake.'

'And did you let it go at that, sir?' asked Dave, looking up from his pocketbook.

'No, I didn't. For God's sake, she was in her underwear at three o'clock in the afternoon, and I knew damned well that the steward had come out of our stateroom. Diana had played away before, so to speak, so I put it to her straight.'

'What did she say?' I asked.

'She eventually admitted, somewhat shamefacedly, that she'd had sex with the steward. She burst into tears and said that she was terribly sorry, and that it wouldn't happen again. But I knew that it had happened before, and I'd forgiven her on those occasions, but this was the last straw. I told her that that was the end of the marriage, and that when we got home to Chelsea I'd be leaving her, and that I'd file for divorce.'

'But you didn't, I take it?' queried Dave.

'No.' Barton took a sip of his whisky. 'There's no fool like an old fool, so they say, and I really did love her very dearly. So I relented. Although I left the marital home for a few weeks, I eventually returned. It was a tearful reunion. She said, yet again, that it wouldn't happen again. And I forgave her, yet again.' He sighed, finished his whisky, and beckoned to a waiter for another.

'Have you any idea who this steward was, sir?' asked Dave.

'Yes, he was our personal steward, and his name was Hendry.'

'Did you do anything about it, Mr Barton?' I asked.

'I most certainly did,' said Barton vehemently. 'I complained to the captain about Hendry's conduct. I asked, rather sarcastically, if it was company policy that stewards were allowed to take advantage of vulnerable women on his ship.'

'What did he say?'

'He was extremely annoyed, and said that he would deal with the matter. As a matter of fact, he didn't seem at all surprised when I mentioned the name of Hendry, and I got the impression that it wasn't the steward's first lapse.'

'And did the captain deal with it?'

'Yes. He made a point of seeing me the next day and telling me that he'd dismissed the steward. To be honest, I felt rather sorry for the fellow because I knew how persuasive Diana could be.'

'Do you recall the captain's name, sir?' asked Dave.

Barton paused in thought for a moment. 'Yes, I think he was called Richards. Captain Richards.'

'And the name of the cruise line?'

Barton ferreted about in his pockets, eventually producing a card. 'There it is. You can keep that, Sergeant.'

It was not unknown for cruise-line stewards to take advantage of willing women on their ship. The most notorious case, one that was described to us on the junior CID training course by a senior detective from Hampshire, was that of James Camb, a steward on the RMS *Durban Castle*. In 1947, he'd murdered an actress called Gay Gibson, and pushed her body out of a porthole. Camb's thinking at the time was that he couldn't be convicted of murder without a body. He was wrong. Although escaping the scaffold – Parliament was debating the death penalty at the time – he served eleven years for his crime.

'You mentioned that your wife had had other affairs,' I said. 'Are you willing to give me details?'

'I can, but is it necessary?'

'One of them might have murdered her, Mr Barton.'

'Oh, I see.' Barton leaned back in his chair, and thought. 'About three years ago I was supposed to be attending a board meeting in Norwich at the company's head office there, but it was cancelled, and I went home. It was about two thirty in the afternoon. I let myself into the house—'

'This was your house in Tavona Street, was it, sir?' asked Dave.

'Yes. Diana and I had lived there for about seven years. Since our marriage, in fact. I'd lived there for longer, much longer, and I'd shared it with my first wife until she died. Now, where was I?' Barton looked vague, and sipped at his whisky. 'Ah, yes.

I got home, and found Diana in bed with this man.' He gave a humourless laugh. 'He was the manager of this very hotel. Ironic, isn't it. Anyway, I threw him out, and sacked him the next day.'

'What was his name, sir?' Dave's pen was poised over his pocketbook.

'Gaston Potier. He was French.'

'Have you any idea where he lived, Mr Barton?'

'In this hotel, of course.' Barton stared at Dave, as though he'd asked a question to which the answer was obvious.

'Yes, I understand that, but do you know if he had a private address, or where he went after you sacked him?'

'Oh, I see. No, I'm afraid not.' Barton passed a hand over his forehead. 'I am really rather tired, Mr Brock,' he said, turning to face me. 'I wonder if we could continue this another day.'

'If we need to,' I said. 'Just one other thing: were there other affairs, apart from Potier and the steward?'

'I'm sure of it, but I never found out who the men were.'

'Well, thank you for your assistance, Mr Barton,' I said, as Dave and I rose from our seats. 'As I said, I don't suppose we'll have any more questions for you, but I'll keep you informed of any progress. Incidentally, you said you'd been abroad on business, and arrived back here to find your house had burnt out.'

'That's correct.'

'Where had you been?'

Barton frowned, and for a moment I thought he was going to refuse to reply. But he relented. 'Cyprus. To Paphos. We only have the one hotel there at the moment, but we're hoping to expand. I was looking at one or two so-called promising prospects.' He shrugged. 'But I'm not sure any of them will do. We'll probably finish up building our own.'

'He's not having a lot of luck, is he, guv?' said Dave as we walked out of the hotel's main entrance.

'Neither are we, Dave,' I said, glancing at my watch: it was nearly nine o'clock. It had been a long day. 'Incidentally, I don't intend telling the press that the death of Diana Barton is now a murder enquiry. Not until we've dug a bit deeper.'

'Good idea, sir,' said Dave.

THREE

I arrived at Curtis Green at nine o'clock the following morning. Dave was already at work.

'I've tracked down Captain Richards, guv,' he said, as he followed me into my office. 'He's on leave at the moment, and I've made an appointment for us to see him at three this afternoon.'

'On leave where? And don't tell me the French Riviera.'

'He's at home, *sir*,' said Dave, in response to what he regarded as a fatuous question. The implication was that if Richards was in France, he couldn't have made the appointment. 'He lives at Grace Darling Street, Southampton.'

'Good. That gives us time to see those two people at Tavona Street.'

'Porter's at number twenty-five, guv. He's the bloke who complained about the disturbance. And Baxter, opposite at twenty-four, is the guy who called the fire brigade.'

'I'm retired now, otherwise you wouldn't have found me at home,' said Frank Porter, as he ushered us into his living room. 'I don't know how I ever found the time to go to work,' he added with a laugh. 'Do sit down. I expect you'd like a cup of tea. I'll just give my wife a shout.' Before we had time to refuse, he disappeared.

'What did you retire from, Mr Porter?' asked Dave, when Porter returned. Far from being an unnecessary question, such information helps to establish the status of a potential witness. Status is all-important when it comes to his being cross-examined by defence counsel. A man of professional standing is more likely to be believed by a jury when compared to a yobbo with a string of previous convictions, an earring and tattoos all over him. One has to think ahead in matters concerning a trial. If ever there was one. That said, it was unlikely that Porter had witnessed anything of evidential value.

'I was a chartered accountant,' said Porter. 'Now, gentlemen, how can I help you?'

'Last Saturday night you called the police to a disturbance next door at number twenty-seven,' I began.

'That's correct,' said Porter. 'The noise was quite deafening. I was surprised because the Bartons are normally such quiet people. And apart from anything else, these old houses have very thick walls. One doesn't usually hear one's neighbours.'

'Do you know the Bartons well?'

'Not what you'd call intimately, but enough to pass the time of day, and visit each other for a drink at Christmas.'

'What sort of noise was it?' asked Dave.

'There was a lot of loud music, and shouts and screams from time to time. I really thought someone was being murdered, and from what I read in the papers, Mrs Barton was found dead.'

'That's correct,' I said. 'Mrs Barton was the victim of a murder, but I'd be obliged if you kept that to yourself. Otherwise there'll be a constant stream of journalists hammering at your door and plaguing the life out of you for anything you can tell them. They can be very persuasive.'

Porter shook his head. 'I don't know what the world's coming to, Mr Brock,' he said. 'And poor James Barton was away. If only he'd been there, it might not have happened. Or if I'd called the police earlier.' Personally, I didn't think that that would have made any difference.

'Did you see any of the people arriving at this party, sir, or leaving it?'

'No. We keep ourselves to ourselves usually. I wasn't aware that there was a party until the noise started to develop.'

'And what time was that, when you first noticed the noise?'

'It must've been around eleven o'clock, I suppose. I'd heard a bit of music before that, but nothing very disturbing. One doesn't like to complain, particularly about such good neighbours as the Bartons, but it eventually became quite intolerable.'

'So you called the police.'

'Yes. A nice young constable called, and said that he'd speak to whoever was making the noise, but it had all quietened down by then.'

I'm not sure I'd've described Watson as 'a nice young constable'. I didn't think he'd done his job as well as he could've done, but I'd be the first to admit that it's easy to be wise with hindsight.

The door opened, and an elderly woman came into the room

carrying a tray. She was tall and slender, and her iron-grey hair was cut severely short.

'This is my wife Sheila,' said Porter. 'They've come to see us about that awful business next door, dear. Apparently poor Diana's been murdered. It wasn't the fire that killed her after all.'

'Oh my God! What a terrible thing,' said Mrs Porter. For a moment she stood still, staring at me, but eventually she set the tray down on a coffee table, and began to pour the tea.

'I was just talking to your husband about the events of last Saturday night,' I said. 'Or early Sunday morning to be precise.'

'The noise was dreadful.' Sheila Porter handed round cups of tea, and sat down beside her husband on the sofa. 'It was so noisy I couldn't get to sleep. It was unusual, too, because the Bartons have always been very quiet people, but we'd never heard anything like it before,' she continued, repeating what her husband had said earlier. 'I eventually told Frank that he'd have to do something. I really began to wonder if the house had been broken into. You hear such terrible things these days about people breaking into other people's houses and holding parties. But by the time the police arrived, the noise had stopped.'

'Did you see anyone entering or leaving the house, Mrs Porter?' asked Dave.

'No, we were sitting in here with the curtains drawn, watching the TV.' Sheila Porter gestured at a large television set in the corner of the room. 'We love those American crime dramas that they have on the TV. CSI and all that. Much better than any of ours.'

I couldn't but agree with her. I enjoyed them too, when I had the time to watch them, but probably because I didn't know when they were making mistakes. There's nothing worse for a London copper than watching a British police 'soap' and spotting the procedural errors in the first five minutes.

I decided that there was little else to be obtained from the Porters. We finished our tea, and crossed the road to number twenty-four.

'I'm afraid my husband's at work,' said Patricia Baxter, as she invited us into her sitting room. 'Can I help?'

'As a matter of interest, Mrs Baxter, what does your husband do?' asked Dave, as ever collecting inconsequential pieces of information.

'He's in IT,' said Patricia.

Given the house in which the Baxters lived, I imagined he was very successful at it, whatever it was.

Patricia saw my puzzled expression. 'Information technology,' she explained.

'I'm told that your husband saw the fire opposite at number twenty-seven last Sunday morning,' I said, 'and called the brigade.'

'That's correct. I was asleep, but he'd got up, and was looking out of the window when he saw the flames.'

'Did you see anyone arriving or leaving number twenty-seven on the Saturday evening, Mrs Baxter?' asked Dave. 'It's the Bartons' house, and police were earlier called to a noisy party that was being held there.'

'No, we didn't hear a thing,' said Patricia Baxter, 'but the double-glazing keeps out most of the noise. We had it put in because there's quite a lot of traffic on this street, even at night. We've been on at the local council for ages to try to have through traffic banned, but we've not had any success so far.'

'So you didn't see anything,' I said.

'No, I'm afraid not,' said Mrs Baxter. 'This is the room in which we spend most of our time, and as you can see it's at the back of the house. We'd watched a bit of television in here, and then played Scrabble. We went up to bed at about a quarter past eleven, I suppose.'

'Exciting lives they lead in Chelsea,' remarked Dave, as we drove back to Curtis Green. 'I wonder if they were playing strip Scrabble.'

Captain Peter Richards was a man in his mid-forties. He had the bearing of a sailor: a little on the short side, about five-nine, with a ruddy complexion, and thinning auburn hair.

'Well, gentlemen, it must be important if you've come all the way to Southampton from London.'

'It is,' I said. 'I'm Detective Chief Inspector Brock of Scotland Yard, and this is Detective Sergeant Poole.' I couldn't be bothered with all this Homicide and Serious Crime Command West nonsense, and we were technically Scotland Yard officers anyway. 'And we're investigating a murder.'

'I see.' Richards crossed his living room to a cabinet. 'Not too early for a drop of Scotch, is it?'

'Thank you. I take it the sun's over the yardarm, then?'

'Depends where in the world you are.' Richards sighed as he poured double measures of malt whisky, and I got the impression that he'd heard the phrase too many times before. He handed us our whisky, and sat down. 'Now, how can I help you with a murder in London?'

'The victim was a Mrs Diana Barton,' I began.

'That rings a bell,' said Richards. 'If I remember correctly, she and her husband were first-class passengers on a cruise last January.'

'That's my understanding,' I said, 'and Mr Barton told me that he'd complained to you about one of your stewards.'

'That's right, he did. That's why I remembered the name. Just hang on a minute.' Richards rose and left the room to return moments later clutching a book. 'My personal log,' he explained. 'I keep kidding myself that I'm going to write a book of my seafaring experiences one day, but I don't suppose I'll ever get round to it.'

'Mr Barton said that the steward was called Hendry,' said Dave.

'That's the fellow. Thomas Hendry,' said Richards, and thumbed through his book. 'Yes, I remember it clearly now. Mr Barton complained that Hendry had forced himself on his wife, and that sexual intercourse had taken place.'

That was slightly different from the account James Barton had given us. 'Are you saying that Mr Barton alleged that his wife had been raped?'

Richards looked up with a twisted grin on his face. 'That was the inference I drew,' he said, 'so I decided to question Mrs Barton when I could get her on her own. But she told me a different tale. She was a bit embarrassed at first, but eventually admitted that she'd encouraged Hendry. Being a virile young man, he didn't hesitate to take advantage of what was on offer.' The captain sighed. 'I'm sorry to have to say that this sort of thing happens from time to time. It must be something to do with the sea air, but young women do some-times fall in love with their steward. Shipboard romances, and all that sort of starry-eyed claptrap. Usually though, the women are much younger and prettier than Mrs Barton. I should think

she was in her late forties.' Richards had the world-weary
approach to life of someone to whom nothing was a surprise
any more.

'She was actually forty-five,' said Dave.

'That sounds about right. Anyhow, in view of what Mrs
Barton had told me, I decided that there was no question of
her having been raped. Nevertheless, I interviewed Hendry,
and he admitted straight away what had happened, but said
that Mrs Barton had led him on.' Richards gave a scornful
laugh. 'But it wasn't the first time that his behaviour towards
women had come to my notice. I'd given him written warnings on the two previous occasions, and so this time I dismissed
him. Our passengers pay a lot of money for these cruises, and
we can't have the menfolk thinking that stewards obliging
lady passengers is included in the package. Apart from
anything else, Barton was a director of a hotel group that has
commercial links with our shipping line, and I didn't want
him complaining to head office. I made a point of seeing him
later and I told him that Hendry would be paid off, dishonourably
discharged if you like, at the end of the cruise.'

'And was he satisfied with that?' I asked.

'Seemed to be,' said Richards, 'but reading between the
lines, I think that his wife made a habit of going over the
side. Not in a nautical sense, of course,' he added, and smiled
at his little joke. 'She probably enjoyed a bit of rough, if you
take my meaning. Hendry was certainly a bit rough, but he
knew how to turn on the charm if there was a big enough tip
on offer. Anyway, Mr Barton said that he wasn't going to take
it any further, and that was that. Case closed.'

'Do you have any idea where Hendry might be now, Captain
Richards?' asked Dave.

'I'm afraid not. But he's bound to be a member of the RMT:
that's the Rail, Maritime and Transport Workers Union. They
might be able to help. Hendry could have given up the sea,
of course. It's a black mark to have got the sack, and he
could've had some difficulty in getting another seafaring job.'

'Would your company hold a photograph of Hendry, Captain?'
asked Dave.

'It's possible, I suppose. All crew members are photographed
when they join the company, mainly for their dockyard passes
and the ship's records, and a copy's held at head office. But it

might have been destroyed once Hendry was dismissed.'
Richards wrote the address of the shipping company on the
back of one of his visiting cards, and handed it to Dave. 'Worth
a try, I suppose.'

Dave examined the card. 'Well, at least it's in London,' he
said.

'It looks like this Hendry guy might be a suspect, guv,' said
Dave, as we journeyed back to London.

'Maybe, unless he's back at sea, and was at the time of the
murder,' I said, 'but from what James Barton said about his
wife having casual affairs, our killer could be just about anyone.
He was only able to name Hendry and Potier the Frenchman,
but he was convinced there were others he didn't know about.'

'Needle in a haystack job, guv,' said Dave. 'So what's next?'

'Two things: find Hendry and find Potier.'

'What about Carl Morgan, the guy who answered the door
to Watson? And Morgan's playmate Shelley. She of the thong.'

'That could be difficult, but we've got to have a go at finding
them, Dave. After all, they could be material witnesses.'

'Or one of them might've topped Diana, guv.'

'Yes, even that,' I said.

This particular enquiry seemed to be generating nothing
but bad news. And when we got back to Curtis Green, there
was even more.

'The report from the lab has arrived, sir,' said Gavin Creasey,
the moment I stepped into the incident room.

'What does it say?' I poured myself a cup of coffee from the
machine in the corner. We're not supposed to have private coffee
machines, and every so often some spotty-faced civilian
jobsworth turns up from an obscure department at the Yard
attempting to find and confiscate such little luxuries. But he's
on a hiding to nothing in attempting to outwit CID officers about
such simple matters as misusing the Commissioner's electricity.

'The semen found in Mrs Barton's vagina doesn't match
any DNA on the database, sir.'

'Wonderful!' I said. 'I wouldn't have expected anything else.'

'There's also the report from the fire brigade, sir,' continued
Creasey. 'Their investigating officer found traces of an accelerant in various parts of the ground floor rooms. Likely to be

an alcohol-based liquid, but he can't define it any closer than that. But he's confident that it's arson.'

'No surprise there,' I said.

'What do we do now, guv?' asked Dave.

I glanced at my watch: it was nearly eight o'clock. 'Go home, Dave. I don't want to get into trouble with your Madeleine. Tomorrow we'll call on the shipping office.'

I'm never very happy wandering around the City of London. For one thing they have their own police force; in my view, an unnecessary extravagance in this day and age. However, we finally located the offices of the company that owned the liner in which the Bartons had sailed for their January cruise.

After a number of false starts, we were eventually shown into the office of a young lady who, we were assured, could assist us. I explained who we were, what we were looking for, and why.

'I'll just check for you,' said the young woman, whose name, she told us, was Kimberley Taylor. 'Call me Kim,' she added. 'Everyone does.' She turned to her computer, her fingers skimming over the keyboard at lightning speed. 'Here we are: Thomas Hendry. Dismissed by Captain Peter Richards on February the seventh this year for gross misconduct, having previously received two written warnings.' She stood up and turned to a filing cabinet. Pulling out a file, she opened it on her desk, and glanced through its contents. 'You're in luck; we still have a photograph of him. It should have been destroyed, but I'm not awfully good at weeding the files,' she added, with a shy smile. 'Would you like a copy?'

'Please,' said Dave. 'While we're here, do you, by chance, have an employee named Carl Morgan?'

'Just a tick,' said Kim, and addressed herself to her computer once again. 'Yes, we do. He was a steward on Captain Richards's ship. The same one that Hendry served on, of course.'

'At the same time?' queried Dave.

'Yes, and he's still there. Actually, he's on leave while the ship's undergoing a partial refit. Should be ready for sea again in a fortnight's time. Would you like a photograph of him too?'

'Yes, please, Kim,' said Dave, who'd obviously taken a shine to the girl, and it appeared that she had taken a liking to him. But then he is a six-foot hunk of rippling muscle.

Kim disappeared from the office and, by some arcane process that I couldn't even begin to understand, returned minutes later with copies of the photographs of Thomas Hendry and Carl Morgan.

'Anything else I can help you with?' asked the helpful Kim.

'Their home addresses would be useful, Kim,' said Dave.

Armed with photographs and addresses, we returned to Curtis Green.

'Why did you ask about Carl Morgan, Dave?' I asked.

'That was the name of the guy who PC Watson spoke to when he was called to the disturbance, guv,' said Dave, as though it was obvious. At the time, I didn't realize why Dave had asked that question, but as I've often said, he thinks of things I don't think of.

'Ah, so it was. Where do these guys live?'

'Southampton.'

'Sod it!' I said.

'Yes, sir,' said Dave.

'Give Chelsea nick a ring, Dave, and ask Watson to call in here to have a look at that photograph of Morgan that we got. If it's the same guy, we might be getting somewhere.'

At half past three, Dave bounced into my office. 'Guess what, guv?'

'What?'

'I showed PC Watson the photograph of Carl Morgan, and he said it wasn't the guy who answered the door of twenty-seven Tavona Street.'

'Why am I not surprised?' I said. I tossed Dave a cigarette, and lit one myself, contrary to all the Commissioner's little regulations, and some ridiculous Act of Parliament.

'But then I showed him the photograph of Thomas Hendry, and he positively identified the guy as the one who'd answered the door.'

'But Watson said that he gave the name of Carl Morgan.' I was slowly getting lost.

'So, he gave a false name, guv,' said Dave. 'I'd call that guilty knowledge.'

'Maybe,' I said, 'or he didn't want to get involved in something that he guessed would turn very nasty. Mind you, if this guy had just topped someone, it takes balls for him to calmly confront a uniformed PC calling at the house.'

'The only problem now, guv,' said Dave, wrinkling his nose at my split infinitive, 'is to find Hendry, and I'll bet a pound to a pinch of snuff that he's done a runner.'

'Well, like it or not, it looks as if we're off to Southampton again.'

'What, now?' Dave obviously didn't like the sound of that.

I kept him waiting for a moment or two. 'No, tomorrow morning.'

Leaving Dave to look up train times, I turned to Linda Mitchell's report of the results of her examination of the murder scene.

Her team had found numerous fingerprints, some of which had been put through the system already. One set matched those of the dead woman, others tallied with James Barton whose prints one of Linda's assistants had taken, but the remainder had no match in national fingerprint records. Except one. Thomas Hendry had a previous conviction for theft when he was aged eighteen. He was now thirty-two years of age, and that conviction was 'spent', otherwise he wouldn't have got a job as a steward on board the cruise ship in which the Bartons had sailed. And Hendry's prints had been found on an empty bottle lying on the sitting room floor. So what? He'd probably poured himself a drink at some time during the evening. PC Watson had mentioned that the man he'd spoken to had been drinking.

But one fourteen-year-old conviction for theft doesn't necessarily lead to murder. In any event, we already knew that the DNA that had been recovered from Mrs Barton did not match any in the database.

However, when the young Thomas Hendry was arrested, fourteen years ago, the police did not take a specimen of his DNA. A DNA database had only been established once the full potential of the science was confirmed as an invaluable aid to criminal investigation.

It was just possible, therefore, that we had discovered our killer. I couldn't wait to arrest Hendry, and get a DNA sample.

But, knowing my luck . . .

I walked through to the incident room. 'Dave, I've just had a thought.'

'Excellent news, sir,' said Dave.

'Go out to that Bayswater hotel where James Barton is staying, and show him the photograph of Carl Morgan. It's just possible that he might recognize him. I know he said he didn't know any of the other men with whom his wife had a fling, but—'

'But there's an outside chance that it might just turn up something,' said Dave, completing my sentence for me.

FOUR

At twenty minutes to eight that evening Dave returned from Bayswater, and came straight to my office.

'There's a problem, guv,' he announced.

'Not another one,' I said wearily. 'What is it this time?'

'James Barton seems to have gone missing.'

I waved Dave to a chair. 'What's the SP?'

'I spoke to the receptionist at Barton's hotel and she told me that he was out, and had gone out at about half ten this morning. As far as she knew, he hadn't returned. She said that that was unusual because he'd always taken all his meals in the hotel since he'd arrived last Monday when he booked in.'

'I suppose he could've been visiting relatives, or attending a business meeting. He does seem to travel all over the place.'

'I don't think that's what happened on this occasion,' said Dave. 'In case the receptionist had missed Barton coming in, I checked with the restaurant manager, and he said that Barton was in the habit of speaking to him at breakfast time. He would make a point of ordering lunch and dinner, and specifying what he wanted, whether it was on the menu or not. But being a director, I suppose he could have whatever he liked.'

'And did he do so this morning?'

'Yes. But I was right about the receptionist. She had missed him, but that's not surprising particularly when the hotel is busy. Apparently a tour party booked in at about half past twelve, forty of them. It so happened that Barton *did* have lunch in the restaurant, but he didn't show up for dinner. And he always had dinner at seven o'clock on the nail. What we don't know, and neither does the receptionist, is what time he went out again. He certainly wasn't in his room when the duty manager checked for me.'

'I suppose he could have met someone. Maybe dropped into his club – he seems the sort of guy who would belong to one – and decided to stay there for dinner. I think it's a bit early to start worrying about him.'

'Yeah, maybe,' said Dave. 'Anyway, I've asked the hotel

manager to ring the incident room if Barton doesn't turn up later on this evening.'

'It seems rather odd, but I daresay he'll reappear. Frankly, I don't see anything sinister in it. After all, he's not a suspect because we do know that he was in Cyprus trying to buy a hotel at the time his wife was murdered. Well, I suppose we do. That has been verified, hasn't it?'

'Yes, guv, Miss Ebdon checked it out.'

'In that case, I don't see that it's relevant, Dave. Showing him the photograph of Morgan's not really going to prove anything. In any case, he's a free agent, not a suspect, and he can do whatever he wants. He might've got held up arranging for his wife's funeral. He could be anywhere, or doing anything. Everyone's got to be somewhere.'

And he was somewhere, but he wasn't doing anything. He was dead.

At ten o'clock, Gavin Creasey, the night-duty incident room sergeant, had received a telephone call from the duty manager at Barton's hotel to say that Barton hadn't returned.

Then, at eleven fifteen, a call came into the incident room from the CID at Paddington reporting that James Barton's body had been found in the gardens in the centre of Sussex Square, just to the north of Bayswater Road. He had been brutally attacked, and stabbed several times. Both the Bartons' names were on the PNC showing me as the officer in the case, and Paddington CID had reported the murder to HSCC as a matter of routine. The commander had been informed, and promptly directed that it was down to me. He came to that decision simply because 'there seems to be a connection with the Diana Barton case', he told Creasey. I think the commander's got it in for me.

All this was imparted to me at about midnight, an hour after Gail and I had gone to bed.

When my mobile rang, Gail's only comment was: 'Oh, not again!'

I know how she felt.

Having consumed a couple of whiskies, and half a bottle of wine over dinner, I felt it unwise to drive myself to the scene. The Black Rats, as the traffic boys are affectionately known

to those of us of *the* Department, delight in finding a CID
officer with a positive breathalyser reading. Instead, I decided
to wreak a little revenge. I rang the Yard and arranged for a
traffic car to take me to Sussex Square. The crew got me there
in about twenty-four minutes. Frightening!

The scene of James Barton's murder had been shrouded in a
tent, and floodlit with Metrolamps. Henry Mortlock was
already there, as was Dave Poole. Linda Mitchell and her
forensic technicians were waiting in their vans, now bearing
the impressive title 'Evidence Recovery Unit', for the pathologist to finish his initial examination. A detective inspector
from Paddington was also there, together with a detective
sergeant. 'Did anybody search the scene?' I asked.
    'I carried out a brief visual, guv,' said the DS. 'There was
no sign of a weapon, but I didn't want to foul up the scene
by going any further.'
    Thank God! A CID officer who knew the routine.
    'Probably took it with him and chucked it in the river,' I
said. 'Who identified him?'
    'I did, guv,' said the DI. 'He had his photo driving licence
on him, but there weren't any credit cards or cash, so I s'pose
the motive was robbery.'
    'If only it was that simple,' I said, but that was too much
of a coincidence in my book. I told the local DI about the
murder of James's wife. 'What about his mobile phone? Did
he have that with him?' We knew he had one; he'd told us.
    'No, guv. That was probably nicked as well.'
    'Who found him?'
    'A Traffic Division crew.' The DI waved a hand at two PCs
standing beside their car.
    Like me, the Paddington DI obviously could not get out of
the habit of calling it Traffic Division, but it was now known
as the Traffic Operational Command Unit. If you're wondering
why, the best people to ask are the boy superintendents who
believe that their way to the top is to come up with clever
titles, and who staff the funny names and total confusion squad
at Scotland Yard. After all, what was wrong with calling it
Traffic Division?
    'OK. You might as well get back to the nick. There's nothing
more you can do here. It's all down to me now.'

The DI grinned. 'Be lucky, guv,' he said, and he and his DS departed, no doubt pleased to be shot of what appeared to be a random mugging that had ended up as a murder. And we both knew that they're bloody difficult to solve. But I didn't believe it to be random.

'What's the verdict, Henry?' I asked, when Mortlock emerged from the tent wherein lay the victim.

'I'm fairly certain that death was due to multiple stab wounds, Harry, but I'll confirm that once I've cut him open.'

'Time of death?'

'You'll have to wait for that. He's been here for some time, I should think.'

I introduced myself to the traffic PCs. 'What's the SP, lads?'

'We were on our way back to the garage and passed through here, sir,' said the driver of the car. 'My mate spotted what seemed to be a bundle of clothing just inside the gardens in the centre of the square.' He waved at the tent. 'That was at twenty-two fifty hours. But when we took a closer look it turned out to be a body, and he was well dead. It was obvious that he'd been stabbed, because there was blood all over him. That's when I put up a shout to Paddington nick.'

'Had you patrolled this area previously during this tour of duty?'

'No, sir. Well, yes, but not since about four this afternoon.'

'So there's no telling how long the body had been there,' I mused aloud.

'I suppose not, sir.'

'It wasn't really a question. Was there any sign of a weapon?' I'd asked the Paddington CID officers, but they acknowledged only to having made a cursory examination, and I like to make sure.

'No, sir. And we had a good look round while we were waiting for the local lads, but we didn't see one,' said the PC, confirming what the Paddington DS had said.

'OK. Thanks. DS Poole will take a statement from you, and then you can get back on patrol. Or are you finished?'

'Should've booked off at eleven, sir,' said the driver's colleague.

'Oh well, that's a couple of hours overtime.'

'Be nice to have the time to spend the money,' muttered the driver. He was not pleased.

'I wonder where Barton was between lunch and when he was found, Dave.'

'Despite what the restaurant manager said, Barton might've had dinner somewhere else, guv. And if the killer had phoned him, we know that the call would eventually be connected to Barton's mobile. But as far as timing's concerned, I reckon we're up a gum tree.'

And there was no arguing with that. I turned to Linda Mitchell who had now started work on the scene. 'Anything important, Linda?'

'We found what looks like a few strands of head hair clasped in the victim's right hand, Mr Brock. With any luck it might belong to his attacker. If there are some roots attached. I'll get it off for DNA analysis.'

'But I don't suppose it'll be on the database,' I commented gloomily. We'd not had a great deal of luck so far.

It was nearly half past two in the morning by the time we'd finished at Sussex Square, and there was nothing else that we could do at the scene.

'Go home, Dave,' I said, 'and don't come in before midday.' It was meant to be an order.

'Right, guv, thanks,' said Dave, but I knew damned well that he'd be at Curtis Green before me in the morning.

I decided not to go back to Gail's house. Leaving her at midnight was one thing; returning at gone three in the morning and disturbing her was quite another, something that would be guaranteed to destroy what little domestic bliss we shared. Even though she was remarkably tolerant, I thought it best to go home to my flat in Surbiton.

It seemed to have been an age since I was last there, but everything was in order. I tend to hang up my clothes on the floor, and leave my shoes where they can be tripped over. But the previous day's chaos had been restored to normality, the breakfast things had been washed up and put away, the bed made, and everything cleaned and polished.

This is all thanks to my cleaner Gladys Gurney. She is an absolute gem, and why she puts up with me is a mystery. But I'm glad she does. Still, I ought to try mending my disorderly ways otherwise she might quit.

There was a charming little note on the worktop in the kitchen. Beside it, carefully washed and placed in a plastic bag, was one of Gail's thongs. My girlfriend seems to make a habit of leaving items of underwear about the flat. It obviously doesn't faze Mrs Gurney; she just washes them and leaves them for me to return to Gail.

> Dear Mr Brock
>
> I found a pair of Miss Sutton's backless knickers by your bed, so I've washed them for her. Also I found a pair of your shoes what needed the heels doing so I took them to the snobs. They will be ready next Monday. It will cost seven pounds the man said. Perhaps you'd leave it for me. Hope that's all right.
>
> Yours faithfully
> Gladys Gurney (Mrs)

I think that Mrs Gurney is the only person I know who still uses the term 'snobs' for a shoe repairer.

I turned in, and set the alarm for nine o'clock.

I arrived at Curtis Green at ten that same morning, and had the misfortune to meet the commander in the lift.

'What progress have you made in the death of James Barton, Mr Brock?' he asked, bowing his head to sniff at the carnation in his buttonhole.

Strange how he always asks questions about the things I don't want him to ask me about.

'Enquiries are in hand to determine why he was found in the middle of Sussex Square at just before eleven o'clock last night, sir.' At least, I hoped that I could rely on the team to have done something to that end. 'It seems he'd been missing from his hotel from some time after two o'clock yesterday afternoon.'

'Mmm! Yes, good. Keep me informed, Mr Brock.'

'Of course, sir.'

Despite my admonition, Dave was already at work. 'I've been on to the hotel in Bayswater where Barton was staying, sir, to see if they could shed any light on his movements yesterday. All they could come up with was a check of the switchboard records, which showed that Barton made a telephone call at two o'clock yesterday afternoon. We can only assume that he left the hotel at some time after that. And that fits in with what the restaurant manager had told me earlier, that Barton had lunched in the hotel restaurant.'

'Any clue as to who he phoned, Dave?'

'No, they just note the time and duration so they can put it on his bill. And it was too late to do a trace this morning, if ever. But I'm wondering if someone lured him out of the hotel for the express purpose of killing him. And, if so, why.'

'Post-mortem's at eleven thirty, sir,' said Colin Wilberforce from behind his desk. 'Will you be attending?'

'No. Where's Miss Ebdon?'

'Here, guv,' said Kate, appearing in the incident room holding a cup of coffee.

'Dave and I are going to Southampton to follow up on the two stewards who were on the Bartons' cruise liner, Kate. Perhaps you'd cover the post-mortem.'

'No worries, guv,' said Kate. As usual, she was wearing a man's white shirt, and a pair of tight-fitting jeans. That should ruin the commander's day if he happens to catch sight of her. But at least she was wearing high-heeled shoes.

First of all, however, I had a telephone call to make to a friend of mine in Hampshire.

Jock Ferguson is a detective superintendent in the Hampshire Constabulary, and when he and I were inspectors, we'd wasted three months together at the Police College at Bramshill.

The Police College, which is regarded by its devotees as the Holy Grail of policing, is an establishment in the depths of Hampshire that has the audacity to convince itself it's the policeman's university. In an attempt to prove how clever they are, the instructors all talk their own gobbledygook and write in strangulated prose that no one else can understand. And they spend valuable time trying to persuade their students to do likewise. And they seem to be very successful at it, but perhaps I'm a cynic.

Fortunately, being a Hampshire copper, Jock knew all the decent pubs in the area, and that's where we'd spent a great deal of our time. When we weren't listening to lectures on subjects we knew more about than the lecturers, that is. The only benefit to accrue from those three months was that I'd made a lot of friends and contacts. On the downside, I probably did my liver irreparable damage.

A few years ago, Jock and I had worked on a murder case

that involved an Aldershot-based soldier and his wife, along with many others. But I knew that he had since been transferred from Aldershot to Southampton, and that might just prove to be useful.

Having got through to Jock, I told him that I was coming down to the city later on that day, and briefly explained about the two murders.

Typical of Jock, he immediately named a pub where he would meet us.

It was almost half past twelve by the time Dave and I arrived at Southampton Central railway station. From there we went straight to the pub mentioned by Jock Ferguson and found him holding up the bar. After the customary exchange of insults, we settled for a pie and a pint: the policeman's usual substitute for a midday meal.

Once we'd finished discussing the appalling state of the Job and had criticized a few senior officers, Jock left us, but told me to get in touch with him if we needed any help.

Half past two found us at Birley Road, the last known address for Thomas Hendry, sometime seagoing steward. It was a short street of old houses close to the city centre.

The woman who answered the door was in her late twenties, had shoulder-length black hair, and bits of metal embedded in various parts of her face and ears. There was a gap between her crop-top and her jeans, presumably to give us a good view of the two butterfly tattoos homing in on her navel. She looked at us with a puzzled expression on her face. Perhaps she thought we were peddling encyclopaedia or religion, but I soon disabused her of that. From the brief description PC Watson had given us, there was little doubt that she was the Shelley he saw in a thong on the night of the disturbance.

'I'm a police officer,' I said, but that was all I had time to say. Unfortunately I'd said it too loudly.

There was a crash from the rear of the small house, as if a table had been overturned, followed by the sound of breaking glass. It was apparent that the man we'd come to interview had taken flight, assuming that it was Thomas Hendry. This, of course, is something CID officers know all about. Fleeing felons are an all too frequent occurrence in the humdrum life of a detective.

Dispensing with the niceties of asking if we might come in, Dave and I sped through the house. In the kitchen, we found that the table had been turned on its side, and the large window-pane had been smashed. There were smears of blood on the jagged edges of the broken glass. I presume that Hendry had scarpered the moment he heard me announce who we were, and had taken a header through the window.

'Where does that lead to?' I asked the startled woman, pointing at the paved area at the back of the house.

'To the garage at the back. It's where we keep the car. There's a service road from there out to the main road.'

As if to confirm what she'd said, I heard the sound of an engine starting, and a vehicle driving away at speed.

Well, that was something. This woman obviously wasn't too worried about telling me how the man had escaped. I tested her even further.

'D'you know the registration number of the car?'

Without a pause, she reeled it off.

'Have you got a telephone here?' I asked, forgetting that my mobile was in my pocket.

'Yeah, of course. It's in the lounge.'

I moved rapidly into the tawdry sitting room that she'd dignified with the term 'lounge', and dialled 999. Having identified myself, and assured the police control room operator that Detective Superintendent Ferguson knew what we were doing, I relayed the details of the car, and the fact that our man could be bloodstained. Now we could relax and hope, and obtain as much information from the helpful woman as she was prepared to give.

'What's your name, Miss?' asked Dave.

'Shelley Maxwell,' she said, confirming that she was the woman who'd been seen by PC Watson. 'What's this all about?'

'And I presume the guy who just disappeared out of the kitchen window was Thomas Hendry,' continued Dave.

'Yeah, that was Tom.'

'Why did he make such a hurried exit, Shelley?'

'I haven't got a clue. He's never done nothing like that before.'

Dave showed the girl the photograph of Hendry that we'd obtained from the shipping office. 'Is this your man Tom?'

'Yes, that's him.'

'You and he were at twenty-seven Tavona Street last Saturday night.'

'I don't know what you're talking about.'

Dave seemed to be doing all right without my intervention, so I let him get on with it.

'I think you do, Shelley,' persisted Dave. 'But if you'd rather, I can take you down to Southampton Central police station, and I'll send for the officer from London who spoke to Tom early last Sunday morning about a riotous party at the house. He recalls that you were scantily dressed at the time. It could all take time, of course,' added Dave, implying that Shelley Maxwell could finish up spending a lot of time at the nick.

'We never had nothing to do with it,' Shelley blurted out.

'Nothing to do with what?'

'The dead woman.'

'What dead woman is this?' asked Dave, affecting an air of innocence.

'Diana. It was her party.'

We were getting close to having to caution Shelley Maxwell, but she might just have a little more to tell us before we resorted to arresting and charging her with murder. I decided to take a hand.

'Shelley, we are investigating the murder of Diana Barton whose body was found at twenty-seven Tavona Street the night you and Thomas Hendry were there.'

Predictably, Shelley Maxwell burst into tears. 'It was nothing to do with us,' she protested, in between sobs that might even have been genuine.

I made a decision, a bit of a rarity for me. 'Miss Maxwell, I'm taking you to Southampton Central police station where I shall question you further. That interview will be recorded for your protection.'

More tears followed this announcement and I got the impression that Shelley Maxwell was in this affair over her head, and couldn't really cope with the resulting stress.

I called Jock Ferguson on my mobile, and asked him to arrange transport to the nick.

Once the plethora of forms had been duly completed, a procedure necessary whenever anyone is brought into a police station, we got down to business in one of the interview rooms.

'You and Thomas Hendry live together, do you?' I asked for openers.

'Yes,' murmured the girl.

'Where do you work?' I was thinking that she was probably an exotic dancer, or a striptease artiste, or even a prostitute. But I was wrong.

'I'm a supermarket check-out assistant.'

Well, that was a first.

'And you were both at a party at twenty-seven Tavona Street, Chelsea on the night of Saturday the twenty-seventh of July.'

'Yes,' said Shelley, her voice almost inaudible.

'You must speak up,' I said, 'otherwise the tape recorder won't pick up your answers.'

'Yes,' she said again.

'What time did you arrive there?'

'About half past four, I suppose.'

'And was Thomas Hendry with you?'

'Yeah, course he was.'

'So, you travelled all the way up from Southampton just to attend a party in Chelsea.'

'No, not exactly. Tom had booked us into a hotel for the Saturday night. He said as how we was going to have the weekend in London. But he did say we was going to a party an' all.'

'And which hotel did you stay at?'

'We never. See, Tom changed his mind, and said we'd come back here.'

'Why was that?'

'I don't know. He just said we ought to go home.'

'Why did he give police the name of Carl Morgan when the officer spoke to him?'

'Did he? I didn't know that. I suppose it was because he didn't want to get mixed up in this business.'

'Did he set fire to the house before you left?'

There was a pause, long enough for me to know that she was going to lie.

'No. I don't think so.'

'Where's Tom gone?'

'I've no idea.' Shelley sniffed.

'If he wasn't involved in the death of Diana Barton, why did he run away when we arrived at your house?'

'I don't know.'

'Do you know the names of any of the other guests at this party?'

'No.'

I imagined that to be a lie, too.

'Why did Mrs Barton hold a party?' I continued to press the girl even though I thought she perhaps didn't know any of the answers to my questions. 'From what I heard, she was a quiet sort of woman. Not the type to have a party where loud music was being played to such an extent that the neighbours complained to the police. And where half naked girls were running about.'

Shelley dabbed at her eyes with a tissue, and then blew her nose. 'She said she wanted to celebrate having a new kitchen installed. We all had to have a look at it, and say wow.'

'*A new kitchen?*' I'd heard of some strange reasons for holding a party, but that was a new one on me. I went on to a different tack. 'Were you aware that Thomas Hendry had had sexual intercourse with Mrs Barton?'

'When? On Saturday?'

'No. I'm talking about the beginning of this year. That's why he was sacked as a steward.'

'Oh that. Yeah, Tom told me about that. I thought you meant last Saturday. He said that when he was on the cruise this woman paid him to screw her. He said it happened about six times. I think it was very unfair of them to sack him for something that was the woman's fault.'

'Did you know that that woman was Diana Barton?'

'No, he never said who she was.'

'I suggest that he murdered her out of revenge for having lost him his job.'

'No, of course he never. He was annoyed about getting the push, but he wouldn't kill no one. That'd be a daft thing to do. Anyway, like I said, I never knew it was Diana.'

I doubted that somehow, but I nodded to Dave, and let him take over.

'How long have you and Tom been living together?' asked Dave.

Shelley paused for a moment. 'About a couple of years, I s'pose. Mind you, he's at sea a lot. Or was.'

'And you didn't mind him having sex with other women?' Both Dave and I knew, from what Captain Richards had said, that Hendry had made a practice of bedding willing women passengers.

'No, of course I never. He was away for long periods at a time, and you can't expect him to go without,' said Shelley with a candid admission of her tolerance. 'That last cruise he was on, when he got the sack, lasted over a month. So he has it off when he can get it.' Shelley paused again. 'And the same goes for me when he ain't here.'

'Are you sure you don't know where he's gone, Shelley?' I took the questioning back.

'No, I don't.'

'Does Tom have any relatives, any friends, where he might've gone?'

'I don't know.'

'Where was Tom yesterday evening?'

'He picked me up from the supermarket when I finished me shift, just after four o'clock that was, and took me home. We went out for a pizza at about eight, had a drink at a pub and then went back home.'

'What time would that have been?'

'About eleven, maybe quarter past.'

That might have been the truth, but there again it might not. However, I concluded that there was little else that we could obtain from Shelley Maxwell. I admitted her to police bail, and sent her home. I told her that she should advise the police if and when Hendry returned home. But I doubted that she would.

FIVE

I came to the conclusion that we had wasted our time talking to Shelley Maxwell. She hadn't told us anything useful about the party. Furthermore, I had great difficulty in believing that anyone would hold a party to celebrate the installation of a new kitchen. There again, it was Chelsea, and all manner of strange things go on there.

I could tell that, for the most part, Shelley had been avoiding the truth in an attempt to shield her live-in lover. If that were the case, she hadn't done a very good job. Even so, I was fairly certain that she knew where Hendry would have gone following his dramatic flight, and I just hoped that one of the Hampshire Constabulary patrols would pick him up. I thought it highly likely he would make for London, there being a fallacy harboured by villains that they can get lost there. It ain't so.

We moved on to Tadley Street, which was not far from Birley Road.

'Are you Carl Morgan?'

'Yes, that's me. Who are you? Are you from the company?'

'No. Mr Morgan, we're police officers. May we come in?'

'Yeah, sure. What's it all about?' Morgan took us into the front room of the house.

Once there, I introduced Dave and me, and explained that we were from Scotland Yard.

'I'm investigating the murder of a Mrs Diana Barton last Saturday in Chelsea.'

'Who? I've never heard of a Diana Barton. And I've never been to Chelsea. In fact, I never go to London. Are you sure I'm the bloke you want to talk to?'

I was certain we had got the right man, but didn't bother to say as much.

'I understand that you were a steward on the same cruise liner as Tom Hendry.'

'Yes, that's right. Look, what's this all about?'

'Bear with me, Mr Morgan,' I said. 'Were you aware that he was dismissed in early February?'

'Yes, it was the day we docked here at Southampton. He was stupid enough to have sex with a woman passenger. He was always doing it, but on this occasion her husband complained, and the skipper put Hendry ashore. Permanently.'

An elderly grey-haired woman entered the room. 'What is it, Carl?' She stared suspiciously at Dave and me as we stood up. 'Who are these people, son?'

'They're police officers from London, Ma. They want to talk to me about a murder up there.' Morgan glanced at me. 'This is my mother,' he explained.

'A murder? You don't know anything about a murder, do you, son?' asked his mother, as she sat down on a sofa beside him. She glared at the two of us.

'No, Ma.'

I gave Morgan the brief details of the murder, and told him that when officers called at the house in Tavona Street, the man who answered the door gave the name of Carl Morgan. 'But,' I said, 'I can see that you're not him.'

'I'll bet that was Hendry,' said Morgan, clearly annoyed. 'It was the best thing the company did when they got shot of him. He was always in trouble.'

'Really? What sort of trouble?'

'Fiddling, mainly. For example, he'd nick a bottle of champagne from the bar, keep it and then put it on a passenger's bill. All the passengers were given company credit cards at the start of the voyage. Most of them never bothered to check their account at the end of the cruise, and settled up. Or if they queried the champagne, the purser would just knock it off.'

'Is that all?' asked Dave.

'No way,' said Morgan. 'For a while, Hendry doubled as a cocktail steward in the Coconut Bar, but he was fiddling passengers' chits there, too. Usually by bunging a few tots on the bill of a passenger who was three sheets to the wind. But the purser could never prove it, and when he spoke to the passengers they always said they couldn't remember how much they'd had to drink the night before. It was only simple stuff, like putting an extra tot of spirits – whisky, brandy, gin or vodka – on the chit. But it all added up, and when Hendry had fiddled enough tots to make up a bottle – that's twenty-six tots – he'd have a bottle away from the store. Anyway, the purser banned him from bar duty just the same. He was pretty switched on, was the purser.'

'How d'you know all this?' asked Dave.

'There are a lot of fiddles going on, and being a steward you don't miss much, believe me. But I never did it,' added Morgan, keen to distance himself from Hendry's nefarious activities. 'It wasn't worth getting the sack for the sake of a few quid. Anyway, if you looked after the first-class passengers, they always gave you a good tip at the end of the cruise. Some of them even bunged you each time you served them.'

'Where were you last Saturday night, Mr Morgan?' I asked. 'And last night?' Despite his protestations of innocence, I still wanted to make certain that Morgan was telling us the truth.

'He was here with me,' said Morgan's mother. 'He's hardly left the house since he got back from his last trip.'

'That's right,' agreed Morgan. 'I don't go out much when I'm on shore leave. My father slung his hook years ago, so my mother's by herself most of the time. It's bad enough leaving her on her own when I'm away, so when I'm at home I spend as much time with her as I can.'

Dave and I stood up. 'Thank you for your time, Mr Morgan, and you too, Mrs Morgan,' I said. 'We'll not need to trouble you again.'

'It's Mrs Marsh,' said Morgan's mother. 'I remarried, but I'm a widow now.'

'If you're looking for someone who did your murder, I'd start with Hendry,' said Morgan, as he saw us to the front door. 'He's a bad 'un if ever I saw one.'

I reckoned he was probably right. So, all we had to do now was find Hendry.

But that too was resolved for us. As we were walking back towards the police station, my mobile rang.

'Harry, it's Jock Ferguson. You'll be happy to know we've got your boy for you.'

'Splendid, Jock. Where is he?'

'On his way back from Southampton General hospital as we speak. He was captured by a traffic unit. Apparently they spotted him on the M3, and he took off. Speeds of up to a hundred miles an hour.'

'Bloody hell! What was he driving, Jock, a Ferrari?'

'Would you believe an R-reg Ford Escort? Anyway, our traffic lads called in other units in an attempt to box him in, but he swung on to the A31 at Shawford Down, and started making his way back to Southampton. But they put a stinger down at Otterbourne. He tried to go on, but eventually he lost it and crashed into a tree.'

'Was he injured in the crash? You mentioned that he was in hospital.'

'Surprisingly no, Harry, but he had a nasty gash on his right forearm, so they took him in to Southampton General to get him stitched up.'

'That was probably caused when he did a header through his kitchen window,' I suggested.

'Maybe, Harry. Anyway, he'll be back here at Central nick very shortly.'

'Thanks for your help, Jock. I'll see you there.'

It was six o'clock by the time that Thomas Hendry arrived at Southampton Central police station. Having had very little sleep, Dave and I had been on the go from first thing this morning. It had been a long day, but interviewing Hendry couldn't wait.

'Hendry will be charged with dangerous driving, and failing to stop for police,' said Jock Ferguson. 'But if you charge him with murder, I doubt the Crown Prosecution Service will worry too much about taking him to court for driving offences.'

Hendry carved a pitiful figure when he was brought into the interview room. He was wearing a bloodstained tee shirt and jeans, and his right arm was bandaged and in a sling. God knows how he managed to drive with an injured arm, but desperation will often summon a hitherto unknown resourcefulness among those attempting to escape the police.

'I'm Detective Chief Inspector Brock of Scotland Yard, and this is Detective Sergeant Poole,' I said. 'This interview will be recorded.'

Hendry stared at me, but said nothing.

'Why did you run away the moment you heard us at your front door in Birley Road?' I asked.

'I thought you were going to arrest me,' said Hendry, leaning forward and resting his injured arm on the table between us.

'Why should you think that?'

'It's what you do, innit? The police, I mean. You find someone and fit 'em up with a job what they ain't done.'

I knew Hendry had one conviction behind him, but I wondered how many others he'd avoided. He seemed to have a contemptuous view of the police that was not warranted by a single entry on his criminal record.

'You were at twenty-seven Tavona Street, Chelsea, on the night of Saturday the twenty-seventh of July.'

'Who says I was.'

'Shelley Maxwell.'

'You don't want to listen to what that silly moo says. Half the time she doesn't know what she's on about.'

I produced the photograph we had obtained of Hendry from the shipping office.

'The police officer who called at twenty-seven Tavona Street has seen this photograph, and positively identifies you as the man to whom he spoke that night.' I hoped that Dave would be impressed by my sentence construction. 'He also mentioned that Shelley was wearing a thong and nothing else.'

Hendry smirked at that, and leaned back, grimacing as his injured arm came off the table. 'OK, so I was there, but I didn't have nothing to do with Diana's death.'

'Who said anything about a death?'

'Well, that's what this is all about, innit?'

Dave shot a warning glance in my direction. I knew that look; he was implying that I should caution Hendry. But I didn't think so. Not yet.

'Yes, it is,' I said. 'The dead body of Diana Barton was indeed found there shortly after your departure, but I suppose you maintain that you didn't kill her.'

'I didn't kill her.' Hendry drew the words out, emphasising each one.

'Then who did?'

'I don't have a clue, mister.'

'When did you discover that she was dead?'

'It was just before that copper came knocking at the door. The party had more or less wound up by then, and everyone had gone home except Shell and me. I didn't know where Diana had gone, and so I had a look round the house so I could say cheers and thanks for the thrash. When I got to her bedroom, I saw her body. There was blood everywhere, and I could see she'd been stabbed a lot.'

'If you had nothing to do with it, why didn't you call the police?'

Hendry sighed again. There was a long pause before he answered. 'We've got history, Diana and me,' he said eventually.

'Care to explain that?' I guessed what was coming, but we knew nothing beyond the fact that Hendry had been dismissed in February for having sexual intercourse with Diana Barton on the cruise.

'I got to know her on a cruise in January. I was a steward on the liner she was on, and she and her husband occupied a stateroom that was serviced by me.'

I glanced at Dave, hoping that he wouldn't laugh. He had a different definition of 'servicing' in this context.

'Yes, go on,' I said.

'It was obvious that she'd taken a fancy to me. You get a lot of women like that on cruises. A bit of sun, and some sea air, and they get horny. She wasn't bad looking for her age, neither, and I could see what she wanted; you can always tell. And her husband was an old guy, well past it, I should think. I doubt that even a treble dose of Viagra would have helped him much.' Hendry laughed, but it was a cynical laugh. 'So it became quite regular, and I s'pose I must've laid her about six or seven times during the cruise. She'd always give me a tip, usually fifty quid, but I knew what she was really paying for.'

'But you finished up getting the sack.'

'Yes, thanks to her bleedin' husband. He told the skipper that I'd raped his wife. The skipper took it seriously because it turned out that old man Barton was a director of the line, or was tied up with it somehow. That was all on the day before the cruise ended. So, the skipper sent for me the next day and gave me the boot.'

'Which annoyed you, presumably?'

'What d'you think? Of course it bloody annoyed me. I haven't been able to get a job at sea since.'

'Annoyed you enough to want to kill Diana's husband.'

Hendry stared at me. 'Don't tell me he's dead an' all.'

'Yes, he was murdered last night.'

'Bloody hell! Well, I can't say I'm sorry. It was him what

lost me my job. Even after Diana admitted to the skipper that she'd been willing.'

That was a fascinating example of self-delusion. Hendry obviously refused to see that it was his own misdeeds that had resulted in his dismissal.

'Where were you yesterday?'

'Here in Southampton, all day, and all night.'

'Can anyone vouch for that?'

'I picked Shell up from the supermarket when she finished work at four o'clock, and took her home. We went out for a pizza at about eight, had a few drinks in a pub, and then went back home again at about eleven.'

'Where did you have this pizza?' asked Dave.

Hendry furnished the name and address of the restaurant. 'They'll remember us; we're often in there.'

'I hope they do,' said Dave, as he wrote down the details. 'For your sake.'

Hendry's account of his movements the previous evening had been a little too perfect, and tallied precisely with what Shelley had told us. Although neither of them was very bright, they were still devious enough to have arranged that alibi in advance.

'How come you went to a party at Diana's house, then?' I asked.

'The last time I bedded her on the cruise was the day before we docked. That was about twenty-four hours before I got the push,' Hendry added bitterly. 'And that was all because her old man had seen me coming out of their stateroom. But Diana had said that she wanted to see me again, in London. She give me her address and phone number, and I went to see her a few times.'

'For more of the same, I suppose?' put in Dave.

Hendry gave a sly grin. 'Well, it wasn't for afternoon tea and biscuits, mate.'

'Why did she have a party in Chelsea?' I asked.

'She said she wanted to celebrate having a new kitchen fitted. That was all bullshit, of course. Just an excuse. Not that she needed one. She said her old man was away, so there wouldn't be no problems with him. If he'd been there, I wouldn't have gone nowhere near the place.'

'And presumably he was away on the previous occasions when you went there.'

'Too bloody right. But I was still a bit doubtful about
going to a party because before that it had been one on one,
if you take my meaning, but she said to bring a bird if I
wanted to. I said I'd take Shell. And Diana said OK, because
there'd be some other guys there who'd keep Shell amused
while Diana and me were having fun.'

'What did Shelley say about that?'

'She was all for it. We might live together, but we go our
own ways when it suits us.'

Now we were getting to the crunch. 'And who were these
other guys who were there?'

Hendry's chin dropped to his chest, presumably in thought.
'I remember a geezer called Gaston,' he began.

'Was he a Frenchman?' asked Dave.

'Yeah, I think so. He spoke with a funny accent anyhow.
Oh, and there was a bloke called Bruce. He was an Aussie.
And there were two other guys: Dale and Barry.'

'Surnames?' I asked.

'No idea,' said Hendry.

'What about the women?'

'There were three of them, I think, apart from Shell.' Hendry
paused in thought again. 'Liz, Debbie and Charlene. That Liz
was some bird, I can tell you.' He looked wistful. 'Long blonde
hair and big boobs.'

'And were they all in a state of undress, like Shelley was
when the police came to the door?'

Hendry grinned. 'Yeah, they'd all got their kit off by the
time the party got going.'

'What did Diana Barton think of all that?'

'It was her idea. She said it wouldn't be a party if it wasn't
un . . . er, unhib something.'

'Uninhibited?' suggested Dave.

'Yeah, I think that's what she said.'

'And was Diana dressed like that?'

'Yeah, she was the first to get her gear off. All of it.'

'And did you have sex with her?'

'Of course. That's why I was there. She was bloody good
in the sack was Diana.' It was interesting that he'd admitted
that. Shelley had claimed not to know that her boyfriend had
been intimate with anyone at the party.

'And did the other men?'

'Did they what?'

'Have sex with her?'

'Probably. It was a bit of a free for all, if you know what I mean. I lost track of who was doing it with who.'

'I get the picture,' I said. 'These other women, did they come with the other men who were there?'

'I s'pose so, except for Bruce, the Aussie. He come on his tod.' Hendry paused and wrinkled his brow. 'Or did he bring Charlene? That's an Aussie name, innit? But I'm not sure. I know that Liz was Gaston's bird. He knew how to pick 'em all right.'

'Whose idea was the music?' I asked.

'One of the guys brought an iPod player and a docking station. That was Barry, I think. Yes, it was him. I s'pose that's what upset the guy next door. But Diana didn't give a stuff, and told Barry to turn up the volume.'

'Was there much alcohol at this party?'

'Stacks of it. Diana laid it on, and some of the guys brought bottles. Well, you do, don't you?'

'What about drugs?'

'Dunno nothing about that.'

'And were you drinking?' asked Dave.

'I know what you're thinking. Yeah, I had a few bevvies, but Shell don't drink, and she was going to drive us back to the hotel.'

'Except you didn't go to the hotel, did you?'

'No, not after what we'd found. I never had anything to do with Diana getting done in, but I thought it best to get the hell out of it as quick as I could.'

'When did the party end?' I asked.

'About midnight. Everyone pushed off together, except Shell and me. And, like I said, I went to find Diana to fix up for coming to see her again. Believe me, the fifty quid she gave me each time came in very handy now I'm out of work, and we couldn't live on what Shell gets down the supermarket.'

'Before you left, who was the last to leave?'

'Well, no one. They all left together. I remember because they was laughing and shouting outside in the street, and I thought that the law would turn up. And they did.'

'The fire officer's report said that the fire was started with an accelerant.'

'Do what?'

'It means that something flammable was used to spread the fire quickly. What d'you know about that?'

Hendry stayed silent for a few moments. Like politicians who find themselves in deep shtuck, I imagine he was considering his position. But I was surprised at his next statement.

'That was down to me.'

Dave looked at me with that same expression as he had used before. This time I nodded, and Dave quickly cautioned the ex-steward.

'Why did you do it?' I asked.

'I was sure the police would find out that I'd known Diana, and would reckon I'd topped her. So I thought that to get rid of all the evidence would let me off the hook.'

'Where did the flammable liquid come from?'

Hendry smiled. 'There was plenty of Scotch and brandy and vodka in the house. I know it was a terrible waste, but I used that.' He seemed more upset by the profligate use of the alcohol than he did about setting fire to the house. And his statement tallied with the empty bottle that Linda found with his fingerprints on it. Not that that meant anything; he'd admitted drinking at the house.

'I'll ask you again: why didn't you immediately call the police? You had ample opportunity when the officer called at the house minutes later.'

'Because I knew you'd put it on me.'

I was still having difficulty in believing Hendry's account. He had motive, opportunity and means, and setting fire to the Bartons' house appeared to confirm his guilt. But even so, none of that constituted enough evidence to secure a conviction for murder. We needed more.

'Are you willing to provide a sample of your DNA?' I asked.

'What for?' Hendry's tone implied refusal.

'I can always get an order from a senior officer to take it.' I knew that Jock Ferguson, holding the requisite rank, would sign the authority without hesitation.

Hendry shrugged. 'Yeah, OK.'

Dave produced the necessary kit from his briefcase. Using a special cotton bud, he took a sample of Hendry's saliva, placed it carefully in a small container, and labelled it.

'Thomas Hendry, I am arresting you for committing criminal

damage by fire at twenty-seven Tavona Road, on or about the twenty-seventh of July this year. You will shortly be taken to London where you will be charged with that offence.' And although Dave had cautioned him, I cautioned him again. At long last, I'd learned the words.

'Yeah, well, like I said, it was down to me.'

Dave wrote that statement in his pocketbook.

Once Hendry had been placed in a cell, I spoke to Jock Ferguson, and told him what had happened.

'You'll be wanting to charge him in London, I suppose, Harry.'

'It'll be more convenient, Jock,' I said. 'And it's the venue of the offence.'

'OK. We'll keep him here until you can arrange an escort. I'll let the CPS worry about the driving charges. But I don't suppose they'll bother about them in view of what you've nicked him for.' Jock Ferguson was a realist.

SIX

On Friday I assembled my team in the incident room for a briefing, firstly to follow up on what Thomas Hendry had told us, and secondly to review what else we knew about the two murders. It was obvious that our priority was to trace the people who'd been at Diana Barton's 'kitchen' party. But how we were to do that presented a problem. Several, in fact.

'First of all,' I began, 'When Thomas Hendry gets here later today, I shall charge him with arson at twenty-seven Tavona Road on the night of Diana Barton's murder. He strongly denied committing her murder, but held up his hands to setting fire to the house.'

'Has he got an alibi for James Barton's topping, guv?' asked DI Ebdon.

'I'm fairly satisfied that the murder of James Barton is not down to him, Kate, but I'll come to that later. However, I haven't dismissed the possibility that he murdered Diana. And that means that we could be looking for two murderers.'

'But if he set fire to the Bartons' house on the night of the murder, he must've topped Diana, surely,' said Kate, unwilling to give up a promising suspect. 'Why else would he have done it?'

'Yes, I know,' I said, 'but I'll get to that. Hendry gave us the first names of some of the people who were at Diana Barton's party.' I waved a hand at the whiteboard upon which Colin Wilberforce had recorded them. The use of a whiteboard was one thing about which the commander and I were in agreement; probably the only thing. He did not trust computers any more than I did, and said that he wanted to see information cast in stone. That, of course, would be difficult, but a whiteboard was the next best thing.

'Didn't he provide us with any surnames, guv?' asked DC Nicola Chance, a note of desperation in her voice as she realized the futility of trying to trace anyone by their first names alone.

'No. He claimed that he didn't know them, but there is one glimmer of hope. Hendry said that one of the guests was called Gaston, as you can see.' I waved a hand at the whiteboard again. 'And that he was possibly French. The chances are that he is Gaston Potier. He was, past tense, employed as a hotel manager by the company that had James Barton on its board. When we interviewed Barton he said that he'd arrived home one day and found Potier in bed with Diana. He sacked Potier next day, but didn't know where he went after that.'

'Do we know where Potier is now, guv?' asked Nicola.

'Not at the moment. It's possible, however, that Diana kept in contact with Potier, and that he was the Gaston at the party.' I glanced at DS Tom Challis, an ex-Stolen Car Squad officer. 'Try the Driver and Vehicle Licensing Agency, Tom, and see if they've got an address for him. If you don't have any luck with the DVLA, you could try the Border Agency, although with the free movement of EU citizens I don't suppose they would have a record. Failing that, I'll have to call in a favour from the *Police Judiciaire* in Paris.' Henri Deshayes, an *inspecteur* with the Paris police was always willing to help me out. For the price of a bottle of cognac. 'It's possible that Potier's now resident back in France, and came over just for the weekend of Diana's little get-together.'

'Any more joy on the fingerprints, guv?' asked DS Charlie Flynn.

'Yes, but first things first, Charlie.' I thumbed through the latest report to have arrived from the forensic science laboratory via Linda Mitchell, the senior forensic practitioner. 'The good news,' I began, 'if you can call it that, is that the DNA of the semen taken from Diana Barton's body matches the DNA of the hair that James Barton was clutching in his hand. So it looks as though the same guy was responsible for both murders. Maybe. But at least we can be certain that James Barton's killer was at Diana's party.'

'So it was one of the four men whose names are up there, guv,' suggested DI Kate Ebdon.

'Not necessarily, Kate. We don't know that we have a full list of all the guests yet. As you already know, Linda's team lifted a whole load of prints from Tavona Street, and they're still being processed. And you also know that she has eliminated those of James and Diana Barton, and that one set tallies with Thomas Hendry. Fingerprint Branch has now turned up another, by the name of Barry Pincher.'

Colin Wilberforce crossed to the whiteboard, and added Pincher to the name of Barry, and Potier to Gaston. Then he put question marks after each of them. Very careful is Colin.

'Pincher has several previous convictions for theft and burglary, and one for armed robbery. His last recorded address was in Lambeth. While you're on to the DVLA, Tom, you might as well see if they've got a different address for him than the one in records. The one we've got might be false.'

'Right, guv.' Challis made a note.

'Kate, hang on until Tom Challis has made his phone call,' I said to DI Ebdon, 'but if he doesn't turn up anything, take a DC to Pincher's last known address and bring him in.'

'Got it, guv,' said Kate.

'I think that'll do for the time being,' I said.

As I was about to send the team on its way, Colin Wilberforce replaced the receiver of his telephone. 'That was the head office of James Barton's bank, sir,' he said. 'Half an hour ago, someone attempted to draw money with Barton's debit card from an ATM in Kensington High Street.'

'But we advised the bank of Barton's murder, didn't we?' I said. 'And they put a stop on the account,

'Exactly so, sir,' said Wilberforce. 'The withdrawal was refused, and the card retained by the machine.'

'Where's the card now?'

'The bank's head office has made arrangements for it to be held by the Kensington branch until we collect it.'

'And everyone will have put their bloody fingers all over it, I suppose,' said Dave gloomily.

'Doubtless,' I agreed, 'but the experts might just be able to do something with it.' I turned to DC John Appleby. 'Get up to this Kensington bank straight away, John, and take the card direct to Fingerprint Branch.'

Tom Challis returned from making his phone call to the DVLA. 'I've got addresses for both Gaston Potier and Barry Pincher, guv,' he said, referring to a slip of paper. 'Pincher lives at Hake Road, Lambeth, which was the one we already had, and Potier was last resident at Rawton Way, Harrow on the Hill.'

'So Potier's still here,' I said. 'Excellent. That'll save me the cost of a bottle of brandy for Henri Deshayes. OK, Kate, away you go to Pincher's drum. Take Ray Furness with you, and feel Pincher's collar for him.' Ray Furness was an experienced DC, and he and Kate were more than capable of bringing in a suspect. 'You might as well turn over his drum while you're at it.'

'Of course, guv,' said Kate, a slight lifting of her chin indicating that she was going to search his house anyway, and didn't need to be told what to do.

'Finally, there might be some benefit in tracing Diana Barton's first husband. According to James Barton, he was married to Diana about seven years ago.' I looked at DC Nicola Chance. 'Perhaps you'd take that on, Nicola.'

'Right, sir,' said Nicola, and made a note.

'Dave, you and I will pay M'sieur Potier a visit, but I think that'll keep until later today. You never know, he might be in gainful employment.'

'Yes, sir, you never know,' said Dave pointedly. He held the view that villains were unlikely to work for their living, and he had already classified Potier as a villain.

At two o'clock that afternoon, Kate Ebdon telephoned from Charing Cross police station to announce that Barry Pincher was being held there. She also mentioned that he was complaining about having had his house searched, and being wrongfully arrested and falsely imprisoned. He also wanted a lawyer. Knowing his form, I wasn't surprised that Pincher knew the sort of noises to make when he was nicked.

It was a lovely sunny August day, and to Dave's undisguised horror, I decided that we'd walk up Whitehall to the police station in William the Fourth Street, a matter of half a mile or so. Unfortunately, Whitehall was thronged with tourists, and anyone who looks like a native of London will be stopped and asked inane questions. But luck was with us, and it didn't happen until we were almost at Trafalgar Square.

'Excuse me, sir,' said the speaker, a well-fed German with a thick, halting accent, and a limited command of English. 'Are you happening to know of the way at Buckminster Castle?'

I debated with myself, albeit briefly, whether he was interested in the location of Buckingham Palace, Westminster

Abbey or Windsor Castle. As he was in Whitehall I guessed that he wanted the nearest: the Queen's London residence.

I declined to show out that I spoke fluent German, about the only benefit of having been married to Helga for sixteen years. Helga Büchner was a physiotherapist at Westminster Hospital who, years ago, had pummelled my shoulder into working order again after a punch-up with a group of yobs in Whitehall. Following a whirlwind courtship, we were married. But she insisted on continuing to work even after our son Robert was born. One day she left him with a neighbour, and the little chap fell into the pond and drowned. He was only four. I was on the Flying Squad at the time, and I'll never forget that awful day. The guv'nor called me into his office and broke the news. Then he told me to take as much time off as I needed. The Job's good like that. But that tragedy, followed by blatant adultery on both sides, signalled the end of the marriage.

'I think you want Buckingham Palace,' I explained to the German. 'Go through Admiralty Arch over there,' I said, pointing, 'and you'll find it at the other end of The Mall.'

'Is that so far?'

'About three-quarters of a mile.' I knew this because I'd walked a beat along The Mall when I was a young PC. 'Very nearly a kilometre,' I added, trying to be helpful.

'Ach! So far? Is it that you can call for me a taxi?'

'No, I can't,' I said. I indicated a passing black cab. 'All you need to do is wave at one of those, and he'll take you there.' I had a feeling that the cabbie might take our German friend on the scenic route via Piccadilly Circus, Oxford Circus and Hyde Park Corner. Taxi drivers always seem to think that foreign tourists want to see as much of London as possible.

We reached Charing Cross police station without further interruption. Kate was with Barry Pincher in the interview room, but she had sent Ray Furness back to Curtis Green.

'I'm Detective Chief Inspector Brock of Scotland Yard,' I announced.

'Oh yeah, and what you going to stitch me up with this time, then?' Pincher was sprawled in a chair, and appeared unimpressed by my awesome announcement. 'An' I wanna know why I've been nicked.'

'You haven't been arrested,' I said, and turned to Kate. 'You didn't arrest Mr Pincher, did you, Inspector?'

'Certainly not, sir. I asked him to accompany me to the police station in order to assist us with our enquiries. And he did so, willingly.'

'Like bloody hell I did,' exclaimed Pincher. 'She had me arm up me back quicker than that. Anyway, if I ain't been nicked, I can go, yeah?'

'There's no hurry,' I said. 'Now then, Pincher, you were at a party at twenty-seven Tavona Street, Chelsea, on Saturday last, the twenty-seventh of July.'

'Who says I was?' Pincher attempted to sound confident, but the fact that we knew of his presence at the Bartons' house had clearly thrown him.

'Several of the other people who were also there told me,' I said.

'So what? It was a party. T'ain't illegal having a party, or going to one.'

'No, but murdering the hostess is,' put in Dave.

''Ere, bloody hold on.' Pincher sat bolt upright. 'I ain't had nothing to do with no murder. D'you mean someone topped Diana?' He contrived, not very successfully, to look surprised.

Dave raised his eyebrows to the ceiling at Pincher's use of a treble negative. I imagine he was regretting that there was no law against the use of bad English. 'Don't you ever read the newspapers?' he asked, and then answered his own question. 'No, I don't suppose you get any further than the sports section. Or, in the case of the *Sun*, page three.'

'I don't know nothing about no one getting topped. Diana was all right when I pushed off.' Pincher was beginning to sound a little desperate now.

'At what time did you last speak to her, Barry?' I asked.

'I can't rightly remember.'

'What my guv'nor means,' said Dave, 'is whether you spoke to her again after you'd screwed her.'

'Now look here—'

Kate Ebdon decided to take a hand in the questioning. 'Look, mate,' she began, her Australian accent becoming more menacing than usual, 'we know you didn't go there for canapés and a glass of plonk. You went there because Diana Barton liked a bit of rough, and I reckon they don't come much rougher than you. So, if I was you, I'd tell Mr Brock exactly what went down.' She opened her pocketbook, and pretended to read

an entry. 'Yes, I knew I'd got something about you here somewhere. I've been listening to the vibes on the grapevine, and
according to my latest information, I hear that the Heavy Mob
would like a word with you.' Police and villains alike invari-
ably referred to the Flying Squad as the Heavy Mob.

'That's a bloody lie. I've gone straight.' Pincher was now
beginning to get very anguished, and the threat of an interview
with the Flying Squad had done nothing to allay his fears that
he was about to be 'fitted up'. I'd read that some of his previous
offences had attracted the attention of the Flying Squad, and
that's never a smart thing to do.

'Who was the bird who came with you?' asked Dave, before
Pincher had had time to recover from Kate's verbal onslaught.

'What bird?'

'That's what I'm asking,' said Dave patiently. 'Liz, Debbie
or Charlene? Take your pick.'

Pincher was slowly realising that we knew more about this
party than he thought. 'It was Charlene.'

'Charlene who?'

'Charlene Hoyle. What d'you wanna know that for?'

'Because we intend to talk to her,' I said. 'Where does she
live?'

'With me.'

I glanced at Kate, and raised a questioning eyebrow.

'She wasn't there when we invited Mr Pincher to come
with us, sir,' said Kate.

'Well?' I turned back to Pincher.

'She's working, ain't she?'

'Where?' This was like pulling teeth, but there was nothing
unusual in that with a villain of Pincher's calibre.

'Some place up Mayfair.'

'And I don't suppose you know the name of this place.'

'S'right. I dunno.'

'And what do you do for a living? Assuming you do something in between your spells as one of Her Majesty's guests.'

'I'm a short-order cook down a burger bar. In the evenings,
six to midnight.'

'God help us,' muttered Dave. He glanced at Pincher's dirty
fingernails and probably decided that he would never eat a
burger again.

'At what time did you leave this party?' I asked.

'About midnight, I s'pose.'

'Weren't you short-order burgering that night, then?' asked Dave.

'How could I be if I was partying?' asked Pincher, a puzzled expression on his face. He seemed to think that Dave was a bit slow on the uptake. Bad mistake.

'To repeat my previous question,' I said, 'when did you last speak to Diana Barton?'

'Must've been about nine. I never saw her after that. She stayed in her bedroom for most of the evening. Leastways, from about nine o'clock onwards.'

'And I suppose each of the men went up to give her a seeing-to from time to time,' said Kate.

'Well, if they did, I don't know nothing about it.'

'Did you have sexual intercourse with Diana Barton at any time during the evening?'

'What, with Charlene there? You must be bloody joking, lady.'

'Have you ever had intercourse with Diana Barton?'

'No, of course I ain't.'

'Why did she ask you to her party, then?'

'I done a bit of decorating for her, an' she said she likes to have young people around the place. So I got an invite.'

'So, who were the other men at this party?' Kate knew what I'd been told by Tom Hendry, but it was a racing certainty that he'd not included everyone. Even if he knew.

'There was some smarmy French git called Gaston something, a bloke called Dale, and a couple of others. But I don't remember their names.'

'What was the name of the girl with Gaston?' asked Dave.

'That was Liz,' said Pincher promptly. 'She was definitely a fancy bit of stuff was that one. Long blonde hair and big boobs,' he added, confirming word for word what Hendry had told us.

'And presumably you sampled her,' suggested Dave.

'No. I told you, Charlene was there.'

I decided that we had got as much out of Pincher as we were going to get. At least for the time being.

'Very well,' I said, standing up. 'I shall admit you to police bail to return to this station in one month's time, or earlier if we send for you. Is that clear?'

'Why should I?'

'Because you're very close to being charged with the murder of Diana Barton, Pincher, that's why.'

'I told you that I never had nothing—'

'Shut it,' said Dave.

How on earth Diana Barton had gathered such a collection of low-lifes around her was a mystery. But we knew why she had. Given what her late husband had told us about her, Pincher's story that Diana simply liked to have young people around sounded a trifle specious. The question remained: could all of these men have had affairs with her in the past, or would she actively solicit any available man? If so, we were about to descend into a veritable cesspool of depravity.

Once out of Pincher's hearing, I asked Kate to arrange an observation on his house, and find out where Charlene Hoyle worked.

'D'you think she might've topped Diana then, guv?' asked Kate.

'Not necessarily, but she might know who did.'

Having left the custody sergeant to deal with the vast amount of paperwork that is involved in bailing an individual, Dave and I made for Harrow on the Hill and, we hoped, an interview with Gaston Potier. It was now five o'clock.

Rawton Way, Harrow on the Hill was a pleasant street of neat detached houses, each with white fencing and beautifully manicured front lawns. The driveways of these houses were occupied, for the most part, by top of the middle-range of family cars. Clearly Rawton Way was *the* place to live if you wanted to be regarded as a success, but I couldn't begin to imagine what mundane lives they must lead. Unless they were like Potier, or what I suspected him of being. There again, one never quite knows what goes on behind the Laura Ashley curtains of quiet London suburbs.

'Yes, what is it?' The woman who answered the door was of angular build and tall, as tall as me. Her short brown hair was cut in an unfashionable style, and she regarded us with a mixture of curiosity and apprehension. I wondered what was passing through her mind at the sight of two large men on her doorstep, one white and one black.

'We're police officers, madam,' I said. 'We'd like to speak to Mr Gaston Potier.'

'How do I know you're policemen?' the woman asked, a question doubtless prompted by the useless sticker on the glass panel of the door proclaiming the Potiers to be believers in Neighbourhood Watch.

I produced my warrant card. 'Detective Chief Inspector Brock of Scotland Yard,' I said, 'and this is Detective Sergeant Poole.'

'You'd better come in,' said the woman, apparently satisfied that we were the real thing, and showed us into a fussily furnished sitting room that abounded with all manner of ghastly ornaments. 'Sit down. I'll fetch Gaston for you.' Judging by her accent, this woman was English, and was definitely not the well-endowed, long-haired blonde called Liz that both Hendry and Pincher had enthused about.

Gaston Potier was a short man, shorter than the woman I presumed to be his wife. He was, I imagined, in his late thirties or early forties, with thinning black hair, and a moustache that was little more than an erratic line above his top lip. He certainly didn't look like the sort of French Lothario who I thought would have attracted Diana Barton, or even less, the woman called Liz.

'My wife tells me you are from Scotland Yard,' said Potier confidently, as he sat down opposite us. Seconds later his wife joined him.

'We are investigating the murder of James Barton,' I began, although that was not the principal reason we were there. I realized that any mention of the pneumatically constructed Liz in the presence of Mrs Potier was likely to be difficult. Not for us, but for Potier. I had, however, foreseen that eventuality, one I'd faced many times before when dealing with adulterous husbands, and had written two names on a piece of paper. I handed the slip of paper to Potier. The next move was up to him.

'I was wondering if you are in a position to help us with this matter, Mr Potier,' I said.

Potier scanned the names – Diana Barton and Liz – and a brief expression of anxiety flitted across his face before he regained his composure. He turned to his wife.

'You remember that I used to work for James Barton before

I got a better job, my dear, but that was some time ago. I
doubt whether I'll be able to assist these officers, so I shouldn't
waste your time listening to all this. You might as well get
on with whatever you were doing.' Potier might be French,
but he had an excellent command of English, and was smooth
and masterful with it.

Mrs Potier obviously didn't take kindly to being summarily
dismissed. Nevertheless, she rose from her seat, nodded briefly
in our direction and left the room.

'You were at a party at Diana Barton's house last Saturday
evening.' I made the statement confidently, in a way that
brooked no denial.

'What makes you think that?' Potier cast a furtive glance
at the sitting room door, even though it was now firmly closed.

'Other people who were there told me,' I said, now fairly
sure that we'd got the right Gaston. Nevertheless, even though
he'd admitted having once worked for James Barton, it didn't
necessarily mean he was the Gaston at the party. But it was
a pretty safe bet.

'But what has this to do with James Barton's murder.'

'I don't know, but it certainly had something to do with
Diana Barton's murder.'

'Diana is dead? *Mon dieu!*' Potier finally resorted to his
native language.

'Didn't you read about it in the newspaper?' I asked, amazed
that he should have been unaware of her death.

'I read of the fire there, of course. When did she die?'

'The night of the party.'

'But she was all right when I left.'

'Where is Liz?' asked Dave suddenly.

'Liz? Who is Liz?'

'Oh come on, Mr Potier,' said Dave. 'For a start her name
was on that piece of paper that you're still clutching in your
hand, and it was doubtless that name that gave you a bit of
a nasty turn. Furthermore she was at the party that Mr Brock
mentioned. What's her surname, and where does she live?'

Potier's shoulders slumped, and his face assumed an expression of despair. 'If my wife gets to hear of this—'

'Not from us, she won't,' I said. 'Perhaps it would be easier
for you to speak to us elsewhere,' I suggested. 'Where d'you
work?'

'I am the manager of a restaurant in the West End,' said Potier, and quoted the address.

'And Liz?'

'Liz Edwards is my *maîtresse d'hôtel.*'

'What time do you start work tomorrow?'

Potier thought briefly. 'On Saturdays I begin at about half past eleven in the morning,' he said.

'Very well. I'll expect to see you at West End Central police station at ten o'clock tomorrow morning. That'll be the nearest station to your restaurant. You know where that is, do you?'

'Yes, of course,' said Potier.

'Good. Well, don't make it necessary for me to come looking for you.'

'I will be there, Chief Inspector, I promise you. And thank you for your consideration.'

'Well, guv, what d'you think?' asked Dave as we walked back to the car. 'Think we should've nicked him?'

'On what grounds? Going to a party with a bird who's not his wife. The prisons would be full to overflowing, Dave.'

'Thought they were already, guv,' said Dave. 'Unfortunately they let the buggers out too soon.'

I rang Kate Ebdon on my mobile. 'Kate, I've made an appointment to see Gaston Potier tomorrow morning at ten o'clock. Can you go to Westminster Magistrates Court tomorrow with Tom Hendry?'

'No probs, guv,' said Kate.

'Good. Ask for a remand in custody on the grounds that he might interfere with witnesses.'

SEVEN

On Saturday morning, John Appleby brought me the result of the Fingerprint Branch officer's examination of the debit card that had been recovered from the ATM at Kensington. But it was negative. Although Appleby had placed it in a plastic bag, there were no discernible fingerprints on it. The bank staff had handled it carefully; they were apparently aware that any fraudulent use of a debit card could have the user's prints on it. It seems that police 'soaps' on TV do have some value, after all. But whoever had attempted to use the card had been careful, too. It looked very much as though he'd worn gloves, or had wiped the card clean after stealing it, and then inserted it into the ATM holding the edges. We all knew that the ATM itself would not produce any fingerprints capable of comparison; dozens of people would have used it after our villain.

However, it looked as though James Barton's killer had forced his victim to part with his PIN before murdering him. Assuming, of course, that it was the killer who'd attempted to use the card. On the other hand, it was possible that someone had chanced upon Barton's body after his murder, and before it was discovered by the traffic police, and had stolen his credit and debit cards. But that was irrelevant: the cards would've been of no value without the PIN, unless Barton had been stupid enough to make a note of the PIN in a diary. There hadn't been a diary or any form of notebook on his body when he was found. He may, however, have been in possession of a BlackBerry, or some similar technical gimmick, but if he had, that had gone too. Such are the complexities that frequently confront detectives in the course of an enquiry that had all the hallmarks of a random killing.

As John Appleby left, Nicola Chance came into my office. 'I've got details of Diana Barton's first husband, sir.'

'Well done, Nicola. What have you found out?'

'His name's Maurice Horton, sir, and he divorced Diana just over seven years ago. Diana was then married to James Barton a month later.'

'She didn't waste any time in getting hitched again,' I said.

'Perhaps Diana's new husband was another of her studs, sir,' said Nicola. 'For all we know he might've been screwing the arse off her for ages before they were married. And we know she'd hop into bed with anyone who was prepared to shaft her.'

I was always amused, and slightly taken aback, when Nicola Chance came out with a bawdy comment of that nature. She always gave the impression of being a demure young woman to whom such language would be completely alien.

'If that was the case, it must've been going on for a long time before her divorce from Horton,' I said. 'We know James Barton was seventy-two and probably past it when he died. Any indication of Horton's whereabouts, Nicola?'

'The address given on the divorce papers is Roget Drive, Pinner. The house is called En Passant. I've done a check on the electoral roll, and Maurice Horton appears to be living there along with a Faye Horton. I then did a check with the General Register Office at Southport. Maurice Horton is fifty years of age, and four years ago he was married to the said Faye Horton, who is thirty-five.'

'Good work, Nicola.' I made a note in my daybook. 'I shall have a word with him whenever I can fit it in.'

When Dave and I arrived at West End Central police station at ten o'clock, Potier was already waiting in the foyer. We conducted him to an interview room.

'I understand from our conversation with the late James Barton that you had an affair with his wife, Mr Potier.' I decided to get straight to the point.

'Mr Barton told you that?' Potier expressed surprise.

'He said he returned home one afternoon and found you in bed with Diana.'

'It was a mistake that he found us.'

'I imagine it was,' I said. 'Why on earth did you visit her at her home?'

'When we made the arrangement, she'd told me that James was attending a board meeting in Norwich that day, and that he would be away overnight. I got there at about two in the afternoon, and we went straight upstairs. It seemed safe enough, but while we were in bed – by then it was about three o'clock – the door to the bedroom was suddenly thrown open, and there was James. He seemed to be very furious, you know.'

I suppressed a laugh. 'I imagine he would've been,' I said. 'What happened next?'

'He told me to get out of his house, so I grabbed my clothes, ran downstairs and dressed, and then I left. But the next day he came to the hotel and fired me. I was the manager of the company's hotel in Bayswater at the time.' Potier didn't seem at all embarrassed by his admission. In fact he shrugged, as though it were one of the little misfortunes that occasionally befell an adulterer. 'Previously Diana had always come to the hotel, usually in the afternoon, and we would use one of the guest rooms. It was easy for me to arrange, being the manager. The staff wouldn't dare to ask questions.'

'Pity you didn't make such an arrangement on that occasion,' commented Dave.

Potier nodded sadly. 'You are so right, Sergeant Poole,' he said.

'How long have you been married?' I asked.

'Eight years. I met my wife when I was the assistant manager of one of the hotels in Ibiza. She was there on holiday by herself.'

'Was that one of the hotels owned by James Barton's company?'

'Yes, it was. I'd been with them for ten years. I started with the company as a reservations clerk and worked my way up to become a manager. It was a terrible shock when Mr Barton dismissed me.'

'But you didn't tell your wife that you'd been sacked, did you? Or the reason.' I guessed that to be the case from the brief conversation he'd had with her when we called at Rawton Way.

'Of course not. I told her I'd resigned. Shortly afterwards I got my present position as a restaurant manager.'

'But you maintained your affair with Mrs Barton even after you were sacked by Barton.'

'Yes. She was an attractive woman, and we enjoyed each other's company. She would take a room in a hotel for the afternoon, and I would join her there for a few hours.'

'D'you mean that she paid for the room?'

'Of course. Diana was a very rich woman.'

I thought it was more likely that James Barton had footed the bill, albeit unwittingly, and I found that rather amusing in a sadistic sort of way.

'So, what did she think when you turned up at her party with Liz Edwards?'

Potier smiled. 'She didn't mind. She was a very broad-minded woman.'

'So I gather,' I said.

'How long have you been conducting an affair with Miss Edwards?' asked Dave. 'Or is it Mrs Edwards?'

'Yes, she's married, but it's not an affair.'

'What is it, then, if it's not an affair?' queried Dave.

'Just an occasional flirtation. We meet at a hotel from time to time.' Potier spoke as though this was normal behaviour, and that there was a subtle difference between an affair and a flirtation. 'Sometimes it's just a quickie in my office at the restaurant.' He'd obviously mastered a few English colloquialisms.

'Does your wife know?'

Potier expressed shock. 'Of course not,' he protested. 'But I work long hours, and late. She does not suspect.'

'How old is Mrs Edwards?'

'She's twenty-two.'

'About this party,' I said. 'What was that for?'

Potier laughed. 'Diana said it was to celebrate her new kitchen, but it was a joke. She didn't need an excuse for a party.'

'She'd had other parties at her house, then?'

'Possibly, but if she had, I wasn't invited.'

'What time did this so-called kitchen party begin?'

'Four o'clock.'

'Four o'clock?' Diana Barton obviously believed in social and sexual marathons.

'Yes. It was a good time.' Potier spoke as though this was not out of the ordinary.

'Presumably you had sexual intercourse with Diana at some time during that evening, Mr Potier.'

'Of course. At about six o'clock. Then at half past eight Liz and I went to the basement. We both got undressed and spent an hour in the Jacuzzi. That's where we met a girl called Shelley. She was there by herself, but a few minutes later a man called Tom joined her.'

'Didn't Liz object to you having sex with Diana?' I asked.
'If she knew.'

'Of course not.' Potier smiled. 'She was hardly in a position to object, was she?'

This guy seemed to have no conscience at all. 'When was the last time you saw Diana, or spoke to her?'

'She went upstairs at eight o'clock, and as far as I know she never came back down again.'

This was getting much too complicated for my liking, and I was glad to see that Dave was taking copious notes. Potier's recollection of the times conflicted with Pincher's statement that Diana had gone upstairs at nine o'clock and didn't return to the party. But, there again, Potier admitted having gone to the Jacuzzi at eight thirty and staying there for an hour, so Diana might have come back downstairs while he and Liz were cavorting in the whirlpool. None of that surprised me however; it is rare to find two witnesses who tell the same story.

'Are you certain of those times?'

'Of course. In my job I have always to be aware of details, Mr Brock.'

'As you're so aware of details, Mr Potier,' said Dave, 'perhaps you can tell us the names of the other people who were at this party.'

'I know only the first names of some of them. There was a man named Dale who came with Debbie, an attractive girl who spoke a little French. We talked for a while of the Loire Valley. I come from there. I was tempted to make a date with her, but Dale never left her side, and I wasn't able to arrange anything. Then there was Barry with Charlene, and the man Tom I mentioned who was with Shelley, the girl in the Jacuzzi.' Potier sighed, and glanced at the ceiling. 'In no time at all Charlene was walking about with almost nothing on. She was a very attractive girl, too.' Potier sighed, presumably at a lost opportunity. 'They were all attractive girls.'

This was getting us nowhere, except to underline that both Gaston Potier and Diana Barton had the morals of alley cats. And in Potier's case an inflated concept of his appeal to women. But then, at last, came something important.

'Also there was a man called Bernie. His girlfriend was Samantha I think, but I'm not sure. I didn't pay much attention.'

'Do you know their surnames?' These were people whose names hadn't cropped up in our enquiries so far, and there was nothing to say that they'd used their real names anyway.

'I'm afraid not. Everyone seemed to be at pains only to use first names.'

'How old were these two people? Bernie and Samantha.'

Potier thought about that. 'He was quite old, fifty perhaps, and the girl was twenty-five or thereabouts, I should think. But there was another man there. His name was Bruce. I think he was from Australia, perhaps New Zealand. Even South Africa, or maybe from the north of England. It is hard for me to tell different English accents.'

'Did he bring a girl?'

'Possibly. It was difficult to know who had brought whom.'

Dave nodded his approval at the construction of that sentence.

'And did this Bruce go upstairs with Diana?'

'Yes, I think so. Yes, he did. I remember now that she took his arm and said that it was his turn.'

'What time was that?'

'Eight o'clock,' said Potier without hesitation.

'And did you see him again?'

'Yes, just after Liz and I came up from the Jacuzzi at half past nine. That's when we left. I drove Liz home, and then went to my own place.'

'Wasn't Liz Edwards's husband surprised that you drove his wife home?'

'No, not at all. It often happens. I think I told you that she is my *maîtresse d'hôtel*. We both work late, and I don't like her to take public transport at that time of night, and a taxi that far is expensive. It's not a problem because she only lives in Lisson Grove. It's on my way.'

This was another variation from what we'd been told by Hendry. Hendry was adamant that all the guests left at the same time, just before the police arrived. But, as he hadn't mentioned Bernie and Samantha, we had to accept that his recall might be flawed, or downright obstructive.

I asked Potier for Liz Edwards's address, in the hope that she would have something to add to what Potier had told us.

'It would be better if you spoke to her at the restaurant, Mr Brock. For the sake of propriety, you understand.'

'Of course. You said just now that you work late at your restaurant. How did you manage to get to Diana's party at four o'clock in the afternoon? And you were at home yesterday when we called in the early evening.'

'I have a very good assistant manager,' said Potier. 'And Liz has a deputy,' he added, forestalling my next question. 'We have a shift system, I think you call it.'

'Thank you for coming in, Mr Potier,' I said. 'Should there be anything else, we know where to find you.'

'Of course. I'm very sad to hear of Diana's death. But if you wish to speak to me again, perhaps you would be so good as to contact me at my restaurant. And, as I said, that goes for Mrs Edwards as well.' Potier smiled apologetically, and handed me a business card. 'You would be welcome to have a meal there any time. On the house, of course,' he added with a wink.

'Thank you,' I said, but it was dangerous practice for a detective to accept free meals from someone who could turn out to be a suspect. I knew of detectives who'd come unstuck over what the Job regards as bribery and corruption. I was fairly sure that Potier had not been implicated in Diana Barton's murder, but you never know.

Dave and I called in at Curtis Green to see if anything of consequence had occurred. Nothing had.

'I got a remand in custody to Kingston Crown Court for Hendry, guv,' said Kate. 'Monday the second of September.'

'Is it in the diary, Kate?'

'Of course, guv.' Kate gave me one of those looks.

It was now half past one on a Saturday, I was hopeful that Maurice Horton would be at home, and that he might be able to shed some light on Diana's life before she married James Barton.

Roget Drive, Pinner, overlooked Pinner Park. The house – En Passant – appeared large enough to have at least six bedrooms, and was probably worth a million pounds at least. It was set back from the road in its own grounds, and a winding, hedge-lined, gravel driveway, shielded from the road by a row of leylandii conifers, led to the front door. A Mercedes CL 65 AMG, definitely top of the range, was parked close to the house.

'Funny name for a house, Dave,' I said, as we alighted from our bottom-of-the-range police car.

'It's French, guv. It means "in passing",' said Dave. 'I suppose it means that he'll be moving on before long.' Such is Dave's whimsical logic.

The woman who answered the door studied us carefully before enquiring what we wanted.

'Is Mr Horton at home?' I asked.

'Who is it what I shall say?' The woman, an attractive girl in her twenties, spoke haltingly, and with a thick accent, possibly East European.

'We're police officers.'

'Just step inside the house, thank you.'

We followed the woman, presumably a housekeeper or maid, into a large entrance hall from which a broad sweeping staircase wound its way up one side.

The woman entered a room on the left of the hall, only to reappear moments later. 'Please this way come,' she said, and led us into a spacious sitting room with tall windows that looked out on to the drive.

A tall man dressed in tan linen slacks with an open-necked shirt and brown loafers, stood in front of a massive York stone fireplace.

'Mr Horton?' I asked.

'Yes, I'm Maurice Horton.' We knew that Horton was fifty years of age, but he looked older. 'Katya tells me you're from the police.'

'That's correct, sir,' I said, and introduced Dave and me.

'How can I possibly help the police? Is there something wrong? My wife's out shopping for clothes. She's not had an accident, has she?' Horton asked the question with a worried expression. But he probably didn't know that detective chief inspectors don't call to tell someone of a road accident.

'Not as far as I know, Mr Horton. I rather wanted to talk to you about your first wife.'

'Diana? Why on earth d'you want to ask me questions about her?' Horton invited us to take a seat, and sat down opposite us. 'We were divorced over seven years ago.'

'I'm sorry to have to tell you that she's dead, sir.'

'Really? Well, I'm sorry to hear that, but our marriage is

all in the past. I've moved on, and remarried. What happened,
a road accident?' Horton did not seem unduly concerned at
news of his ex-wife's death.

'No, sir, she was murdered.'

'Good God! But there was nothing in the papers about it.'

'No, we deliberately withheld that information from the
press, Mr Horton.' Nevertheless, I was surprised that he hadn't
read of the fire, but perhaps he hadn't made the connection
even if he'd known Diana's current address.

'How can I help, then?' asked Horton again.

'We're trying to establish a motive for Diana's death, sir.'

'What happened to her?'

'A week ago she held a party at her house in Tavona Street,
Chelsea, apparently to celebrate the installation of a new
kitchen.'

'You're joking.' Horton gazed at me with a half smile on
his face. 'She hated parties, and why on earth should she have
held a party for something as banal as that?'

'I have to say I found it rather odd,' I said, 'but that's the
information I've received from several sources.'

'What an extraordinary thing to do.' Horton appeared as
mystified as I'd been when first told of the reason for the
party. But I now knew that the kitchen story was merely an
excuse for what had probably been planned as an orgy in the
first place.

'However,' I continued, 'at just after midnight last Sunday
police were called because of the noise, although by then the
noise had abated. But a short while later the house caught
fire, and the fire brigade found Mrs Barton's body in the
master bedroom. She'd been stabbed.'

'And you've no idea who was responsible?'

'Not at this stage, Mr Horton, no.' I thought it unnecessary
to tell this man that I'd arrested Thomas Hendry for setting
fire to the Bartons' house. And there'd been no mention of it
in the press.

'How d'you think I can assist you, then?'

'It would help if you could start by telling me what sort of
person Diana was, and what led to your divorce?'

'I don't see how that can help, but it was . . .' Horton paused.
'I imagine it's best described as incompatibility. For one thing
I play a lot of golf. But my golf – an obsession, I suppose you'd

call it – combined with a love of frequent exotic holidays, in particular the Caribbean, or touring in France, didn't interest Diana and led us to split up after twenty years of marriage. We really had nothing in common.'

'Were there any children?' I asked.

'Yes, just the one, a son Gregory. He's a mining engineer and lives in Australia. He married an Australian girl, I believe, and it looks as though he's settled there for good now.'

'Do you have an address for him, Mr Horton?'

'No, I'm afraid not. We've not been in touch with each other since I divorced Diana. I got the impression he thought I shouldn't have left her.'

'Would I be right in thinking that Diana wasn't interested in being little more than a housewife, then?' I asked, reverting to my original line of questioning.

'Very much so. That and helping out at a charity shop twice a week. She got involved in a lot of charity work. Oh, and she belonged to the Women's Institute when we lived in Wiltshire. Took a great interest in organising the annual WI flower competition while we were there.' Horton took out a packet of cigarettes and lit one. As an afterthought he offered one to Dave and me, but we both declined. 'I suppose the best way to describe her was domesticated.'

This was an entirely new slant on the character of the adulterous, fun-loving Diana Barton. I hesitated before posing my next question.

'Were you aware of any extra-marital affairs Diana might have had?'

'Affairs?' Horton laughed scornfully. 'Who, Diana? Good heavens no. Whatever makes you ask that?'

I outlined what we had learned about Diana's sexual activities, including the affair on the cruise, and the one with Gaston Potier, although I didn't mention the names of either of her paramours. Neither did I tell Horton what we'd heard had taken place at the kitchen party.

'Well, I have to say I'm surprised. This doesn't sound at all like the woman I was married to. Are you sure we're talking about the same person, Inspector?'

'It's *chief* inspector, sir.' I was always irritated by TV detective chief inspectors who not only allowed themselves to be

addressed as inspector, but sometimes introduced themselves
as such. There is quite a difference: about eight grand a year,
in fact.

'Oh, I'm sorry, Chief Inspector,' said Horton, but his slight
smile gave the impression that he didn't think it all that
important.

It crossed my mind that Diana might have had affairs during
her first marriage, but had been sufficiently devious to keep
them from Horton.

Dave produced a copy of a studio portrait of Diana Barton
that we'd recovered from James Barton's smoke-filled study
on the first floor of the house at Tavona Street. 'Is that her?'
he asked, handing the print to Horton.

Horton glanced at it. 'Yes, that's the Diana I was married
to.' He shook his head. 'Unbelievable. She wasn't the slightest
bit interested in sex,' he said suddenly. 'That was another of
our problems.'

I'm glad Horton had said that. It wasn't the sort of intrusive
question that I'd been prepared to ask, but it was useful to know,
even though it conflicted with what we knew of the woman.
Or thought we knew.

Horton paused for a moment. 'I understand that she married
again. We've not kept in touch, you see.'

'Yes, she did, to a James Barton. He was murdered last
Thursday.'

'Good God!' Horton shook his head, as though trying to
come to terms with what I'd told him. 'It's not the James
Barton who was involved in hotels, is it?'

'Yes. Did you know him?'

'Not all that well,' said Horton. 'Our paths did cross occasionally. I'm a venture capitalist, you see.' He gave a diffident
smile, and waved a hand in the air. 'As you can see from this
house, I've been rather successful at it.' He paused to stub out
his cigarette. 'Do you think the same person was responsible
for both murders?'

'We don't know at this stage,' I said, although the DNA
evidence seemed to point to it. But I had no intention of telling
Horton that.

There was a sound of a car approaching the house, and the
crunching of gravel. I glanced out of the window in time to
see a woman alighting from a white Lexus that she'd parked

next to the Mercedes. Moments later, the front door slammed, and a woman's voice called out 'Hello, darling.'

'Ah, that'll be my wife,' said Horton as the sitting room door opened.

The woman who entered was obviously much younger than Maurice Horton; in fact, we knew there to be a difference of fifteen years in their ages. She had cropped blonde hair, and was stylishly dressed in an elegant trouser suit. It looked expensive, and I'm sure my girlfriend would've been able to put an exact price on it. Mrs Horton carried two large bags bearing the names of well-known West End fashion houses.

All three of us stood up, and she gazed at Dave and me. 'I see we have company, darling. I didn't recognize the car on the drive.'

'These gentlemen are from the police, Faye.' Horton turned to us. 'This is my wife Faye,' he said.

'Are we in trouble?' Faye Horton shot an engaging smile in our direction, put her shopping bags on the floor near the door, and sat down in an armchair opposite her husband.

But it was Maurice Horton who replied. 'They're enquiring about Diana. She's been murdered.'

'Your first wife, you mean?'

'Yes, and her husband has been murdered as well.'

'Well, you haven't seen her since the divorce, have you?' There was an element of suspicion, accusation even, in the glance Faye Horton gave her husband. But apart from that the news had no impact on her.

'Of course not. I didn't even know where she lived until these officers told me.'

We had learned a little more of the enigma that was Diana Barton, but it didn't help very much.

'Thank you, Mr Horton,' I said, as Dave and I stood up.

'D'you know where and when the funeral will be held?' asked Horton.

'Not at the moment.'

'You're not thinking of going, surely?' asked Faye Horton sharply. It sounded like an order.

'Er, no, not really, darling.'

I got the impression that all was not well in the Horton marriage, and wondered whether Maurice Horton had had a different reason for divorcing Diana. A reason he'd not

furnished. But that was of no concern to me or my enquiry.
Maybe.

'Thank you, Mr Horton,' I said, as Dave and I stood up. 'I
don't think either of you can help us further.' But in that I was
wrong.

EIGHT

'**D**'you remember the two people that Potier said were at the party?' I asked, as Dave and I drove back to Curtis Green. 'The ones that no one else mentioned: a young woman and a much older guy.'

'Bernie and Samantha,' replied Dave promptly. 'Are you thinking what I'm thinking, guv? That they might've been Maurice Horton and Katya?' he suggested. 'She's a good-looking girl, and that wife of Horton's looks to be one very cold bitch. I wouldn't blame him if he was having a fling with Katya.'

'I must admit that the same thought occurred to me, Dave. It's a pity we didn't ask Potier whether the girl called Samantha spoke with a foreign accent.'

'I'll give him a bell,' said Dave. 'Of course, if he didn't speak to her, we shan't know.'

'No, but Hendry or Pincher might remember them.' I waited until Dave had negotiated a tricky roundabout. 'I agree with you about Faye Horton. I formed the opinion that she was a bit of a tartar.'

'And some,' said Dave. 'I reckon she leads Maurice a dog's life. And if those shopping bags were anything to go by she hits his bank account something rotten.'

It was getting on for six o'clock by the time we got back to the office, and I checked the incident room to see if anything of consequence had occurred in our absence. Nothing had.

'I think we'll call it a day, Dave,' I said. 'In fact, there's nothing more we can do until Monday. Is Madeleine working tomorrow?'

'No, sir,' said Dave. 'Ballet dancers don't dance on Sundays as a rule.' There was an element of restrained sarcasm in his reply.

'Take the day off, then.'

It was nearly half past seven when I knocked at Gail's door.

'Hello, stranger,' she said, as she invited me in.

'I thought I'd take you out to dinner, darling.' I'm incredibly generous when the mood takes me. 'There's a new place opened in Kingston that I think might be worth a try. By the way,' I added, handing her a small package, 'my cleaning lady, Mrs Gurney, has washed your thong.'

Gail took the package with a smile, but without comment. 'Come in and help yourself to a drink,' she said. 'I'll just go up and get changed. Perhaps you'd bring me a gin and tonic in a minute.'

'Why d'you need to get changed?'

'I can't go out looking like this, my love. I'll just find something casual to put on.'

Gail was wearing 'something casual' now: jeans, a white tunic and a wide black leather belt. And she looked really good.

'I don't see anything wrong with what you've got on,' I said.

'No, you wouldn't, Harry,' said Gail cuttingly. 'Won't be a moment.'

Ten minutes later, I delivered her G and T, but she'd made little progress other than spreading a variety of clothes on the bed.

The 'moment' she'd said it would take turned out to be half an hour, but it was worth the wait. She looked terrific in a white trouser suit with a silver circle suspended on a slender chain around her neck, and for once her long blonde hair, usually held back in a ponytail, was worn loose around her shoulders.

'I thought we'd walk,' I said.

We crossed the Portsmouth Road and strolled along Queen's Promenade for the mile or so into Kingston town centre. Other couples were walking along the river bank enjoying the sunny weather of early August, and I noticed how many of the men shot admiring glances in Gail's direction. It's good for a man's ego to have his girlfriend admired, provided that's as far as it goes.

During our meal, which wasn't as good as I'd hoped, Gail raised the subject, once again, of trying for a part in a forthcoming play in the West End.

'It's a revival of J.B. Priestley's *An Inspector Calls*,' she said.

'Which part are you after, the inspector's?' I asked. 'If they're updating it, you should have a word with Kate Ebdon. She'll tell you how a real woman inspector carries on. Then again, perhaps not,' I added hurriedly, recalling what I'd heard about the reputation Kate had acquired on the Flying Squad.

I got one of those looks. 'No, it's the wife's part,' said Gail.

My reaction to this was lukewarm. If Gail went back to the stage, I would see even less of her than I saw now. It wasn't as if she needed the money; her father George Sutton, a property developer who lived in Nottingham, gave Gail a substantial allowance. I'd met George a few times. He was a charming man, and his only character flaw was his boring passion for Formula One motor racing and the land speed record, about which he would talk incessantly. Until his wife Sally stopped him.

I put my thoughts into words. 'Do you have to go back on the stage?' I asked. 'It'd mean you'd be late turn six days a week, with matinees on Wednesday and Saturday.'

'Would you give up the police force?' Gail asked. It was her usual irrefutable counter to my objections.

'That's different,' I said. 'What else could I do?'

'You needn't do anything. You could live on my allowance and become a kept man,' said Gail impishly. 'Then I'd have you all to myself all day.'

'Except when you were on stage,' I said.

And so we reached our usual impasse. But I hoped that Gail's occasional yearning for a return to the footlights was but a passing fancy, and that she'd forget all about it. Or maybe, I thought selfishly, someone else would get the part.

We spent Saturday night and Sunday at Gail's town house. We rose at eleven, showered and spent a lazy day lounging about listening to CDs and eating when we felt like it.

'It's time we had a holiday,' said Gail suddenly.

'I'm in the middle of a complicated murder enquiry,' I said. 'I shouldn't really be here now. I'm sure there are things waiting for me at the office.'

'I sometimes think you create work for yourself,' said Gail, who really had no understanding of what a detective's professional life entailed. 'Why don't we have a week in Paris? We could meet up with your old friend Henri and his wife. That'd be fun.'

I knew exactly what that would mean. As I mentioned earlier, Henri Deshayes is an *inspecteur* in the *Police Judiciaire* with whom I had liaised from time to time. That part of it was all right; all Henri wanted to do was talk about the Job and drink cognac in some pleasant pavement cafe. But his wife Gabrielle, a former dancer at the *Folies-Bergères*, was an ardent clothes shopper, and that spelled trouble. Believe me, there's nothing more taxing for men than following a couple of fashion conscious women around the highly priced haute couture establishments of Paris.

I arrived at the office at nine o'clock on the Monday morning, Gail's suggestion of a week in Paris still unresolved.

Colin Wilberforce had added to the whiteboard the names of Bernie and Samantha, the two partygoers Potier had mentioned. And having read Dave's statement, Colin had also listed Maurice and Faye Horton, and Katya Kaczynski, as 'persons of interest'. Colin, by some assiduous search of police records, had discovered Katya's surname, and that she was Polish.

On reflection, I didn't think that either the Hortons or Katya were of any real interest. As Dave and I had discussed, it was possible that Maurice Horton was having an affair with the shapely Katya, but that would only concern us provided neither of them was murdered. I always think of these things; Pinner falls within the area for which HSCC West is responsible, and the commander would be bound to see a connection. He loved making connections.

At ten o'clock, Kate Ebdon came into my office.

'We've discovered where Charlene Hoyle works, guv,' she announced, and handed me a slip of paper with the details. 'D'you want to interview her?'

I glanced at my watch. 'Why not?' I said. 'We'll see her at wherever she works. What does she do there?'

'She's a receptionist at a hairdressing salon.'

Charlene Hoyle, Barry Pincher's girlfriend, was seated behind a computer, and glanced up with a welcoming smile as Kate and I entered. Judging by the decor and location of the salon, in the heart of London's West End, I guessed that the prices would be astronomical, and the fact that no tariff was exhibited confirmed my suspicions.

Charlene gave me a strange questioning look, probably wondering what a man was doing in a woman's hairdressing establishment, and then turned her attention to Kate. 'How may I help you, madam?' she enquired politely, but without managing to disguise her native Essex accent.

I'd already decided to let Kate do the talking. Without a word, she held her warrant card in front of Charlene's nose, and sat down in the chair provided for clients.

'It's about the party at twenty-seven Tavona Street on Saturday the twenty-seventh of last month.'

Charlene was clearly alarmed by this terse introduction. 'What party?' she blurted out. Obviously a knee-jerk reaction.

'We can do this here, or down at the nick,' said Kate quietly.

'Barry said you'd been to see him.'

We'd already decided that Charlene Hoyle would have nothing to add to what we knew already, but we were keen to discover more about Bernie and Samantha, the mystery couple mentioned by Gaston Potier.

'There was a guy there called Bernie who was with a girl called Samantha. What d'you know about them?'

'Excuse me a minute.' Charlene took a credit card from a departing customer, and ran it through her machine. Once the woman had entered her PIN, and been given her receipt, Charlene turned her attention once more to Kate. 'Bernie was an old guy, about fifty at least, I should think. He kept trying to chat me up, but Barry threatened to chin him if he didn't clear off, and he never bothered me again.'

'And what about Samantha?'

'Stupid cow, she was.'

'How old?'

''Bout my age, I s'pose.'

'Which is?'

'Twenty-nine.'

'Did you speak to her? Did she have a foreign accent?' Having read the statement of my interview with the Hortons, Kate was obviously making a connection with Katya Kaczynski.

'Dunno. I never spoke to her.'

Another client entered the salon, and Charlene spent a few minutes dealing with her.

'What d'you reckon, guv?' asked Kate.

'Waste of time,' I said.

'OK, Charlene, that'll be all,' said Kate, once the girl had finished with the latest client. 'For now.' She always managed to leave a threat hanging in the air.

We walked out into the sunlight of Oxford Street, and I hailed a cab. I wasn't going to risk another walk through the tourist-thronged West End.

'What d'you think, guv? Could they have been Horton and Katya?'

'No idea,' I said. 'Seems unlikely, but Horton could've been lying when he said he hadn't seen Diana since the divorce. Somehow, I can't see Faye Horton letting her husband off the leash that easily. In my experience women who are married to millionaires are loath to let them out of their clutches.'

'Mind if I do a bit of digging on the Hortons?' asked Kate.

'Not at all, but I don't know what you expect to find.'

But in the event, the result proved to be surprising, and turned the enquiry on its head.

As we were in the West End, I decided to take the opportunity to speak to Liz Edwards, with whom Gaston Potier enjoyed what he called 'an occasional flirtation'.

The restaurant had an air of catering mainly for the upmarket business expense customer. The white napery was of the finest linen, the chairs – at first sight – very comfortable. And the premises were carpeted with thick pile throughout.

The young woman who glided toward us was tall, blonde and endowed with a splendid figure. From the description given us by Tom Hendry and Barry Pincher, who'd both enthused over the woman's long blonde hair and big boobs, this was obviously Liz Edwards.

'A table for two, sir?'

'Are you Mrs Edwards?' I asked, wanting to make sure.

'Yes, I am.' A frisson of concern crossed the woman's face.

'We're police officers, Mrs Edwards. Would it be possible to have a word with you in private?'

Liz Edwards glanced around and beckoned to a waiter attired in a long white apron.

'Charles, would you take over for a minute or two. I have to speak to this lady and gentleman.'

'*Oui, madame.*' Charles nodded, and turned to deal with two men who had followed us in.

Mrs Edwards led us through the restaurant to a small office at the rear. Once inside, she closed the door. 'Are you the officers who spoke to Gaston?'

'That's correct. I take it he's not here today.'

'No, he's taken the day off,' said Liz Edwards. 'Please sit down, but I'm sorry that the chairs are not very comfortable.' She smiled an apology and sat down behind the desk.

'Mr Potier probably told you that we're investigating the murder of Diana Barton, Mrs Edwards,' I began, as Kate and I sat down. 'I'm told by Mr Potier that you accompanied him to a party at her house the night she was killed.'

'Yes, that's right. What a dreadful thing to have happened.'

'We're anxious to trace everyone who was at the party, Mrs Edwards, and I was hoping that you might be able to fill in some of the gaps for us. Mr Potier has provided us with a few of the names, but are you able to help?'

'Not really. I was horrified at some of the people there, and the things they were doing. Most of the women were wandering about half naked. It's not the sort of party I'm accustomed to. To be perfectly honest, I did my best to distance myself from them. In fact, it seemed to be getting so out of hand that I asked Gaston to take me home.'

'What time was that, Mrs Edwards?' asked Kate.

'Half past nine or thereabouts.' Liz Edwards seemed to be very self-assured, and her poise tended to confirm her claim that it was not her 'sort of party'.

But it was at that point that Kate decided to burst Mrs Edwards's bubble. 'Mr Potier told us that at half past eight you and he went down to the Jacuzzi in the basement, and that you were both naked. Is that true?'

Liz Edwards blushed scarlet, and looked down, staying silent.

'Mrs Edwards?' said Kate.

'Yes, it's true. I wasn't wearing anything,' said Liz quietly, and flicked a strand of hair out of her eyes.

'And I understand from Mr Potier that you didn't object when he earlier disappeared to Mrs Barton's bedroom for the purpose of having sex with her.'

'I was hardly in a position to object, was I?' snapped Liz defiantly.

Kate smiled. 'I suppose not.'

I got the impression that being questioned by a woman officer was discomfiting Mrs Edwards, and that she would far rather have spoken to me alone. I've noticed in the past that women are far more open with a male officer when talking about their adulterous relationships and sexual proclivities.

'And you're adamant that you didn't know the names of any of the other guests at the party. What about a man called Bernie?'

'Oh, yes, I do remember him. He was about fifty, I should think. He had a worn expression about him, as though he'd seen life. Which was more than could be said for the others there. There were a couple of men who were quite rough diamonds, not at all sophisticated. I wouldn't have been surprised to learn that they worked on a building site.'

'But you didn't discover their names,' I said, although I was certain that she was referring to Hendry and Pincher.

'No. As I said, I tried to avoid the other people there, and I spent most of the time talking to Gaston.'

'What about the girl you met in the Jacuzzi? Mr Potier said you went there at about half past eight,' said Kate. 'D'you remember her?'

'A tart,' said Liz dismissively. 'I think she was called Shelley, or some TV soap name like that. One of the rough men joined her later on, and that's when we left.'

'And presumably they were naked too?'

'Yes.' But then there was a spark of fire. 'Look, is all this really necessary? I mean does it help you find whoever murdered Mrs Barton?'

'We never know until we ask, Mrs Edwards,' I said smoothly. 'Do you recall an Australian man called Bruce?'

'I didn't talk to him, but I do remember hearing an Australian accent. A rather uncouth man. Muscular, with a good conceit of himself.'

'What about a girl called Samantha?' asked Kate. 'Do you recall seeing her?'

'The name doesn't mean anything.'

'Thank you for your assistance, Mrs Edwards,' I said, finally deciding that this woman couldn't, or wouldn't, help. 'I doubt we'll need to trouble you further.'

Liz Edwards gave a curt nod, and showed us to the door of the restaurant without another word.

'Stuck up bitch,' said Kate as we reached the street. 'I wouldn't mind betting she was up for it. All this nonsense about the wrong sort of people, but she was quick enough to get her kit off and jump into the Jacuzzi. I think she knew more than she was telling.'

'Probably, Kate,' I said, 'but I doubt if it would've been of any assistance to us. And if her attitude is what she professed it to be, I wouldn't give much for Potier's chance of continuing his "flirtation" with her. Particularly since he'd told us about their naked frolics in the Jacuzzi.'

'I telephoned Gaston Potier at home, guv.' Dave was in the incident room when Kate and I returned. 'He didn't talk to either Bernie or Samantha at the party, so he doesn't know whether the girl had a foreign accent. So, it's still possible that it was Maurice Horton and Katya.' He was clearly loath to abandon that idea.

'No more than I expected,' I said. 'Any luck with tracing the other people at the party who we haven't yet identified?'

'Not so far,' said Dave. 'It's virtually impossible with only their first names to go on.'

It was what Nicola Chance had implied, and I knew it to be true.

It was on Tuesday morning that Kate Ebdon came up with the information that changed the course of the enquiry.

'I spent yesterday afternoon on the computer to Companies House in Cardiff, guv. I thought it might be interesting to find out a bit more about Maurice Horton.'

'And did you?'

Kate sat down and balanced a pile of computer printouts on her knee. 'Certainly did.' She glanced at the first page. 'Among other interests, Maurice Horton's venture capitalist outfit owns a property development company that doesn't seem to be doing much in the way of business. But here's the interesting bit. Horton is a majority shareholder of that company, fifty-five per cent, and Diana Barton owns the other forty-five per cent. And they're both directors.'

'And he claimed not to have seen her since the divorce,' I said.

'That might be true,' said Kate. 'According to the latest

figures the dividends, which were substantial up to two years ago, are paid into her bank account, but the address shown for her in the company records doesn't exist. Not that it matters; being the majority shareholder, Horton would be able to make all the decisions without reference to Diana. At a guess, I'd say that the false address was deliberately to hide her whereabouts from Horton.'

'Providing a false address could be an offence.'

Kate glanced up and laughed. 'Bit difficult to prosecute her now, guv,' she said. 'Anyway, I called in a favour from a guy I know in the Divorce Registry at Holborn.'

'What did he have to say?' I wondered briefly what sort of favour this individual owed Kate, but thought it best not to pursue it.

'It appears that Diana Barton's retention of her shares and her directorship were part of the divorce settlement. On her marriage to James Barton, her name was changed in the records from Horton to Barton. But there was no provision for her to cede the shares to Horton on her remarriage.'

'And because he had access to the records, Horton must've known that Diana had married again.'

'Looks like it,' said Kate.

'And yet he claimed not to have known, or at least was vague about it.'

'I reckon it's a thorn in his side,' suggested Kate. 'And I think that he'd be very keen to lay hands on those profitable shares all for himself.'

'Or even more likely that Faye Horton was keen for him to do so.'

'Exactly,' said Kate. 'It's a funny thing about millionaires: they always want even more money than they've got.'

'Strange that a man with his resources wasn't able to find out where Diana lived,' I said.

'Maybe he did try, and maybe he did find out, guv.'

'But if he did, it poses the question of why he bothered. I doubt that Diana would've parted with the shares in any event. I think we'll need to have another word with Maurice Horton, Kate, and try to discover what dark secret he's hiding. But I'm loath to drive all the way to Pinner on the off-chance that he's there.'

'When were you thinking of going?'

'Right now if possible. But he might not be there.'

'I'll make a phone call, guv,' said Kate, and disappeared to her own office. She returned a few minutes later. 'He's at home, guv.'

I laughed. 'I suppose you did your wrong number trick, did you?' Kate's ploy was to make a call and immediately start talking as though she was connected to the right number. When eventually the person at the other end identified himself, usually in desperation, Kate would claim it was a wrong number. In that way she knew he was at home.

Kate laughed too. 'Always works,' she said.

NINE

The Mercedes and the Lexus were parked side by side when we arrived at En Passant.

Once again it was Katya Kaczynski who answered the door. 'Oh, it is you,' she said. 'It is Mr Horton you are wanting to speak at, yes?'

'Yes,' I said, and Kate and I followed Katya into the house.

Faye Horton was alone in the sitting room, watching television. She crossed to the set and switched it off as Katya showed us in.

'I suppose you're wanting to speak to Maurice again,' she said, a measure of irritation in her voice.

'Yes please, Mrs Horton.'

'He's working in his study. I'll get him,' said Faye, but instead of leaving the room, or sending for Katya, she picked up the handset of an internal phone from the table beside her chair, and summoned her husband. She spent the intervening moments carefully appraising Kate's outfit. Fortunately it was one of those rare days when she'd opted for a light grey business suit, court shoes and gold earrings.

'Good afternoon.' Horton, attired in a white shirt and designer jeans, his bare feet in expensive sandals, exuded confidence and charm. 'Please sit down, and tell me how I can help you.'

'This is Detective Inspector Ebdon, Mr Horton,' I said, appreciating that Horton had not met Kate before. 'I'll come straight to the point. I understand that Diana Barton was a shareholder in your property company. A substantial shareholder.'

'My goodness, you have been doing your homework, *Chief* Inspector.' I noticed that he emphasized the 'chief'. 'Does this have some relevance to her murder?'

'I don't know. Does it?'

Horton smiled. 'You tell me, Mr Brock. You're the one investigating this matter.'

'I was wondering why you hadn't told me this when I was here last.'

'Perhaps my husband didn't think it was relevant,' said Faye Horton. 'And I have to say I can't see that it is.'

'Leave this to me, Faye,' said Horton sharply.

'Well, it seems that this is an unnecessary intrusion into your affairs, darling,' said Faye, clearly not intending to be silenced.

'I have to agree with my wife, Mr Brock,' said Horton. 'Why are you so interested in this business of the shares?'

'Was there any provision for the disposal of them on your wife's death?'

'Not that I know of. To be honest, I never visualized that she would die before me. I suppose it's a possibility I should have considered. As a matter of interest, have your enquiries revealed what happens to them now?'

Kate decided to make a contribution, and I was happy for her to do so; she'd done the search of company records and was more familiar with the set-up than me. 'Presumably her entire estate would have passed to her husband James. But as he died within twenty-eight days of her demise, his estate will go to Diana. Providing it's a standard form of will, Diana's estate – including what James left her – will revert to her nominated heirs. We don't know who they are at this stage, but I suppose it's likely to be her son. Of course, details of the legacies won't be known until both the Bartons' wills are proved at probate. However, specific provision might have been made for the shares to revert to you, Mr Horton.'

Both Horton and his wife stared at Kate, apparently surprised that a detective, and a woman detective at that, should be so familiar with testamentary law.

'I see,' said Horton eventually. But he'd probably had as much trouble as me in following Kate's explanation.

'Did you have any contact with Mrs Barton after the divorce, Mr Horton?' I asked.

'No, I didn't,' snapped Horton. 'I told you that the other day.' He was beginning to get a little rattled.

'I understand that the shares were part of the divorce settlement,' I said.

'Yes,' said Horton.

'You never told me that, Maurice,' said Faye, shooting her husband a withering glance. 'Why on earth did you do such a stupid thing?'

'There were a lot of tiresome negotiations about the divorce, my dear, and that was the agreement that was eventually arrived at,' said Horton patiently, but it sounded defensive, and I thought that he was in for a bit of a rough ride once Kate and I had left.

'Did you at any time attempt to buy the shares from Mrs Barton, Mr Horton?' queried Kate.

'I didn't know where she was,' replied Horton.

'Did you attempt to find out where she was living?'

There was a distinct pause before Horton answered, and he gave the impression of a man who was being backed into a corner. 'I did have someone make a few enquiries, yes. I wanted to approach Diana, and make her an offer for the shares.'

'And did your representative find her?'

'No, he didn't.'

'Was this person a private detective?' Kate continued to press the venture capitalist.

'As a matter of fact, he was. A chap called Simkins I think, with offices in London somewhere. I can't exactly remember now. I might even have got his name wrong.' Horton realized that he'd spoken too quickly, and pretended ignorance of the address. But we'd find him.

'Well, that seems to have cleared things up, Mr Horton,' I said, as Kate and I stood up. 'I'm sorry that we had to bother you again, but we're never quite sure what relevance these matters might have until we're able to clarify them.'

'Not at all,' said Horton warmly. 'Only too glad to assist.' He appeared relieved that we were going, and escorted us to the front door.

'Miss Kaczynski seems a pleasant girl,' said Kate. 'She's Polish, I believe.'

'Er, yes, she is,' said Horton, but I could see he was wondering how the hell we knew her full name and nationality.

We walked out to our car. Kate paused briefly to admire Faye Horton's Lexus LS600hL. 'Nice car for shopping, guv,' she said, and sighed enviously.

'Well, what d'you think, Kate?' I asked, as we drove back to London.

'That Faye Horton is a right bitch. I almost felt sorry for Maurice. She didn't miss a word of our exchange, and I'll wager that she's giving him a right ear-bashing at this very moment.'

'See whether you can track down this enquiry agent called Simkins, Kate. We might be able to get something out of him, but he'll probably plead client confidentiality.'

'I think I'll be able to persuade him to tell us what we want to know,' said Kate.

I had no doubt about that. If I were a recalcitrant witness I wouldn't want to be interrogated by Kate.

Private detectives are not difficult to find. Because it's a highly competitive game they have to advertise to survive. Countless ex-coppers think that becoming an enquiry agent is an easy way to supplement their police pension. They set up business, usually in well-appointed offices with a good address that they can ill afford, and have business cards and headed stationery printed that proclaim them to be ex-Scotland Yard, whether they are or not.

In the heyday of contested divorces, where infidelity had to be proved to the hilt, they prospered. But now that divorce is much easier for those couples that bother to get married in the first place, it is much harder for the private eye to make a living. Gone are the days when a prostitute would be provided – at an exorbitant fee, of course – to be photographed in a compromising position with a husband keen to be parted from his wife. But in these enlightened days, most of these 'confidential investigators' eventually give up, and try to work out how to settle the debts they've accrued since retiring from the police force.

Arnold Simkins was one of the survivors. Kate Ebdon had thumbed through Yellow Pages, and found that he had an upstairs office in a back street of Clapham, sensible fellow. There was no receptionist, no fancy furniture, no carpet, and no gold lettering on a glass-panelled door. In fact, there were no frills of any sort, and Simkins's office was nothing like the American TV portrayal of a PI. This was clearly a work-shop. And it was cold, even at this time of year.

'Mr Simkins?' I asked.

'At your service.' Simkins glanced at Kate and me, and stood up to shake hands. 'What can I do for you?'

I told Simkins who we were, and he nodded as though he'd already worked it out.

'I'm ex-Job myself,' said Simkins. 'Did most of my time down the East End. Finished up as a DS. Have a pew.' He was slightly stooped, and was wearing a faded woollen cardigan, a striped shirt and a tie. His unfashionable wire-framed spectacles had a piece of sticking plaster across the bridge holding the two halves together. He would not have inspired confidence in his clients, but I knew that he was the type of detective sergeant who, whilst lacking ambition for promotion, was totally dedicated to the Job. And to the career he now pursued. I was sure he'd approach any enquiry like a terrier.

We sat on the black bentwood chairs that Simkins had provided for his clients. From their lack of comfort I deduced that clients were not meant to tarry here for long.

'I'm investigating two murders, Mr Simkins,' I began, and went on to tell him about the death of Diana Barton, the subsequent fire at 27 Tavona Street, and followed all that by mentioning the killing of James Barton.

'So it was Diana Barton, then. I read about the fire, and recognized the name. The press reports implied that she'd died as a result of the fire, but I suppose you wisely kept the fact that she was murdered to yourself for the time being.'

'You knew that's where she lived, then, Mr Simkins.'

'Call me Arnie, guv.' I could see that old habits died hard with ex-DS Simkins. 'I was always known as Arnie when I was in the Job. Yes, I knew that's where she lived.'

'I don't know how much you're able to tell me, Arnie,' I said. 'Client confidentiality being what it is.'

'To hell with that, guv. My loyalty's to the Job. Always has been. What d'you want to know?'

'Maurice Horton was your client?'

'That's right,' said Simkins. 'Didn't take to him too much. Not a likeable bloke at all. A stuck-up bastard actually, begging your pardon, miss,' he said to Kate.

'Did you tell him that that's where Diana Barton lived?'

'Yes, of course. That's what he was paying me for.'

'How long ago did you tell him?'

Simkins flicked through a few pages of a large desk diary. 'Six months ago,' he said. 'I sent him some photographs of Diana Barton, and a report saying that she was married to James Barton, a director of a hotel chain.' He looked up. 'I also told him that the two of them lived at twenty-seven Tavona Street, Chelsea, and that she'd been there for the preceding six and a half years. I think that Barton himself had already lived there with his previous wife until she died.' He crossed to a filing cabinet, and took out a folder. 'There it is,' he said, handing me a copy of the report.

I glanced through it, but it only contained what Simkins had just told me in summary. 'You say you sent the original of this to Maurice Horton.'

'That's right.'

'So, anyone could've read it, like his wife Faye for instance.' I had doubts about Faye Horton and her interest in money.

'What he did with the report was down to him, guv,' said Simkins.

'Was there anything else?' asked Kate.

'Like what?'

'We've had a report of a riotous party, Arnie.' Kate went on to tell Simkins about the gathering that had concluded with Diana's murder and the fire. 'I wondered if you'd noticed anything else when you were near the premises, like people coming and going. Regular parties, maybe. We've learned that she seemed to be pursuing a lifestyle that was contrary to what we've been told by James Barton, and her first husband who, of course, was Maurice Horton.'

'Hang on a mo.' Simkins opened a drawer and took out a thick A4-sized book. 'My daybook,' he explained. 'Always kept one in the Job. You never knew when someone might come asking questions.' He thumbed through it until he found the right page, and then looked up. 'I only kept a brief obo on the Barton pad. There was no point in doing anything else once I'd established that that's where Diana lived. That's all Horton wanted to know. By the way, he has a son Gregory who lives in Australia. Horton told me he's a mining engineer, and is married to Elizabeth aka Beth née McDonald. From what Horton told me the lad's settled there now.' He closed his daybook. 'I don't know if it's of any interest, but there was a sign outside from some firm doing a kitchen installation.'

'Did you take a note of the name, Arnie?' queried Kate. 'Or a phone number.'

Simkins gave Kate a crooked smile, and tapped the side of

his nose with a forefinger. 'Like I said, guv, you never know when these things might come in handy.' He wrote the details on a slip of paper, and handed them over. 'You making progress with this topping, guv?' he asked, turning his attention to me.

'Not a lot,' I said. 'So far, Horton seems to be the only one with motive, but we're a long way from proving it.'

'In my experience it was ever thus,' said Simkins, a realistic statement clearly based on years of trying to solve unsolvable crimes. 'Well, be lucky, guv. If I hear anything else, I'll give you a bell. Got a card, have you?'

We now had the address of the company that had fitted Diana Barton's new kitchen, but whether that would advance our enquiries remained to be seen. But you've got to try. Kate and I set forth.

Tucked away in a street near World's End, Fulham, the front office of the kitchen company was the usual set-up: a desk, a computer, and a disinterested girl. She had spiky blonde hair and her heavy arched eyebrows had been painted on, giving her the appearance of a startled porcupine.

'Help you?' asked the girl listlessly, and moved her chewing gum from one side of her mouth to the other.

I told the girl who we were, and asked to speak to whoever was in charge.

'You'll be wanting Mr Barnes. It's through there.' The girl pointed at a door on the far side of the office, and carried on reading a magazine and filing her nails.

'Good morning.' The man behind the large desk was poring over a sheaf of plans. 'How can I help you?'

Once again, I explained who we were, and said that I'd learned that his company had installed a kitchen for Mrs Diana Barton.

'Yes, I remember that job. Number twenty-seven Tavona Street, if memory serves me correctly.'

'That's the one, Mr Barnes,' I said.

'Is there a problem, then?'

'Yes, but it's my problem, not yours,' I said. 'Mrs Barton's been murdered.'

'Blimey!' This information produced an interesting reaction. Barnes hurriedly tapped a few details into his computer before looking back at us with an expression of relief. 'That's all right,' he said. 'She settled the account.'

'What was the name of the man who did the installation, Mr Barnes?' asked Kate.

'Bruce Metcalfe, an Australian. He was a good worker, and completed the job single-handed.'

'From when to when?'

Barnes referred to his book again. 'Seventeenth to the twenty-third of June, but I eventually had to sack him. Pity really because, like I said, he was a good worker. In fact, he was more than that. He came in one morning and said he'd approached Mrs Barton – what we call a cold call in the trade – and persuaded her to have a new kitchen put in. And that was only four days after I'd taken him on. Not bad during a recession. You don't get many workers like that, I can tell you.'

It was easy to understand how Metcalfe could have persuaded Diana Barton that she needed a new kitchen. Knowing what we did about her, Metcalfe would have had no problem in sweet-talking the willing Diana straight into bed. But why had he picked on her?

'Why did you sack him, then?'

'He was on drugs.'

'How did you know?'

'I caught him in the stockroom one morning when he was supposed to be putting together the gear he needed for that day's work, and he was snorting the bloody stuff. Bold as brass. So I gave him the push on the spot. I won't have that at any price. They might injure themselves on the job, and then I'd have the health and safety Gestapo down on me like a ton of bricks.'

'What date did you sack him?' It was looking very much as though this was the Bruce who had been mentioned as one of the guests at Diana's party.

Barnes interrogated his computer again. 'Twenty-ninth of July,' he said.

'Do you have an address for this Metcalfe?' I asked. The date was significant, and I tried not to get too excited about the fact that it was the Monday following the murder of Diana Barton.

'Sure do. It was number nineteen Dakar Road, Fulham. It's not far from here. I gather it's a bit of a doss house, but he was a single guy, so I suppose it was good enough for him.'

'It looks to me as though Metcalfe made a point of seeking out Diana Barton, Kate,' I said, as we left Mr Barnes. 'And persuaded her that she needed a new kitchen. But I wonder why he should've picked on her, unless he knew her previously. Or knew of her.'

'I wouldn't mind betting that he bedded her almost immediately, too,' said Kate. 'Food for thought.'

'Talking of which, Kate, I think we'll grab a bite to eat,' I said. 'There must be a half decent pub around here somewhere.' It was now almost half past one.

Number 19 Dakar Road proved to be an old Victorian house with steps leading up to the front door. Three stories high with a basement area, it was in poor condition. Some of the stucco facing had broken away to reveal the brickwork beneath. The windows were dirty, and what used to be the front garden had been concreted over to accommodate an ageing Volvo. A broken wash-hand basin was lying next to a couple of over-flowing wheelie bins.

'Looks like a fun place,' said Kate, as she hammered on the front door.

The balding, middle-aged man who answered was wearing jeans and a singlet, each as dirty as the other. Several compli-cated tattoos adorned his muscular arms.

'We're police officers,' said Kate.

'Oh, and what does the law want with me?' The man gave us a glance that combined apprehension with suspicion.

'Are you the owner of these premises?' Kate asked.

'Yeah.'

'Who are you, then?'

'Fred Makepeace, if it's any of your business.'

'Well, it is my business.' Kate placed a finger firmly on Makepeace's chest and pushed him back into the entrance hall. 'How many rooms have you got here?' It certainly seemed to be the sort of doss house that Barnes had described.

'What's this about? There ain't nothing wrong here. I run a respectable house.'

'You could've fooled me,' said Kate. 'How many rooms?' she asked again.

'Six. All bed-sits.'

'All let out, are they? And am I going to find any toms here?'

'No, you ain't. I wouldn't take no prostitutes or your lot'd be round here quicker than you can say knife. I pay me taxes, and I have the bleedin' council round here about once a month. He's some geezer from environmental health, he is. Makes me life a bleedin' misery.'

'We're looking for a man called Bruce Metcalfe.'

'Gone,' said Makepeace.

'Gone where?'

'Search me.'

'Not without rubber gloves,' said Kate, 'and I haven't got any with me.'

'Mr Makepeace,' I said, finally tiring of the man's churlish lack of co-operation, 'we are conducting a murder enquiry, and I suggest that you assist us to the best of your ability, because right now my temper is shortening quite dramatically. That might provoke me into continuing this little chat down at the nick, and there's no telling what else I might find out about you once I start having a trawl through our records.'

Makepeace took a pace back. 'I don't know nothing about no murder,' he protested. The manner in which he'd replied left me in no doubt that he was familiar with police station charge rooms. He might even know his way round some of Her Majesty's prisons.

'In that case, you'd better tell me where Metcalfe is.'

'I don't know, guv'nor. He never said where he was going.' Makepeace adopted a wheedling tone. 'He paid up to the end of the week, and cleared off. He said something about going back to Australia. That's where he said he came from.'

'What date did he leave?'

'I don't rightly remember.'

Kate took a step towards the recalcitrant boarding-house owner, invading his personal space. 'Then you'd better look it up in your register, hadn't you, sport. I'm sure you keep proper records for the Revenue and Customs people, because they might just come round and do a bit of checking.' She paused. 'And they certainly will if I have a word with them.'

'You'd better come in the office,' said Makepeace hurriedly.

What passed for Makepeace's office was a tip. A dilapidated vacuum cleaner, a couple of buckets and a worn out mop stood in one corner on the bare boards of the room. Under a window so dirty it was difficult to see out of it, stood a table piled high with paper, letters and several copies of the *Daily Mirror*. A mangy tabby cat was asleep on top of a heap of telephone directories.

'It's here somewhere,' said Makepeace, pushing the cat on to the floor, and ferreting through the mess. 'Ah, here we are.' He produced a dog-eared ledger. 'Yeah, he went on the twenty-ninth of July.'

It was the same date that Metcalfe was sacked from his job as a kitchen fitter. He must have returned to Dakar Road straight away, packed his belongings and moved out. Perhaps he *had* gone back to Australia.

'Are you sure you don't know where Metcalfe went from here?' asked Kate menacingly.

'Sure I'm sure.'

'Did any letters arrive for him?'

'Yeah, now you come to mention it.' Once again Makepeace sifted through the piles of paper on his desk. 'Here you are. This was the only one.' He handed Kate a letter bearing an Australian stamp.

'We'll take that,' said Kate, and peered at the postmark. 'It's from Darwin in the Northern Territory. Why am I not surprised.'

I assumed that Kate had no very high opinion of people from Darwin.

'Ain't you supposed to have a warrant to take things like that?' protested Makepeace. 'I mean he might come back for it.'

'Are you trying to tell me my job, mate?' demanded Kate, staring straight at Makepeace with a threatening look in her eye.

'No, but I just wondered,' whined Makepeace, wisely deciding not to fence with Kate.

'Well, I should stop wondering if I was you,' said Kate. 'It'll hurt what passes for your brain. But if he does come back, he can collect it from Scotland Yard. Tell him to ask for Detective Inspector Ebdon.' She turned to me. 'I reckon that's all we can do here, guv.'

And so it seemed to be. It had been a fruitless sort of day. If Bruce Metcalfe was the Australian who'd been at Diana's party, it was possible that he had gone back to Australia as Makepeace had suggested. On the other hand, he could just as well have remained here. But finding an Australian in London is fraught with difficulty. I know; I've tried before.

'Metcalfe might be living in the Bayswater area, guv,' suggested Kate.

'Why there?'

'Well, James Barton's body was found in Sussex Square. It could be that Metcalfe, if he's the murderer, didn't want to stray far from where he's living now. Wherever that is.'

'You're clutching at straws, Kate,' I said.

'What else is there to clutch at, guv?'

TEN

When we returned to Curtis Green, I asked Colin Wilberforce to enter Metcalfe's name on the Police National Computer with a direction that I was to be contacted if he was found. I also got him to pass the information to the drugs section of Revenue and Customs, and to that branch of the Specialist Crime Directorate – another pompous title – that dealt with the enforcement of drug legislation. But I had no great hope that either of these agencies would find Metcalfe for me.

'I don't know if this will help, guv.' Kate handed me the letter she had seized from Fred Makepeace at Dakar Road.

Headed Waimatutu Station, Tamorah, Darwin, and dated Saturday the thirteenth of July, it was signed 'Your loving cousin Ethel.' Kate told me that 'station' was the Australian term for a large farm. The content of the letter described the day-to-day happenings on the station, inconsequential news about nearby neighbours, problems with the weather, and how much the veterinary surgeon's bills had risen since Bruce left there. Finally, in a postscript, it reported that someone called Marlene had given birth to a twelve-pound-seven-ounce boy.

'It might give us a lead, Kate,' I said. 'I'll give Steve a ring.'

Inspector Steve Granger of the Australian Federal Police was an attaché at his country's high commission in the Strand.

'Steve, it's Harry Brock at the Yard.'

'G'day, Harry. What can I do for you?'

'I'm looking for an Australian, Steve,' I began.

There was a guffaw of laughter. 'Aren't we all, mate. I've got a list of wanted Australians as long as your bloody arm. What's this particular mongrel been up to?'

I explained about the murders of Diana and James Barton, and the fact that Bruce Metcalfe could well be the Australian who was at Diana's 'kitchen' party.

'A kitchen party?' queried Granger. 'You pommies sure have some bloody strange customs.'

'It's like a barbecue, but indoors, Steve,' I countered. 'Look, I know it's a long shot, but if this guy has DNA that matches samples we've recovered from the two victims, he's got some questions to answer.'

'You got anything to go on, Harry?'

'We picked up a letter addressed to him at the last place he was known to be living,' I said, and gave Steve the address of Bruce Metcalfe's 'loving cousin Ethel'. 'Any chance you could have enquiries made at this Waimatutu Station? They might be able to tell us Metcalfe's present whereabouts.'

'Sure, Harry, no worries,' said Granger. 'D'you want him arrested?'

'Not at this stage, Steve. On the evidence we've got so far we'd never get a fugitive offender's warrant. All I want to do at the moment is to find out where Metcalfe is now. And there's one other thing, Steve . . .' I explained about Horton, and that he'd got a son in Australia who was married to a woman called Elizabeth née McDonald, known as Beth. 'He's said to be a mining engineer, but I don't know where he lives. Is there a professional association of mining engineers that might have an address for him?'

'Only if he's qualified, Harry. A lot of them aren't, but they still call themselves engineers. Leave it with me. I'll give it my best shot.'

I gave the letter back to Kate. 'It's a case of wait and see,' I said.

'Are we going to have another word with Horton, guv?'

'Not yet, Kate. We need more before we can have another go at him. He's too bloody smart, but if we wait, he might just slip up.' It was a vain hope. I'd no idea if he had anything to slip up about, but it's the sort of thing detectives always say when they haven't a clue what to do next.

It seemed that Kate had been giving some thought to finding the errant Metcalfe. 'Earls Court is a popular place for Australians, guv,' she said when I walked into the incident room. 'And I should know.'

'I hope you're not suggesting we should carry out door-to-door enquiries there,' I said.

'No, guv. But I've got a few informants in the area. It might be worth putting out feelers. If Metcalfe's gone to ground, I can't think of a better place to hide than among a load of other Australians.'

I was not wholly convinced that Kate's suggestion would yield any useful results, but I had to admit that she knew more about Australians than I did. 'Metcalfe is not exactly an uncommon name,' I said. 'Even if we assume it's his real name. Anyway, we don't really know what he looks like.' The description that we had obtained from Barnes and Makepeace might just as well have been of two entirely different men. But it was ever thus.

'And I understand that the name Bruce is quite popular among you antipodeans, guv,' put in Dave, directing a mischievous glance at Kate. 'But we know that quite a few people at Diana Barton's party actually saw Metcalfe.'

'That'll only help once we've got him in custody and can hold an ID parade,' I said. It seemed to me that we were all getting a little desperate in our attempts to find Bruce Metcalfe, and it might turn out, even if we did, that he wouldn't be the man we wanted anyway.

'There is another way,' said Dave. 'Computer-aided graphics might help.'

'What the hell does that mean?' I asked. I was always wary of Dave when he started venturing into the field of computer technology. Mainly because I hadn't a clue what he was talking about.

'If we get one of the Yard's E-fit technicians to interview the people who actually saw Metcalfe, he might be able to produce a composite picture of what the guy looks like.' Dave leaned back in his chair with a satisfied smile on his face, the sort of smile that suggested he'd thought of something the guv'nor hadn't thought of. In this case, it was justified.

'OK, Dave, organize it,' I said.

Dave brought the computer E-fit technician into my office and made the introductions. Rather than being the 'he' that Dave had suggested, the computer expert turned out to be a mature woman dressed stylishly in a scarlet sweater and a black calf-length skirt. A pair of glasses hung from a cord around her neck. And she was called Marilyn Munro.

'Before you ask, it's spelled M-U-N-R-O, unlike the film star,' said Marilyn. 'It was my father's idea. He thought Marilyn

Monroe was the sexiest woman on two legs. Unfortunately for him, our family name was spelled differently, but he was so besotted with the bloody woman that I'm surprised he didn't change it to the same as hers.' She obviously bore a lasting grudge against Marilyn Monroe just for having existed.

Having got that bit of her family history out of the way, I explained to Miss Munro what we required of her.

'Shouldn't be a problem,' she said. 'But I'm not one of those technicians who has a dogmatic faith in what I do. I know from experience that there's only a remote chance of getting a similar likeness from each of your witnesses, but I'll do what I can. I even did one once of a serial burglar that turned out to be the spitting image of the Commissioner. And at the end of the day, it might even be necessary to get a police artist to enhance what I've produced. It sometimes helps.'

'Well, I'm sure you'll do your best, Miss Munro,' I said. It was refreshing to find someone who did not have an undying belief that the system they operated was foolproof and superior to all others.

'Oh do call me Marilyn,' said Miss Munro. It was a name that did not seem to suit this rather academic woman who, I hoped, would eventually help in identifying Bruce Metcalfe.

'One of the witnesses, Tom Hendry, is in prison on remand for arson, Marilyn,' I said.

'Not a problem. It wouldn't be the first time I'd ventured into a nick to knock up a likeness. I think I've done all the London ones: Brixton, the Scrubs, Wandsworth, Pentonville, Holloway and Belmarsh, plus Parkhurst on the Isle of Wight. I even went to Dartmoor once. Lovely views, but a bit bleak.'

'I'll send DS Poole with you,' I said.

'There's no need for that,' said Marilyn. 'I'm a big girl now.'

'I appreciate that, but Tom Hendry might just have remembered something else that's relevant to our murder, and it'll be useful for Dave to put a few questions to him. Apart from anything else, you'll need him to guide you to the places where the other people live. Some are in Southampton.'

It took Marilyn Munro until Monday morning. She arrived in the incident room and handed me a sheaf of prints.

'They're the best I can do, Mr Brock.'

I glanced through the results. Admittedly, there were simi-
larities in the six depictions that Marilyn had produced, but
there were also significant differences. It was more or less the
result that she'd predicted.

'I've made a composite of those six,' continued the helpful
Marilyn, and handed it to me. 'I don't know if it'll be of any
use.'

'It's all we've got,' I said, 'and thank you for your efforts.'

Once Marilyn Munro had departed, I handed the prints to
Colin Wilberforce, and waved a hand at his computer. 'Can
you send those to Inspector Granger at the Australian High
Commission on that machine of yours, Colin?' I asked.

'It's possible, sir,' said Colin doubtfully. 'I could scan them
in and transmit them as an attachment to an email – provided
Mr Granger's software is the same as ours – but it might be
better if they were delivered in person. In that way you won't
lose any of the definition.'

It would have been unwise of me to argue with Colin's
technical expertise, mainly because computers are a foreign
country to me. I telephoned Steve Granger and told him I was
on the way over.

'Good,' said Steve. 'I've got something for you.'

As his office was only in the Strand and less than a mile
away, I decided to walk. Avoiding the inevitable tourists and
their inane questions, I opted to go by way of Victoria
Embankment, up the steps into Lancaster Place, and across
to Australia House.

'The local Northern Territory constable who covers Waimatutu
Station at Tamorah knows the people there very well, Harry,'
Granger began, once I was seated in his office.

'Good news?' I asked hopefully.

'I doubt that it'll help much,' said Granger. 'The station's
run by an old couple called Paterson, Colin and Mary, and
they've never heard of a Bruce Metcalfe. There isn't anyone
on the station called cousin Ethel, and neither is there a
woman in the area called Marlene who's recently had a baby.
I suppose Metcalfe might've been a jackaroo, a casual worker,
for the season. They get plenty of them, but the Patersons
denied ever taking on someone of that name. Of course, if

Metcalfe was there, he might've used a different name. But frankly, I don't think he was ever there. I say that because these local constables keep an eye on itinerant workers. They're often on the run.'

'Like Ned Kelly, you mean?' It wasn't often I got the chance to have a dig at Steve Granger.

'Ha, ha!' said Granger. 'But what it comes down to, Harry, is that we've no idea who wrote the letter. But in my experience, anyone who makes up names and news like that is up to no good, mate.'

'I agree, Steve. Did your people turn up anything on Gregory and Beth Horton?'

'Not so far, Harry. I've got the guys at HQ in Canberra working on it. I'll let you know as soon as I've got something.'

I handed Granger the E-fit prints that Marilyn Munro had compiled from the descriptions given to her by our witnesses. 'There's not much chance that these will help, Steve, but it's the best we can come up with so far.'

Granger glanced at the prints. 'I don't know how useful these things are here in the Old Country, Harry, but in Australia we only use them as a last resort.'

'So do we, Steve. But my DI, Kate Ebdon, is going to show them around the Australian communities in London. You never know, she might strike lucky.'

'If anyone can find your drongo, Harry, it'll be Kate,' said Granger. 'She's a smart sheila, that one. Give her my regards, and tell her she owes me a drink.'

Once back at Curtis Green, I called Kate and Dave into my office and told them what I'd learned from Steve Granger. Which didn't advance our enquiries one little bit, apart from making Metcalfe appear more of a suspect than ever.

'But the thing that puzzles me,' I continued, 'is how the hell a letter comes to be posted from there without the knowledge of the Patersons.'

'Doesn't mean it came from there specifically,' said Kate. 'Darwin is the capital city of Northern Territory. Any letter posted there, or in the surrounding outback, will almost certainly have a Darwin postmark. I reckon that Bruce Metcalfe was in the Darwin area at some time, and that he wrote and posted the letter to himself. The question is why he should have done so.'

'And it was postmarked the thirteenth of July,' I said, 'so he must've been there then, assuming it was he who posted it.'

'If he didn't, he probably got a mate to post it for him,' said Dave. 'By the way, when I visited Brixton prison with Marilyn, I asked Hendry if he knew anything about Bernie and Samantha, the two mystery guests at Diana's party. He didn't.'

'And Barry Pincher and Charlene?'

'Drew a blank there as well, guv. The names didn't mean a thing, although he reckoned he vaguely remembered an older guy who could've been Bernie.'

It was then that I decided to authorize a news release stating that Diana Barton had been murdered. When her body was first discovered, I didn't contradict the newspapers' assumption that she'd died accidentally in the fire as a result of smoke inhalation. Consequently press reports of the incident, in most papers amounting to a column-inch tucked away on an inside page, had appeared on one day only.

I spoke to the press department at the Yard, which some time ago had taken unto itself the fancy name of Directorate of Public Affairs and Internal Communication, and arranged for the news release to go out as soon as possible. In that release, I linked Diana's death to that of her husband, and hinted that the same person might have been responsible for both murders. I made no mention of the DNA evidence we possessed, or of Bruce Metcalfe. I didn't want to give too much away.

Then I sat back and waited to see what would happen next.

I was working on a report at half past six that same evening, when Gavin Creasey, who had not long taken over from Colin Wilberforce for the night duty stint, came into my office.

'I've just had a telephone call from a man named Dale Sims, sir. He saw our piece on Sky News about Diana Barton's murder, and thinks he might have something to tell us.'

'I wonder if he's the Dale who was at the kitchen party. Got the address and phone number, Gavin?'

'Here, sir.' Creasey handed me the details.

'Is Dave in the incident room?' I asked, having scanned the message.

'No, sir.' Creasey grinned. 'He said to tell you that he's downstairs in the car with the engine running. And he's got the E-fits of Bruce Metcalfe with him.'

Tapert Road, Fulham, was in that maze of streets bounded by New Kings Road, Wandsworth Bridge Road and the River Thames. Dale Sims lived on the top floor of number 13, an old Edwardian dwelling that had been converted into flats.

'Mr Sims?'

'That's me. Are you from the police?'

'Yes, we are.' I introduced Dave and me, and Sims invited us in.

'This is my partner Debbie Clark.' Sims indicated a young woman who was reclining on a sofa reading a book.

'Hello,' said the girl. She closed the book, and swung her feet to the floor.

'I understand that you have something you wish to tell me,' I said, as Dave and I accepted Sims's invitation to sit down.

'We were at Diana's party the night of the fire, but we had no idea that she'd been murdered, Mr Brock,' Sims began. 'When we read the newspaper report of the tragedy we assumed that it had been an unfortunate accident.'

'I'm afraid not. Mrs Barton had been stabbed several times, and the house was set on fire deliberately.'

'Oh God, how awful,' said Debbie. It was the sort of shocked reaction that most people express when they hear of the murder of someone they knew.

'I read about her husband's murder, too,' Sims continued. 'But I gather that wasn't at the house, was it? I can't remember.'

'His body was found in Sussex Square in Bayswater,' I said, 'although the two murders might be connected. We're particularly interested in tracing a man called Bruce Metcalfe whom we believe to be Australian. We think he was at the party.'

'Yes, there was an Australian there.' Sims turned to his partner. 'You remember him, don't you, Debs?'

'Yes, I do,' said Debbie. 'I think he was on drugs. I didn't like him at all. He was stripped to the waist and showing off his muscles.'

It was useful to have confirmed what Barnes, Metcalfe's

erstwhile employer, had said, although I wasn't sure if it would be of any help.

'Why were you at the party?' asked Dave.

'Diana had invited us.'

'Yes, I gathered that,' said Dave patiently, 'but why were you invited?'

'Oh, I see. I'm an interior designer,' said Sims, 'and some time ago I'd advised Diana and her husband on a suitable decor for their sitting room. Mr Barton left it to his wife, but she eventually decided against going ahead with my design. Pity really, it would have made a real showpiece of that room. Anyway, she invited us and a few others who'd either installed her kitchen, or done some decorating.'

'At what time did you arrive, Mr Sims?' continued Dave.

'About seven, I suppose. The invitation said the do started at four, but that was too early for me. I was at an up-market fashion outlet in Mayfair until about five thirty, advising the owner on its refurbishment.'

'And what time did you leave the party?'

Again Sims turned to his partner. 'It would've been about ten o'clock Debs, wouldn't it?'

'About then, yes,' said Debbie. 'It wasn't really our scene. We hadn't been there long before several of the women were running about stark naked. We'd only been there half an hour before I wished we hadn't come. They weren't a very nice lot at all, apart from Gaston. He was a Frenchman, and as I speak a little French I thought it was a chance to try it out. He came from the Loire Valley apparently, and we went there for a holiday last year. But he told me that he hadn't been back there for years.'

'I have a rather delicate question to put to you, Mr Sims,' I said. 'Did Diana Barton at any time solicit you for sex?'

Sims laughed outright. 'Good God no. Whatever makes you think that?'

'Just something I'd heard from others who were at the party.' I left it at that, declining to tell Sims what we'd learned of Diana's sexual history.

'She did disappear from time to time,' said Debbie, clearly more observant than her partner. 'And some of the men disappeared at the same time.'

'D'you remember which of the men?' asked Dave, busily making notes in his pocketbook.

'There was a rather louche character called Tom. He had a girl with him called Shelley, one of the naked ones. Tom certainly went upstairs with Diana at one time.'

Dave seemed to be impressed by Debbie's use of the word 'louche'. 'What d'you do for a living, Miss Clark?' he asked.

'I'm a librarian at London University,' said Debbie.

'Really? I graduated from there,' said Dave, 'but I don't remember you.'

'I've only been there for a year,' said Debbie. 'Before that I worked at a public library. Pretty dull.'

'Was anyone else absent at the same time as Mrs Barton?' I asked, steering Dave and Debbie away from their cosy tête-à-tête. 'Apart from Tom.'

'Yes, Bruce the Australian. I recall Diana coming back into the room and taking his arm. I didn't hear what she said, but they both disappeared.'

Dave produced the E-fits that Marilyn Munro had produced. 'Have a look at these, Mr Sims, and tell me if any of them are like the Bruce you saw.'

Sims studied each one of the E-fits carefully. Eventually he selected one. 'That's the nearest,' he said. It was the one that Tom Hendry had compiled.

Dave handed the prints to Debbie Clark. After looking at them closely, she picked out the same one.

'Have either of you seen this man since?' I asked, taking in Sims and his partner with a glance.

'No,' said Sims.

'Nor me,' said Debbie. 'Is he the man who murdered Diana?'

'We don't know,' I said. 'But we think he might be able to assist us with our enquiries.'

Dale Sims laughed. 'You policemen always say that,' he said. 'At least they do on television.'

I declined to dignify that comment with a reply. 'Thank you both for your time,' I said, as Dave and I stood up. 'I don't suppose that we'll need to see you again.'

'I hope you catch him,' said Sims, as he escorted us to his front door. 'Diana was a nice woman.'

It was getting on for ten o'clock that evening by the time we got back to Curtis Green. I told Dave to go home for what we in the CID call an early night.

*   *   *

Although it was nearly eleven o'clock by the time I got back to Surbiton, I was in the office by half past eight on the Wednesday morning.

No sooner had I stirred my coffee and lit a forbidden ciga-rette – to hell with the law – when Colin Wilberforce came into my office with a message form in his hand.

'What is it, Colin?'

'Bruce Metcalfe's been found, sir.'

'Where?'

'Fifty-four Talleyrand Street, Earls Court, sir.'

So Kate Ebdon was right in thinking that he tried to lose himself among fellow Australians, I thought. 'Is he in custody?'

'No, sir, he's dead.' Wilberforce flourished the message form. 'And it's described in this as a suspicious death. The owner of the house identified him, and among his possessions was a credit card in the name of James Barton. Mr Cleaver is acting commander and he directs that you investigate.'

If Alan Cleaver said it was down to me there was no argument. He was a career CID officer, and knew what he was doing.

'As a matter of interest, where is the commander, Colin?'

'He's taken a couple of days off, sir,' said Wilberforce. 'Apparently something to do with refurbishing his caravan,' he added with a grin.

That I could believe. Our illustrious commander always struck me as the sort of individual who'd spend his holidays in a caravan. But to me a week or two in a caravan with Mrs Commander sounded like a holiday to be avoided like the plague. 'What's happened so far?' I asked.

'Local CID are on scene and dealing, sir, but when they did a check on the PNC and found you had an interest they referred it to us. Dr Mortlock's been called, as has Linda Mitchell and her team.'

'Any indication of how he was murdered, Colin?' asked Dave.

'None at all, Dave,' said Wilberforce. 'The message merely said a suspicious death.'

'Looks like we're off again, guv,' Dave said. 'I'll get the car.'

'It's the rush hour, Dave. Get a traffic car to take us,' I said with some misgiving. 'I want to get there before the locals make too much of a mess of our crime scene.'

So once again, I placed my life in the hands of the Black Rats, arguably the finest drivers in the world. That said, there was a story circulating in the Metropolitan Police some years ago that a senior politician, on urgent business, was taken from the Foreign Office to Heathrow Airport at high speed. Conveyed in a police car, he was accompanied by a motor-cycle escort. He had intended to work on his dispatch box during the journey, but by the time he arrived – a bare twenty minutes later – he'd screwed up its contents in sheer terror. On staggering white-faced from the traffic car he expressed the opinion that his life seemed to be in grave danger only when he was surrounded by the police.

I knew how he felt.

ELEVEN

The house at Talleyrand Street was the usual sort of shabby Victorian dwelling common to that area of Earls Court and within walking distance of the famous exhibition centre. Divided into bed-sits, the house was largely inhabited by single people either striving to make a living, or surviving on the generous handouts provided by Her Majesty's government.

The front door was guarded by a policewoman who, although undoubtedly slender, had the misfortune to appear overweight because of the bulky yellow jacket that she was obliged to wear over her stab-proof vest. The jacket was emblazoned with the word POLICE front and back, just in case you couldn't tell by the Metropolitan Police badge on her hat, the chequered cravat, the personal radio and the long truncheon at her side.

Having satisfied a uniformed inspector that we were in the Job, and waited while he laboriously wrote our details on his clipboard, we found the local DI outside a door on the first floor.

'What's the SP?' I asked.

'The short story is that the dead man didn't come down to collect his mail this morning, guv. So the guy who owns the place went up to his room to give it to him, and found your Mr Metcalfe as dead as the proverbial dodo.'

'Where is the owner now?'

'In his office talking to one of my detective sergeants.'

'I'll get around to him later,' I said. 'What's the owner's name?'

'Howard, guv.'

'Right, but first I'd better have a look at the body.'

'The pathologist is in there doing the business, guv.' The DI pointed at an open door. Linda Mitchell was waiting with the DI.

'Good morning, Linda,' I said. 'Nice day for it.'

'Matter of opinion, Mr Brock,' said Linda.

The room that was the scene of our murder was furnished in the sparse way I'd come to expect of cheap rooming houses. A worn carpet, dirty curtains, a chest of drawers on which were a television set and a small mirror, a single unmade bed along a wall, a sink that doubled for washing and washing up, and an armchair. The armchair was occupied by the dead body of my latest victim. A door led to a lavatory.

'Just finished,' said Dr Henry Mortlock. 'I meant that I've just finished,' he added, and pointed at Metcalfe. 'He was finished some time ago.'

I've mentioned Henry Mortlock's black humour before.

'Preliminary findings, Henry?'

'This is an interesting one, Harry. There's an entry wound at the left temple.' Mortlock pointed with a thermometer, presumably in case I couldn't work out where the man's left temple was situated by the hole in his head. 'It's just over ten millimetres across, but if it was an entry wound made by a bullet it must've been a big bullet, and there's no gunshot residue that I can see. Nor does it look as though it was made with a bladed instrument. The murder weapon could have been something pointed and rounded in section, I suppose. And from his post-mortem posture, I'd say that he was taken by surprise. Bit of a strange one altogether. I'll have to get him on the table and carve him up before I can tell you anything else.'

'Time of death?'

'Ditto,' said Mortlock tersely, as he packed the sinister tools of his trade into a little black bag. And with that pithy comment, he wandered off, humming a theme from a Bizet opera. Or so Dave told me later.

'Just to confirm Doctor Mortlock's opinion, have you come across any shell cases?' I asked Linda Mitchell who, dressed in her usual sexy white coveralls, had followed me into the room. The rest of her team was still downstairs in their van.

'We've not had a chance to do a detailed examination yet, Mr Brock, but on my initial quick visual there weren't any signs of any.'

'I'll leave you to it, then.'

Linda leaned over the banister rail and shouted. 'Send my lads up here, someone.'

Dave and I went downstairs, and found the owner. 'I'm

Detective Chief Inspector Brock of Scotland Yard,' I said, 'and
this is DS Poole. What's your name?' I knew what the local
DI had said, but it's always as well to check.

'Seamus Howard.'

The owner of the house was perspiring heavily, although it
was not hot in the room. I wondered if he too was a drug user,
or if the presence of the police had brought him out in a sweat.

'What can you tell me, Mr Howard?'

'I've already told this fellow here,' said Howard, indicating
a youngish man. Howard's accent told me that he hailed from
Liverpool. 'And I told that inspector, too.' He spoke wearily,
as though tired of being asked the same question over and
over again.

'And who are you?' I asked the other man, although the
local DI had told me he was one of his sergeants.

'DS Todd, guv.'

'OK, you can leave it to us now, Skip.'

'Cheers, guv,' said Todd, and departed, doubtless pleased
to be relieved of any involvement in my murder enquiry.
Murder enquiries meant late nights and lost weekends.

'Now, Mr Howard, perhaps you'd tell me what you know.
Again.'

Howard let out a sigh. 'Like I told the other scuffers—'

'The what?' demanded Dave.

'It's what we call the police in Liverpool.'

'Well, not down here you don't,' said Dave in one of his
more threatening voices. 'Go on.'

'Oh, sorry.' Howard seemed bemused by Dave's objection.
'Anyhow, like I was saying, Bruce usually comes in here of
a Wednesday morning to collect his benefit cheque, but he
didn't show. That was unusual because his benefit always
comes on a Wednesday. I thought he might've overslept, so I
went up there. Bloody nasty shock finding him dead in his
armchair, I can tell you.'

'Yes, it must've been quite awful,' said Dave sarcastically.

'D'you know if Metcalfe had a job, Mr Howard?' I asked.
'Regular employment.' Howard had mentioned a benefit cheque,
so I thought it unlikely.

'I dunno about that, but he usually went out around eight in
the morning. I dunno if he had a job, though. P'raps he was
looking for one.'

'And did his benefit cheque arrive today?'

'Yeah, just this one letter.' Howard handed over a buff envelope. 'Like I said, it's the Giro cheque for his benefit.'

I glanced briefly at the letter and handed it to Dave.

Dave ripped it open. 'Yes, sir, it's a handout from our benevolent government. Unemployment benefit. That was quick considering he's only been unemployed since the end of July. I'll bet he was drawing this while he was working for Barnes at the kitchen company.' Dave had an ingrained dislike of people who defrauded the government, and therefore him as a taxpayer. 'If I thought he'd got any estate, I'd make sure the Work and Pensions office clawed it back.'

'What can you tell me about Metcalfe, Mr Howard?' I asked. 'For a start, when did he move in here?'

Howard turned to a large book on his desk, and thumbed through the pages. 'Twenty-ninth of July.'

That, of course, was the day he was sacked by Barnes at the kitchen company, and also the day he left his previous lodgings at Dakar Street, Fulham. I wondered briefly why he'd bothered to move. It was clearly nothing to do with shortage of money. But maybe his sudden move had been prompted by a fear that Barnes might've informed the police about his drug habit.

'And you've no idea where he was working, assuming he *was* working.'

'No idea,' said Howard.

'If he was working, he was defrauding the Work and Pensions people,' muttered Dave, returning to his original theme. 'Did Metcalfe have any visitors, particularly yesterday or early this morning, Mr Howard?' he asked.

Howard shrugged. 'He might've done, I s'pose, but I don't keep a check on who comes and goes.'

'Were you aware of anybody calling on him at any time?' persisted Dave with, for him, remarkable patience.

'Nope.'

And that, I decided, was as much as we were going to get out of Howard for the time being. I returned to the scene of Metcalfe's murder.

'How are you getting on, Linda?'

'We found this in a plastic bag in the lavatory cistern,' said Linda, displaying a number of packets of white powder. 'Very original hiding place, that is,' she added acidly. It seemed that some of the CID's cynicism had rubbed off on her.

'Heroin?' I queried.

'Most likely, Mr Brock.' Linda smiled. 'I doubt that it's talcum powder, but you'll have to wait for the lab report.'

'If it is heroin, is there enough of it to make him a dealer?'

'I should think so. I reckon there's about a hundred grams here which is . . .' Linda paused as she did the mental arithmetic. 'At least five thousand pounds-worth at the current street value. If it's heroin, that is.'

'Bloody hell!' I exclaimed. 'And to think he's on unemployment benefit.'

'Why shouldn't he be, guv?' said Dave. 'I don't suppose that Her Majesty's government recognizes illegal drug dealing as a lawful occupation . . . yet.'

'There was no sign of a struggle, as far as I can tell,' continued Linda, which is what Dr Mortlock had said, 'but we're in the process of lifting a number of fingerprints. However, judging by the general lack of cleanliness of the room, they could belong to the three occupants before Metcalfe, at the very least. But we live in hope,' she added with a smile.

'Any corres?' I asked, using the police shorthand for paperwork of any description.

'Only an Australian passport in his name, and a credit card belonging to James Barton. I gather you'll not be surprised by that.'

'I guessed there'd be something of the sort. He was probably the bloke who tried to use the debit card that the bank seized. Are there any letters?'

'I'm afraid not. But there is an entry stamp in the passport. It seems he arrived in the UK on the third of June this year.'

'I suppose you haven't come across a mobile phone or a BlackBerry, or anything like that. I know that James Barton owned one. He told us that he'd got a mobile.'

Linda picked up a plastic bag. 'There's this mobile phone, Mr Brock, but it's a cheap pay-as-you-go job. I doubt that James Barton would've owned it.'

'If Metcalfe nicked Barton's expensive phone, he'd've flogged it, I expect.' I suggested.

'What about a rent book?' asked Dave.

'Haven't found one, Dave, and we've done a thorough search,' said Linda. 'But there was this.' She produced a small bottle of bright red nail enamel, and a mascara pencil. 'They'd fallen down the back of the chest of drawers.'

'I can't see that a butch Aussie like Metcalfe was in the habit of using those,' I said. 'Any female clothing?'

'No, nothing, Mr Brock.' Linda pointed to a makeshift cubicle, the curtain of which was drawn back. 'I checked his boudoir,' she added sarcastically, 'and as you can see there are only some empty hangers, a pair of jeans and a couple of shirts screwed up on the bottom. All dirty, of course. But I think I detected a whiff of Jo Malone.'

'Who the hell's Jo Malone?' I asked, wondering whether this was another name to add to our list of partygoers.

'It's an expensive line of perfumery, Mr Brock.' Linda shot me a pitiful smile. 'White jasmine and mint at a guess.'

'Oh. Well, if there was a woman living with him, she's made a hurried departure.' I glanced at the narrow bed, and decided that if Metcalfe had shared it with a female, both of them would have been very uncomfortable.

'You happy for the body to be moved now?' I asked.

'Yes, I've done with it,' said Linda. 'DS Wright's here somewhere.'

I sent Dave downstairs to find 'Shiner' Wright, the laboratory liaison officer. His responsibility was to take charge of Metcalfe's body in order to maintain continuity of evidence while the scientific tests were carried out on it.

On our way out, we stopped again at Seamus Howard's office.

'We couldn't find Metcalfe's rent book,' I said. 'Any idea where he keeps it?'

Howard looked shifty. 'I don't know,' he said.

'But you did issue him with one, didn't you?' asked Dave, his antenna telling him that Howard was lying.

'He must have it somewhere,' said Howard, but it sounded unconvincing.

'If you haven't provided him with one you're committing an offence,' said Dave. 'Section Twenty-Four, Rent and Rooming Houses Act 1987 applies. Two years in the nick,' he continued, instantly manufacturing a fictional piece of impressive sounding legislation, secure in the knowledge that

Howard wouldn't know anything about the law regarding rent books. 'So you'd better hope we find one.'

Howard looked rather unnerved at Dave's threat, but said nothing.

'It seems that there was a woman living with Metcalfe at some time, Mr Howard. D'you know anything about that?'

'No, I don't. I never saw no birds coming or going. Anyway, it's only a single bed.'

Howard was definitely a character who under different circumstances would have merited closer scrutiny, but I had no time to waste on him. We waited until 'Shiner' Wright had supervised the removal of Metcalfe's body, and left Linda to make a video and photographic record of the scene. And to gather any other useful evidence she might find in the course of her search.

'I reckon our Seamus Howard's on heroin, guv, and that Metcalfe probably paid his rent in kind,' said Dave, as we left the building.

'I agree,' I said, 'but we don't have the time to mess about with that. We'll hand it over to the Drugs Squad. It'll give 'em something to do.'

By two o'clock Dave and I were back at the 'factory', as we CID officers tend to call our place of work. I now had three murders to solve, and I wasn't happy, even though this latest one might have resolved the other two.

I telephoned Steve Granger at the Australian High Commission, and told him that we'd found Bruce Metcalfe and that he'd been murdered. I also told him that the victim had arrived in the UK from Australia on the third of June this year.

Steve said he'd look into it.

'Any news on Gregory Horton, Steve?' I was still interested in discovering the whereabouts of the son of Maurice Horton and Diana Barton, even though I thought it was unlikely to further our enquiries. But I hate loose ends.

'Nothing yet, Harry. I'll let you know as soon as I have something.'

As I replaced the receiver, Kate Ebdon came into my office clutching a file. 'I've been doing some ferreting, guv, and I've discovered the name of the Bartons' London solicitor.'

'How did you do that?' I asked, although Kate could always be relied on to dig up facts that were pertinent to the case.

'I checked with the hotel company of which he was a director, and they told me. Apparently this firm of solicitors handled all Barton's legal affairs, personal as well as business. And since his marriage to Diana they'd handled her affairs too.'

'So, what have you learned?' I motioned Kate to a chair.

Kate sat down, and opened the file. 'I obtained a copy of both wills from the solicitor. Each was the standard sort of reciprocal settlement that I'd anticipated. On her death, Diana Barton's estate went to James Barton. But as he died within twenty-eight days, it came back to her and went to her son Gregory Horton. And as James Barton had left his entire fortune to Diana, Gregory gets the lot.'

'How much?'

'Give or take a few pounds, Gregory Horton's now worth something in the region of eighteen million pounds. That's made up of deposits, stocks and shares, and the Bartons' house at Tavona Street. And being Chelsea that's worth a few quid on its own.'

'Ye Gods! If that doesn't sound like a motive, I don't know what does,' I said. 'Pity we don't know where Gregory Horton is.'

'Ah, but we do, guv,' said Kate triumphantly. 'The last address the solicitors had for him is in Tandy Road, Blair, in the Northern Territory. I've had a look at the map, and Blair is a small town about five miles from Tamorah and eight miles from Darwin. You'll recall that Waimatutu Station is at Tamorah, the Patersons' place from where someone presumably sent the letter to Metcalfe that we seized from Makepeace.'

'It could be that Metcalfe and Gregory Horton were in this together,' I said, 'and that it was Horton who'd sent the letter.' But even as I expressed that view, I realized that it didn't make a lot of sense.

'Nothing would surprise me with this topping, guv,' said Kate.

I grabbed the telephone and rang Steve Granger again.

'Kate Ebdon's tracked down Gregory Horton, Steve,' I said, and passed on the information she had gleaned from the Bartons' solicitor.

'Leave it with me, Harry. I'll get someone on to it as soon as possible. D'you reckon this guy will still be there? If he's just copped eighteen million, he'll likely have shot through to some place like Sydney for the bright lights.'

'Your guess is as good as mine, Steve, but it'll be a long time before he lays hands on the cash.'

'Any chance that this Gregory Horton's up for your murders, Harry?'

'Not if he's still in Australia, and has been for the last month or so. But if he's adrift, he might be involved. And eighteen million pounds makes for a bloody good motive,' I said, repeating my previous thought. 'But that aside, I'm pretty certain that the murders of James and Diana Barton were down to Metcalfe.'

There was a pause before Granger spoke again. 'I think I'll ask HQ to get one of our people from the local AFP office at Darwin to take it on, rather than the Northern Territory Police. Sounds as though it might be getting serious.'

'How long before you'll get an answer, Steve?'

'It's three o'clock here, so in Canberra it'll be one in the morning. There's only a half hour difference between there and Darwin. So if I get an email off now, and HQ forwards it straight on to Darwin, our man there will probably pick it up first thing tomorrow morning. With any luck, I'll get a reply by Friday. How's that suit you?'

'Fine, Steve, and many thanks.' Although I was impatient to resolve the Gregory Horton end of things, I did have other things to occupy me. At least I knew that the Australian Federal Police would pull out all the stops.

The next piece of good news to arrive was a report from the forensic science laboratory.

'We're getting there, Kate,' I said. 'The lab compared Metcalfe's DNA with the semen found in Diana Barton, and it's a match. And according to this,' I continued, tapping the report, 'that makes it a match with the handful of hair that James Barton was clutching when he was found.'

'Well, I reckon that's two of the murders cleared up, guv. All we've got to do now is find out who topped Metcalfe.'

Colin Wilberforce put his head round the door. 'The commander would like a word, sir.'

'Oh, he's back, is he?'

'Yes, sir,' said Wilberforce, with a perfectly straight face.

I walked down the corridor to where the commander presided over his paper empire.

'You wanted to see me, sir?'

'Ah, Mr Brock, what's the progress on these three deaths you're dealing with.'

'I'm ninety per cent sure that two of them have been cleared up, sir. It's looking as though both toppings are almost certainly down to Bruce Metcalfe.'

'But he's dead.'

'Yes, I'm aware of that, sir,' I said patiently, 'but we've compared his DNA with that found at the scenes of the two Barton murders, and they're a match to Metcalfe's.'

'Yes, that's all very well,' said the commander, pretending to understand, 'but what about the Metcalfe murder?'

'We're waiting on enquiries that have been lodged with the Australian Federal Police, sir.'

'Is there an Australian connection, then?'

'Yes, sir.' I explained, as simply as possible, where Gregory Horton fitted into our enquiries.

'Is this man Horton a suspect?'

'I don't know, sir, but I intend to find out. Of course, if he's in Australia—'

The commander looked alarmed, and fiddled with a paperknife. I knew what he was thinking, and it didn't take long for him to put it into words. 'I hope you're not suggesting that it'll be necessary for you and Sergeant Poole to fly to Australia, Mr Brock,' he said sharply, suddenly realising what a huge cost this would entail.

'Not at this stage, sir,' I said, somewhat blithely. I couldn't see a need to go 'down under' at any time in the future. But I always enjoyed winding up the commander about expenses.

'Well, I shall need to see a substantial reason if you do make such an application, and so will the DAC,' said the commander. He always fell back on what the deputy assistant commissioner might think, rather than offering an objection of his own. 'We do have budgets to consider, you know. I sometimes think that you CID officers believe you can spend as much as you like in the course of an investigation.'

'Yes, I'm afraid you and I tend to think like that, don't you agree, sir?' I said, in a lame attempt to remind the commander that he too was a CID officer. If only on paper. And, it would seem, only when it suited him.

'Yes, yes,' said the commander. 'But if you ever reach my rank, Mr Brock, you'll realize that there are other considerations.' But he said it in such a way that I ruled out any possibility of promotion.

'Did you manage to get your caravan sorted out, sir?'

'How did you know about that, Mr Brock?' The commander frowned.

'I'm a detective, sir.'

Back in the incident room, I learned that the local drugs squad had already struck. They'd found a significant amount of heroin in Howard's own living quarters, and had arrested him.

Well, at least someone was having some luck.

TWELVE

On Thursday morning, Dave and I met Henry Mortlock at his carvery in Horseferry Road. As usual, he'd completed his examination by the time we'd been told to arrive. But Henry had always been impatient to get on with the job.

'I'll put it in layman's language for you, Harry. In short, an instrument of some sort was placed against Metcalfe's left temple and a spigot, for want of a better word, was discharged into the left temporal lobe of his brain. Death would have been instantaneous.'

'Have you recovered this spigot, Henry?'

'No. It's not in his cranium, and Miss Mitchell didn't find anything like it at the crime scene.'

'Any ideas?' I asked.

Mortlock peeled off his latex gloves and tossed them into a medical-waste trashcan. 'I've come across this once before,' he began, as he took off his apron and threw it towards a bench. He missed, and it fell to the floor, but he ignored it. 'Some years ago, I was called in by the Avon and Somerset Constabulary to a man who'd been found murdered on a remote cattle farm. He was the partner of the farmer – who was eventually convicted of the victim's murder – and we found that the murder weapon was a humane killer normally used for putting down animals. The Somerset police searched the farmhouse and found the weapon in a cupboard, and there were traces of the victim's blood and DNA on it. I reckon you're looking for a "captive bolt" humane killer, so called because once the bolt's been deployed, it retracts into the barrel. And that's why I didn't find the bolt, and neither did Miss Mitchell.'

'I wonder if this humane killer came from Waimatutu Station in downtown Tamorah,' suggested Dave in a quiet aside.

Suddenly the likelihood of having to go to Australia had become more of a reality. That would definitely not please the commander.

'If Metcalfe had never been to Waimatutu, it's possible that

Gregory Horton had,' I said. 'According to Kate Ebdon, Tamorah is only five miles from Blair, where Horton lives. But we'll have to wait and see what Steve Granger has to say. If Horton's still in Australia, and has been for the last month, that rules him out.'

'What do these humane killers look like, Doctor?' asked Dave.

'The one that was found in Somerset, Sergeant Poole,' said Mortlock, 'was about ten inches long, with a bolt some two inches in length by half an inch in diameter. The bolt is discharged by either a large percussion cap or a blank cartridge. Look it up on the Internet, you'll find all you need to know about it there. As I said at the scene, I'm fairly certain that your victim was surprised by his murderer. He must've approached him, placed the humane killer against his temple and *bang*! Metcalfe wouldn't have seen it coming, and certainly wouldn't have known what hit him.'

'It's likely, then, that Metcalfe knew his killer,' I suggested.

'That's only my medical opinion, Harry,' said Mortlock with a cynical smirk. 'You're the one who's faced with the problem of working it out.'

'Miss Ebdon said that there are quite a lot of Australians in Earls Court,' put in Dave. 'It's possible, I suppose, that one of them could have been a farmer in a past life.'

'Haven't you been listening, Sergeant Poole? I told you that they're used in this country, too,' said Mortlock irritably, as he put on his jacket. 'Try the local abattoirs.'

'Well, that's given us something to think about, Dave,' I said, as we arrived back at Curtis Green. In the incident room, I told Colin Wilberforce of Dr Mortlock's suggestion that a humane killer was the murder weapon.

'See what you can find out about abattoirs in the area, Colin. It's a long shot, but it's something we've got to pursue.'

'I'll Google it, sir.'

'Whatever it takes,' I said, once again failing to understand what Wilberforce was talking about. It didn't help that I thought he'd said 'gargle' it.

He turned to his computer and played a tattoo on the keyboard. 'There we are, sir,' he said a minute later, and turned the screen so that I could see it. 'There are some in the East End of London, but the rest are in the Home Counties.'

'Nothing anywhere near Earls Court?'

'No, sir, not according to this.'

'Thanks, Colin.' I turned to Dave. 'I can't see anyone bothering to travel all the way from the East End to murder an Australian in Earls Court, Dave.'

'From what Linda found at Talleyrand Street, guv, we're fairly certain that Metcalfe was a drug dealer, and drug dealers must have suppliers. Perhaps Metcalfe reneged on a deal, and the supplier turned nasty.' Dave paused. 'And the supplier might just have worked in an abattoir,' he added, anxious to make his point.

'Thanks for that,' I said, and shook my head. 'I don't know, Dave. We start off with a nice domestic murder in fashionable Chelsea, and now we're looking for a murdering abattoir worker who sidelines as a drug supplier. I think we'll let that one sweat for the time being. Unless you can turn up something.'

Just before midday on Friday morning, I got a message from Steve Granger asking me to call on him at the Australian High Commission. Leaving Dave to puzzle over the abattoir problem, I took Kate Ebdon with me.

After a bit of amusing Australian backchat between Steve and Kate, we sat down in Granger's comfortable office, and accepted his secretary's offer of coffee.

Granger took a sheet of paper from his desk, and sat down in the armchair next to mine.

'Gregory Horton,' he began.

'Got something good, Steve?'

'Depends which way you look at it, Harry. The AFP man in Darwin visited Horton's place in Tandy Street, the address in Blair you gave us. It's a bar, but it's closed, and has been shut since some time in early July.'

'Was Horton still there?'

'No. It looks as though he's gone walkabout. And his wife's disappeared too. HQ in Canberra checked with Immigration, but they've got no record of Horton leaving the country. Mind you, that's not foolproof. There are plenty of ways to get out of Australia without the authorities knowing.'

'But he wouldn't have been recorded leaving anyway, would he, Steve, being an Australian?'

'He's still a Brit, Harry. He never took out Australian citizenship.'

'What's known about this bar of his?'

'According to the local copper, Greg's Bar – that's what it was called – had been going downhill for a long time. Horton was apparently a miserable bastard, and the locals decided they weren't going to drink there anymore. Like everywhere else in Australia, there are plenty of bars in Blair.' Granger looked up and smiled. 'Believe me, Harry, if you don't have an Australian's beer poured and on the counter the moment he walks in, you're in deep trouble.'

'Anything about Beth Horton, Gregory's wife?'

Granger laughed. 'In a manner of speaking. She was born Elizabeth McDonald in Sydney, and is twenty-three years old. According to the locals she's regarded as a bit of a charity moll.'

I glanced at Kate. 'Translate, please.'

'A part-time prostitute, guv. Usually does it for free.'

'Rumour has it that quite a few of the locals have enjoyed her favours,' Granger went on, 'and it seems that it was only her flaunting herself behind the bar that kept the business going. But eventually the clientele even got fed up with her. Or she got fed up with them. The Northern Territory's not exactly the place for a Sydney girl.'

'Horton's father said that Gregory was a mining engineer, Steve.'

'In his dreams,' said Granger. 'The local NT copper learned that he'd worked as a labourer at a bauxite mine in Gove Peninsula for a short while. Before arriving in Blair, that is. I reckon he must've been spinning his old man a yarn. Probably so he didn't look like a drongo.'

'An idiot,' interpreted Kate, before I'd even glanced in her direction. 'A no-hoper.'

'There's some suggestion that at one time Greg – he was known to everyone as Greg – got fed up with his wife hopping into other men's beds,' Granger continued, 'and they split up for a while. But he realized that he couldn't manage without her, and took her back.'

'And there's no indication where they might have gone,' I said.

'None,' said Granger. 'One day the bar was open, but in

the early part of July the shutters went up, and it hasn't been open since. If, as you say, he's just inherited eighteen million pounds, he's probably made for Sydney or Melbourne. And that was very likely his wife's idea. Although I don't see that he would have shot through *before* he got news of his inheritance. That doesn't make sense.'

'There's a lot about this job that doesn't make sense, Steve,' I said. 'You mentioned earlier that the Patersons at Waimatutu Station in Tamorah didn't know Metcalfe, but was there anything to suggest that they might've known Greg Horton?'

'No, Harry. Is there any reason for you to think that they did?'

'Only that Bruce Metcalfe was killed with a humane killer, at least according to our pathologist. And they're used on farms.'

'Well, that's original.'

'I don't suppose Greg Horton had a record, had he, Steve?'

'No chance. Whatever else he was, Horton wasn't a crim. He got involved in punch-ups with customers once or twice a week, but that's par for the course in Australia, and no one bothers about it. Our man did get a warrant, though, and searched his bar. He found a photograph hanging on the wall, and the locals identified the subjects as Greg and Beth Horton.' Granger handed over copies of a photograph of a smiling couple, their arms around each other's shoulders. 'Might be some help in tracking down the guy if you think he's here in the UK now.'

When we got back to Curtis Green, I handed the photograph of Gregory and Elizabeth Horton to Colin Wilberforce, and gave him what details we knew of the couple.

'Get that put on the Police National Computer, Colin, and I think we'll run them in the *Police Gazette*. The usual caveat: establish present location, but not to be questioned or alerted to our interest.'

'What's next, guv?' asked Kate.

'Next, Kate, is we pay the Hortons another visit at Pinner. They might have had recent contact with Gregory.'

The Hortons' two cars were parked side by side outside En Passant, their house in Pinner, indicating that the couple were at home. They didn't strike me as the sort who would ever have walked anywhere. Except, in Horton's case, around a golf course.

'Ah, the policemen,' said Katya Kaczynski. She glanced briefly at Kate. 'And woman,' she added, and opened the door wide.

Faye Horton was exactly as we had found her previously, watching television in the sitting room.

'Oh, not again!' she exclaimed, when Katya showed us in. She cast a critical eye at Kate, now dressed in her usual white shirt and jeans, and clearly did not like what she saw.

'Is your husband at home, Mrs Horton?' I asked.

'Yes, of course. He's working in his study. I suppose you want to speak to him,' said Faye Horton. Without awaiting my reply, she somewhat wearily picked up the internal telephone, and told her husband that the police were here again.

A few moments later, Maurice Horton strode into the room, an expression of annoyance on his face.

'What the hell is it now?' he demanded angrily. 'You'd better sit down,' he added, suddenly remembering his manners.

'Inspector Ebdon has obtained details of the Bartons' wills, Mr Horton. We thought you might be interested.'

'Why should I be?'

'I gather that you were anxious to obtain the shares in your property company that were held by Mrs Barton.'

'It would have been useful,' said Horton. 'And now that Diana's dead, I'm naturally curious to know what's happened to them.'

Kate took the file from her briefcase and opened it on her lap. 'As I'd anticipated, Mr Horton, Diana Barton's will left her estate to James Barton, and his will reciprocated by leaving his estate to her. However, as he died within twenty-eight days of Diana, his estate automatically reverted to her, and the entire combined legacy went to your son Gregory. That estate, in stocks, shares, property and cash, amounts to approximately eighteen million pounds.'

'That's outrageous!' exclaimed Horton, showing some emotion for the first time since we'd met him.

'My God!' muttered Faye Horton, who until then had maintained an attentive silence, but had not missed a word of what Kate had been saying. 'What on earth is that little waster going to do with all that money? It's a great shame you weren't able to find Diana before she died, Maurice.' There was a heavy note of censure in her last comment, tinged with a regret that so much money had eluded them. But I wasn't quite sure how finding Diana would've avoided the money going to Gregory.

'You know I tried, Faye, but that enquiry agent was unable to find her.' Horton made a placating gesture with his hands.

That interested me greatly. Simkins had told me that not only had he traced Diana Barton, but had informed Horton where she could be found. He'd also discovered details of James Barton's directorship, and passed those on as well. I was not about to betray Simkins's confidence, but I found it rather curious that Horton should maintain this fiction.

I could only presume that, for some reason best known to himself, he didn't want his second wife to learn that he knew where Diana was living. That might all be nonsense, of course; Faye Horton could've seen Simkins's report. It was also possible that Maurice Horton had commissioned Bruce Metcalfe to murder Diana, but I couldn't see the point of that; he must've worked out, or guessed, that her estate would go to James Barton.

On the other hand, Horton might have hoped, in the event of James dying before Diana, a good chance given the age difference, that she would have been charitable enough to bequeath the all-important shares to her ex-husband. It was also possible that, despite his denial, Maurice *had* spoken to Diana, and that she'd promised that the shares would be his in the event of her death. If that were the case, she'd virtually signed her own death warrant.

But, all things considered, Diana Barton's murder might've had nothing to do with the shares. Maurice Horton was a rich man, and had perhaps been carrying on an affair with his ex-wife. I'm a pretty good judge of women, and to me Faye Horton looked a touch frigid. Diana, on the other hand, was the complete opposite.

'You might be interested to know, Mr Horton,' I said, 'that we've identified the man who we're fairly certain murdered Mr and Mrs Barton. He was an Australian named Bruce Metcalfe.' I wondered if that would produce a reaction confirming my somewhat doubtful theory that Horton had had something to do with Metcalfe's death.

Horton raised his eyebrows. 'You have? Have you charged him?'

'No, we—'

'Why ever not?' demanded Horton.

'Because he's dead,' said Kate bluntly. 'Somebody murdered him.'

Horton shook his head. 'Who would've done that?' It was a pointless question, and I wondered if Horton was thinking aloud. Or had he murdered Metcalfe, and was putting up a smokescreen?

'We've no idea,' I said.

'Have you been in contact with Maurice's son in Australia?' Faye Horton asked me suddenly. She'd obviously been fretting about the eighteen million pounds her nominal stepson had just inherited.

'He's disappeared, Mrs Horton,' I said. 'I've had enquiries made by the Australian Federal Police, but he's not been seen for over a month.'

'D'you have any idea where he was working, Chief Inspector?' asked Horton. 'I think I told you that he was a mining engineer.'

'He wasn't,' said Kate. 'He ran a bar in Blair, a small township in the Northern Territory, not far from Darwin.'

'But that's not possible,' said Horton. 'He told me he was a mining engineer.'

'I'm afraid he lied to you,' said Kate. 'Our information is that he worked as a labourer in a bauxite mine at Gove Peninsula which is about three hundred and seventy miles from Darwin. But he wasn't there very long. Presumably that's where he made enough money to open his bar in Blair.'

'I'm finding this all very hard to believe,' said Horton. The initial arrogance had dissipated, but might have been a ploy to cover guilty knowledge.

'When did you last see your son, Mr Horton?' I still wondered if Gregory had had anything to do with Metcalfe's murder.

'When he went to Australia about seven years ago. I think I told you that it was just after my divorce from Diana.'

'And you've not seen him since?'

'No. Nor have I heard from him. Why d'you think I might've done?'

'We have reason to believe that your son might be in this country, Mr Horton,' said Kate.

'Are you from the Australian police, Inspector?' asked Faye, at last picking up on Kate's accent.

'No, I'm a Metropolitan Police officer attached to New Scotland Yard,' said Kate.

'Oh, I wondered, considering you're so very interested in Maurice's son,' said Faye Horton, and lapsed into silence again.

'If you should hear from your son, perhaps you'd let us know, Mr Horton,' I said.

'D'you think he's somehow connected to these dreadful murders?'

'We shan't know until we talk to him, but I find it rather curious that he should have disappeared from his bar in Blair a short time before Mrs Barton was murdered.'

'But you said that you knew who murdered her.' Horton gave a wonderful impression of being utterly confused by the whole business. 'A man called Metcalfe, I think you said.'

'Yes, but we don't know who murdered Metcalfe,' said Kate.

'And you suspect my son?' Horton sounded appalled at the very idea.

'You said it, not me, Mr Horton,' said Kate. 'Do you think he's capable of murder? After all, the outcome of the murders of Diana and James Barton is that Gregory Horton is richer by eighteen million pounds.'

I wasn't sure if planting that seed in Horton's mind was a good idea. If Gregory Horton did contact his father, it would be a father's instinct to protect and warn his only son that the police were looking for him.

'D'you think that something might've happened to Gregory?' asked Horton. 'You say he's disappeared, but could he be dead? You hear such awful stories about people being lost in the outback, I think you Australians call it, and never being found again.'

Kate smiled. 'I've no idea,' she said. 'But it's a possibility.'

'What would happen to all that money if Maurice's son *is* dead?' asked Faye Horton, her mind still on the fortune that, in her mind, should have gone to her husband.

'I imagine it would pass to his Australian wife Elizabeth, known as Beth,' said Kate, a statement that afforded Faye

Horton no comfort whatever. 'That's assuming they're still together, of course,' she added. 'We've heard that she was working as a prostitute at one time.' That was gilding the lily somewhat, but I imagine that Kate had said it to annoy the Hortons. And it certainly ruffled Faye's feathers.

'Good God!' she said. 'Surely not.'

Kate and I stood up to leave. 'If Gregory does get in touch, Mr Horton, be sure to let me know,' I said again, and handed him one of my cards. But I had no great hope that he would. The outcome would probably be that Gregory Horton would disappear into that great metropolis called London. I knew from experience that if that happened, it would be difficult, but not impossible, to find him.

THIRTEEN

I t was on the Friday morning that a surprise call was received in the incident room.

'I've just had a man named Bernard Graves on the phone, sir.' Colin Wilberforce came into my office holding a message form. Dave Poole followed him. 'He said he's been abroad on holiday, but has had all his newspapers held for him by his newsagent,' explained Wilberforce. 'Apparently he's a freelance journalist and likes to keep up to date with everything that's going on in the world.'

'That's all very interesting, Colin, but why's he got in touch with us?'

'He said he was at Diana Barton's party at Tavona Street the night she was murdered, sir, but he'd only just read our news release.'

'It's a racing certainty that that's the Bernie we've been looking for, guv,' said Dave. 'The guy who Gaston Potier reckoned was at the party with a bird called Samantha.'

'What's Graves's address, Colin?' I asked.

'Seventeen Coxbridge Road, Golders Green, sir.'

'Is he there now?'

'Yes, sir.'

'Right, Dave, let's go to Golders Green.'

Dave waggled a set of car keys. 'Raring to go, guv.'

Bernard Graves was about fifty but looked older, which accorded with the description of him that Liz Edwards had given us. I can only assume that the life of a journalist had taken its toll in late nights, loose women and alcohol. He was almost completely bald, and overweight. He wore an old shirt, and a pair of ragged shorts that looked as though they'd been cut down from full-length jeans. On his feet was a pair of plastic beach thongs.

'Mr Graves, we're police officers,' I said, and introduced Dave and myself.

'I take it you're here about Diana's murder,' said Graves,

peering at us through a pair of thick horn-rimmed spectacles. 'I telephoned this morning. Come in.' He led us into a comfortably furnished sitting room. On a purpose-built unit in one corner was a computer. A nearby table bore piles of newspapers and magazines next to which was a combined telephone and fax machine. On the adjacent wall to the right of the computer was a small whiteboard on which were scrawled hieroglyphics that I took to be Graves's personal shorthand notes. A framed copy of a tabloid newspaper's front page hung on another wall. The headline read: SOAP STAR IN BUBBLE BATH FROLIC WITH MARRIED FOOTBALLER. The by-line read Bernard Graves.

'I gather you're a journalist,' I said, although Colin Wilberforce had told me he was.

'That's me,' said Graves, seeing that I'd spotted his frivolous exposé. 'But I'm freelance now, and I do quite a lot of work abroad. As a matter of fact, I'm not long back from Iraq, which was not a happy experience. All of which explains why I'm not married. Not any more. Have yourselves a seat, gents.'

'You've been on holiday, you told my officer in your phone call, Mr Graves,' I said.

'Yes, I treated myself to a couple of weeks in the South of France to see how the other half lives. Mind you, I combined business with pleasure. I managed to pick up a few juicy pieces about the rich and famous cavorting on the beaches – and in the bedrooms – of Cannes. That way I'm able to charge part of the cost of the holiday against tax. Now, what can I help you with?'

'You said in your phone call that you were at Diana Barton's house in Tavona Street on the night she was killed.'

'Yes, but I understood from press reports at the time that she'd died as a result of the fire. But now I see from your news release that it's being treated as a murder enquiry.'

'That's so,' I said. 'She was stabbed several times in what you press chaps would doubtless describe as a frenzied attack.'

'God, what an awful way to die. Any idea who killed her?'

'Yes, but it's not for publication.'

Graves held up his hands in an attitude of supplication. 'I do have *some* moral principles, Chief Inspector, even though I'm a hack,' he said.

'We're fairly sure that her murderer was a man called Bruce

Metcalfe who's since been found murdered himself. But that hasn't been released to the press either.'

'Well, Metcalfe's death was no bloody loss,' said Graves. 'D'you know who killed him?'

'Not yet. From what you say, I assume that you came across Metcalfe at Mrs Barton's party.'

'Yes, I did. He was an Australian. Nasty piece of work. It's a sure thing that he was on drugs, and I do know a pothead when I see one, believe me.'

'One of the witnesses suggested that you came to the party with a girl called Samantha. A girl in her middle to late twenties.'

'I wish,' said Graves with a lascivious grin. 'I don't think a broken down scribe like me would have stood a chance with her.' He lit another cigarette from his existing one, and stubbed out the old one in an ashtray that bore the word Belga and a small picture of a girl in a 1920s hat.

'Did you talk to her?' asked Dave.

'Exchanged a few words, but she'd come with this Bruce bloke, the Aussie guy you mentioned.'

That was interesting, and contrary to the information we'd received from Potier and others, all of who had expressed the view that Metcalfe had arrived alone. 'Did she tell you anything about herself?' I asked.

'No. She struck me as a bit of an airhead. Nice body, and probably good in bed. But she'd have failed in the intelligent conversation stakes. She was Australian as well.'

I don't know why Dave did what he did next, but I was pleased that he did. He produced a copy of the photograph that the Australian Federal Police had seized from Gregory Horton's bar in Blair.

'Do you recognize the woman in this photograph, Mr Graves?'

'Yes, that's Samantha, without a doubt. Where was that taken?'

'A place called Blair, a few miles from Darwin in the Northern Territory. She and her husband ran a bar there, and her name is Elizabeth Horton.'

'That Bruce guy wasn't her husband, then. At least, that's not him in the picture.'

'No, he wasn't. Did she mention her husband?'

'Not to me she didn't. I got the impression she was free and easy. Well, certainly the latter. I wonder why she called herself Samantha.'

'Did you notice what perfume she was wearing, Mr Graves?' asked Dave.

Graves laughed. 'You must be joking,' he said. 'I can't tell one scent from another, but she was wearing something. I mean perfume; she wasn't wearing much else.'

So there we had it. Bruce Metcalfe had brought Beth Horton with him to Diana Barton's party, and she had called herself Samantha. But that posed another question: why was she there, and where was Gregory Horton? And, for that matter, where were she and her husband now?

'Did she say how long she'd been in England?' I asked.

'No, she didn't say much at all. I think she took one look at me, and decided that a fat fifty-two-year-old balding divorcé was too far over the hill for her to bother with. She wandered off, and started chatting to someone else.'

'How did you come to know Diana Barton, Mr Graves?' asked Dave.

'We're old friends. As a matter of fact, I met her about five or six years ago in the South of France. I was working for a national at the time, and I was down there to cover some scandal about a Z-list actor having a fling with a German model who was not his wife. The usual sort of muckraking that we journalists indulge in,' Graves added with a self-deprecating laugh. 'The hoot of it all was that the German model turned out to be a guy who was in the process of changing his sex. That must've dampened our soap star's ardour.'

'When you say that that's where you met Diana, how did it come about?' Dave wanted to get to the bottom of this friendship, even though it was probably of less value to our enquiries than it was to his prurient interest.

'We met in a cafe on the front at Cannes. I was enjoying my usual mid-morning brandy, and watching the passing scene. But I noticed her straight away; she was a damned attractive woman dressed in shorts and a bra top. She was having a coffee at the next table, all by herself. She asked me for a light, and we got talking. She told me that she was with her husband, but he was an old guy apparently, and not much fun to be with on holiday. Mind you, I got the impression that he wasn't much fun to be with at any time. She explained that he was something to do with the hotel business, and spent most of his day working, even on holiday. "Some holiday this has turned out to be!" was how she described it. But I know what you're working up to. Yes, we had an affair.' Graves crossed to his workstation, and opened a drawer. After spending a few minutes riffling through its contents, he produced a photograph and handed it to me. 'There, that's her. She was a good swimmer, that girl.'

The photograph showed a woman, who was undoubtedly Diana Barton, attired in a one-piece black swimsuit sitting on a sandy beach with a towel round her shoulders, and smiling at the camera.

'She was staying at the Carlton, of course. Only the best for her,' Graves continued, 'but even so she didn't mind sharing my bed at the crummy two-star I was staying in at the other end of the rue du Canada.'

'And I presume this affair continued after you both got back here,' I suggested.

'Yes.' Graves smiled. 'On and off.'

I handed Graves one of my cards. 'If you should happen to run into Beth Horton alias Samantha again, Mr Graves,' I said, 'perhaps you'd give me a ring.'

'Sure,' said Graves, tucking the card into the pocket of his shorts. 'Is there a story in it?'

'Maybe,' I said, 'but let me know first.' I'd come across journalists before who'd tried to get a story out of a suspect before notifying the police. The worst offender of my acquaintance was known as Fat Danny, crime reporter of the worst tabloid in Fleet Street. Press intervention didn't help.

It seemed that we'd now traced everyone who'd attended Diana Barton's party, but only Graves had identified Beth Horton. If we now showed her photograph to other witnesses, they might recognize her too. But, given that Graves's recognition was so positive, there seemed little point. I doubted that they could've added anything.

The next problem was to discover if she was still in England, and why she had come here in the first place. The question of the letter seized from Makepeace, Metcalfe's former landlord in Fulham, now took on a new dimension. Had Metcalfe written

it and posted it, or had Beth? If so, what was the point? And
had she been having an affair with Metcalfe? The red nail
enamel and the mascara pencil that had been found at Talleyrand
Street certainly pointed to the presence of a woman in
Metcalfe's bed-sit at some time, to say nothing of Linda's
suspicion of the presence of the perfume she'd identified as
one of the Jo Malone range. But Metcalfe was probably the
sort of disreputable character who ran a stable of women. And,
having examined his muscle-bound body in the mortuary, I
could quite see the attraction that he would have held for any
woman, particularly one who was older than he.

I rang Steve Granger again, hoping he wasn't getting too
fed up with my constant enquiries, and asked him if there was
any way in which he could find out if Beth Horton had returned
to Blair, or even Australia. I also asked if he could get as
much background information on her as possible. He promised to give it his best shot.

It would probably be a couple of days before Granger came
up with any answers to our queries, and there was nothing
that we could do in the meantime.

I reported to the commander, and briefed him on the progress
of the enquiry. His response was predictable.

'I hope you're not contemplating going to Australia, Mr Brock,'
he said once again. He seemed obsessed with expenses and
budgets.

I really don't know what he was worried about. There was
nothing more in the Job to which he could aspire. He was
now too old to be a likely candidate for promotion; he had
his pensionable time in, and had been awarded the Queen's
Police Medal for Distinguished Service. I couldn't begin to
visualize what sort of distinguished service had merited that
award, but the dual hierarchies of the Ministry of Justice and
the Metropolitan Police work in mysterious ways.

I decided to take the weekend off, but left a message with
the incident room to say that I was to be contacted if anything
arose that was likely to be of interest to me. I was pessimistic
enough to think that someone else would probably be murdered,
given that I intended to spend the weekend with Gail.

To say that Gail was surprised that I had taken time off in the
middle of a murder investigation was putting it mildly.

'I didn't expect to see you on a Saturday afternoon. Haven't you got any murders to solve? Or have you solved them all?' I'd noticed that the longer Gail spent with me, the more cynical she became. It must be contagious.

I explained briefly why there was a hold up in my enquiries without bothering her too much with the sordid details.

'What d'you fancy doing?' I asked. 'Somewhere quiet for dinner, perhaps? There's that place—'

'Actually, I'd arranged to go for a swim at Bill and Charlie Hunter's place at Esher this afternoon,' said Gail, cutting across my suggestion. 'But I'm sure they'd be delighted to see you again. Bill is always talking about how interesting it was to talk to a real detective. You do remember them, don't you, darling?'

'I'm not sure,' I said, deliberately adopting a pensive expression. 'Isn't his wife Charlie the very shapely brunette who looks terrific in a bikini? An actress, I seem to recall, and Bill does very little in the City, but makes a lot of money doing it.'

'I see you do remember them.' Gail laughed and gave me a playful punch. 'But Bill took a bit of a knock in the depression.'

'I'm sorry to hear that.'

'He had to sell the Rolls Royce and buy a Jaguar.'

'Tough!' I said.

'I'll drive,' said Gail.

It was an exceptionally hot August afternoon, and although the Hunters' secluded pool looked inviting, it was not tempting enough for me. Gail and Charlie spent most of their time splashing about in the water, or just standing chatting and cooling off, but Bill and I sat on the sidelines, drinking whisky sours.

'Gail tells me that you're dealing with the murder of Jimmy Barton, Harry,' said Bill.

'That's right.' My antenna immediately went on the alert.

'As a matter of fact, I knew him. We did a bit of business a few years ago. Bit of a dry old stick. Totally consumed by the need to make money, but he never seemed to give a thought about how to spend it. Didn't really see the point of amassing all that filthy lucre just for the sake of it. If I'd been his age,

I'd've retired long ago. You can have too much of the City, you know, Harry.'

'Did you meet his wife, Bill?'

'First or second?'

'Diana, his second wife.'

Bill Hunter laughed, and took a sip of his whisky. 'Yeah, I met her, old boy. Positively exuded sex. I could see she was a bloody dangerous woman the moment I set eyes on her.'

'I take it you weren't tempted?' I asked, softening the question with a laugh.

'Oh, come off it, Harry. Just take a look at her.' Bill pointed at the figure of Charlie who, together with Gail, was at last emerging from the pool, and squeezing the water out of her long hair as the pair of them walked across to the shower. 'With a wife like that, would I need a woman seven years older than me who was married to a guy I was doing business with? No way.'

'I take it you didn't become friendly with them.'

'Not at all. As I said, Jimmy Barton was as dry as dust. He'd've bored for England, that guy, and I told you what I thought of his wife. They'd've made a dinner party from hell. Have you found out who murdered them yet?'

I waited until Bill had poured me another drink before I replied.

'We think it was an itinerant Australian she was having an affair with. One of many.'

'One of many Australians?'

'No, one of many lovers.' I decided not to say any more. Bill was a nice bloke, but City people are notorious for leaking like sieves when it comes to keeping a secret.

'I'm not surprised. Got him locked up?'

'In a manner of speaking,' I said. 'He's in the mortuary.'

Bill laughed; he laughed easily. 'I like your style, Harry. What happened to him, then?'

'He was murdered,' I said, and left it at that.

Having spent some time chatting under the shower, the girls finally joined us, and stretched out on the recliners next to ours.

'Charlie's invited us to stay for dinner, darling,' said Gail. 'She's a very good cook.'

'Are you sure it's no trouble, Charlie?' I posed the question out of politeness, but was pleased that we'd be spending more time in the Hunters' company. 'I rather feel that we're in danger of wearing out our welcome.'

'Don't be silly,' said Charlie. 'We're delighted to see you both. Anyway, I've got plenty of stuff in, and I'll soon throw something together. Won't be a banquet, though.'

But it was; Charlie proved to be as good a cook as Gail. She and Bill were delightful hosts, and the conversation was light-hearted and non-stop. But then Gail and Charlie started talking seriously about the theatre, and their respective professional careers. Bill looked at the ceiling with an expression of hopeless despair, and took me into his study for a brandy and a cigar.

By the time we took our leave, at nearly one in the morning, I'd had much too much to drink, and I was pleased that Gail had opted to drive. It's not that far from Esher to Kingston, but taxi drivers know how to charge. Especially when they've got a passenger who's smashed out of his skull.

We spent what remained of the night at Gail's town house, and lounged about all day Sunday. I didn't have much alternative: I was recovering from a hangover, a state of health that received no sympathy from Gail.

I arrived at Curtis Green on the stroke of nine o'clock on Monday morning.

'Good morning, sir,' said Colin Wilberforce. 'Inspector Granger's in your office, and I've given him a cup of coffee. He has some information for you, and he said he'd rather give you the details in person.'

'G'day, Harry,' said Granger, as he stood up and shook hands. 'I don't think much of your coffee.'

'I love you too, Steve.' We both sat down. 'What've you got for me?'

'Our man in Darwin's done some digging among the locals. Your Beth Horton's got quite a history.'

'That doesn't surprise me, Steve.'

'I told you before that she was born in Sydney, but her parents, the McDonalds, bought a farm, what we call a station down under, not far from Tamorah. Not long afterwards, the McDonalds, Beth's parents, were killed in a plane crash. Mick McDonald was taking his family for a spin and

the kite just spiralled out of control and hit the ground.
Miraculously, Beth survived unscathed, and from about the
age of five she was brought up by her grandparents who took
over the running of the station.'

'I presume there was nothing suspicious about the crash,'
I said, but only out of policeman's interest.

'No idea,' said Granger. 'However, Greg Horton appeared
on the scene about six years ago and opened his bar in Blair,
having spent a year or so at the bauxite mine in Gove Peninsula
that I told you about. He met up with Beth almost immediately, she was seventeen by then, and they later shacked up
together in Tandy Street. There are living quarters over the
bar. They were married a couple of years later.'

'She'd know how to use a humane killer, then.'

'I guess so, mate. But here's the interesting bit. According
to the then local constable, who's now a sergeant in Darwin
city, your Bruce Metcalfe worked on the McDonalds' station
as a jackaroo for a couple of years. The local gossip is that
he deflowered Beth when she was sixteen, and carried on
screwing her until she met Greg, and perhaps even afterwards.
And she probably kept on seeing Metcalfe until he shot
through. No one's quite sure when he left, and as the
McDonalds, Beth's grandparents, are now both dead, there's
no telling. The present owners of the station haven't got any
records that cover the period the McDonalds were running
the place.'

'And she's not been seen since Greg Horton closed his bar.'

'Neither has Greg, Harry. Not a single trace of either of
'em.'

'Well, thanks for that, Steve,' I said, as Granger stood up
to leave. 'All I've got to do now is to find out if she's still
here in the UK, because anyone who can use a humane killer
has got to be a front runner for topping Bruce Metcalfe.'

'Best of luck, mate,' said Granger, and shook hands. 'If I
can help any further, give me a call.'

When Steve Granger had left, I called Kate and Dave into my
office, and briefed them on what Steve had told me.

'D'you reckon Beth's up for it, guv?' asked Dave.

'It's our most promising lead so far, Dave,' I said. 'We know
from Bernie Graves that she was at the kitchen party. Give

the Border Agency a call, and see if they've a record of when Beth Horton arrived in this country. And more to the point, if they've a record of her leaving.'

'We should be so lucky,' muttered Dave, who had no great faith in the Border Agency's efficiency. 'By the way, should we tell them about Barnes, the kitchen man, employing a guy who was probably only here on a visitor's permit?'

'Forget it, Dave. Barnes did us a good turn. If the Border Agency want to make a federal case out of it, good luck to them, but they won't get any help from me.'

Despite Dave's pessimistic view of Britain's immigration controls, fortune was on our side.

'Beth Horton arrived at Heathrow Airport on Wednesday the seventeenth of July, guv,' said Dave, when he swanned into my office half an hour later. 'There's no record of her departure, for what that's worth. But here's the good bit: she told the immigration officer that she was here on holiday, and would be staying with her in-laws, the Hortons in Pinner.'

'And they'll be bound to deny it,' I said.

'They'll have a job, guv. When Beth Horton arrived, the immigration officer checked with the Hortons and they confirmed that Beth would be staying with them.'

'Well, well, well. Guess where we're going next, Dave.'

Dave sighed. 'The car will be able to find its own way to Pinner if we go on at this rate, guv,' he said.

FOURTEEN

'Don't you people ever give up?' Faye Horton was radiating fury when once again Katya Kaczynski showed us into the sitting room of the Hortons' elegant house. 'I really can't understand why you have to keep pestering us. I'm sure we've answered all your questions, and I'd've thought that that was an end to the matter, particularly now that Diana Barton's murderer is dead. Or so you told us, did you not?'

'Is your husband at home, Mrs Horton?' I asked, ignoring the woman's sarcastic tirade. I guessed that he was: the Mercedes was parked outside.

With a cluck of annoyance, Faye Horton snatched at the internal telephone. 'The wretched police are here again, Maurice. They want to talk to you *yet again*,' she said, and slammed down the receiver.

A full five minutes later, Maurice Horton burst into the room, a pen held in one hand, and a writing pad clutched in the other. The impression that he obviously meant to convey was that we'd interrupted his work.

'What is it this time?' he demanded truculently.

'It concerns your daughter-in-law, Mr Horton,' I said. We'd not been invited to sit down, and remained standing.

'What about her?'

'When did you last see her?'

'I've never seen her. I told you before that my son emigrated to Australia shortly after my divorce from Diana, and has never returned. He married some Australian girl, and I've not met her. I've not been in touch with either of them. There, is that clear enough for you?' Horton put his writing pad on a table, slipped his pen into his shirt pocket and thrust his hands into his trouser pockets.

'We've had a report from the Border Agency,' began Dave mildly, 'that Elizabeth Horton arrived in this country on the seventeenth of July this year. She stated to the immigration officer who dealt with her at Heathrow Airport that she'd been invited to stay with you. The immigration officer said that he telephoned you to confirm this arrangement, and you agreed that this was the case.'

'That's stuff and nonsense.' However, Horton's reaction indicated that he'd been wrong-footed by the thoroughness of our enquiries.

'Are you saying that you did not receive such a telephone call?' persisted Dave. 'I have to point out that serious offences might have been committed if you or your daughter-in-law made false statements to the authorities. The penalties are quite severe.'

'Yes, Sergeant, it's true, but it came to nothing.' In the face of Dave's implied threat, Horton capitulated and sat down, indicating with a wave of his hand that we should do so as well. 'I did receive such a phone call. I have to say that her arrival came as a complete surprise to me. I had no idea that she was coming here, and I'd certainly not heard from her in advance. No letter, no email, no phone call, nothing. But as she was married to my son, I could hardly refuse. Apart from anything else, I was interested to meet the girl who Gregory had married.'

'When did she arrive here, Mr Horton?' I asked. 'At this house.'

But it was Faye Horton, now more conciliatory than before, who answered. 'She never did arrive, Chief Inspector. We're not all that far from Heathrow, as I'm sure you appreciate – fifteen miles or so – and we'd anticipated that she'd be here within an hour at the most. If we'd known in advance, one of us could have driven over to collect her. I arranged for Katya to prepare a room for her, but Elizabeth never turned up. We didn't hear from her, or of her, again. We've no idea where she went, or where she is now.'

'Did this official at the airport mention my son, Chief Inspector?' asked Horton wearily, his mood having changed to one of contrition. 'Was he not with her?'

'No, he wasn't, and we've no idea whether he's in this country or still in Australia. As I told you last time we were here, he's not been seen in Blair since about the middle of July.'

'Why are you so anxious to speak to Elizabeth, then?' asked Horton.

'We've reason to believe that she was having an affair with Bruce Metcalfe, the man who was found murdered last

Wednesday, and whom we believe murdered Diana and James
Barton. We've been told by the Australian police that she and
Metcalfe had a sexual relationship in Australia, although how
long it lasted, if in fact it did, we don't know.' I based that
statement on the information I'd received from Steve Granger.

'A sexual relationship?'

'I don't know why you're so surprised, Mr Horton,' I said.
'The last time we were here, Inspector Ebdon told you that
Elizabeth had a reputation in Blair as a part-time prostitute.'

'And now you're suggesting that she came to this country
to continue the affair with this Metcalfe here as well as in
Australia. After she was married to my son.' Suddenly the
appalling truth struck Horton. His mouth opened, and for a
moment he stared at me uncomprehending. 'Do you think it
likely that she could have had something to do with Metcalfe's
murder?' he asked eventually.

'It is a possibility I'm bound to consider,' I said. 'Scientific
tests are still being carried out.'

'Good God! But what possible reason could she have had?'
Horton glanced at his wife, but Faye just shrugged, as though
such a prospect came as no surprise to her. And Faye's reaction made me wonder whether Beth Horton *had* been here.
Why else should Horton have lied initially? Were he and his
wife covering up for Elizabeth?

'That is something I can only resolve by speaking to her,
Mr Horton. In the circumstances, I must ask you to let me
know if she does contact you.' I handed him one of my cards.

Horton stared vacantly at the card, and thrust it into his
pocket. 'Of course,' he said. And then another thought occurred
to him. 'D'you think something might've happened to Gregory,
Mr Brock?'

'I can only repeat what I said before, Mr Horton. The
Australian police have no idea where your son is, and to the
best of our knowledge he's not been seen since the middle of
July. However, enquiries are continuing in the Darwin area in
an attempt to discover his present whereabouts.'

I could sense what was going through Horton's mind: if
we suspected his daughter-in-law of murdering Metcalfe, she
might also have murdered Gregory. There was a large sum of
money at stake, eighteen million pounds, and murders have
been committed for less of a reason than that.

Faye Horton put it into words. 'That bitch is after your money, Maurice,' she said. 'And I doubt that she'd stop at anything to lay her hands on it.'

But that was a conclusion founded on a false premise. If Beth Horton inherited the money, there was no chance that Maurice Horton would receive any of it.

'Have you any basis for thinking that, Mrs Horton?' I asked.

'Well, it stands to reason, doesn't it?'

That's exactly the sort of female logic that Gail sometimes came up with, and there was no point in arguing with it.

I decided that there was little to be gained by questioning the Hortons any further, and we took our leave. For the present.

'Not a very happy pair of bunnies,' said Dave, as we walked back to our car.

And that seemed to encapsulate the Hortons' reaction to the whole affair.

The moment we got into the car, I received a call on my mobile from Colin Wilberforce.

'Yes, what is it, Colin?'

'Inspector Granger telephoned, sir, to say that he has some important news for you and it's urgent. He'd be grateful if you could call on him at his office.'

I glanced at my watch. 'We're just leaving Pinner now, Colin. Ring Mr Granger back and tell him I'll be with him ASAP.'

I was in a mood of some despair by the time Dave and I reached Australia House. The conversation with Maurice and Faye Horton had been largely fruitless. They could've been telling the truth, but there again, they might've been lying through their respective teeth. However, it was patently clear that we would need to find Beth Horton as soon as possible. But where was she?

And the news, momentous though it was, that Steve Granger gave me only served to complicate the issue further.

'Greg Horton's been found, Harry,' said Steve Granger, the moment Dave and I walked into his office.

'Has he been interviewed, Steve?'

'Be a bit difficult, mate,' said Steve with a laugh. 'He's dead.'

I groaned. 'That's all I need. What were the circumstances, Steve?' I asked.

'There's absolutely no doubt that he was murdered, Harry.

The post-mortem was a bit difficult by all accounts, because
Horton's body had been dumped in the outback not far from
Tamorah. It was spotted by a police helicopter on a routine
patrol. Apparently the dingoes had been at the remains, but
there was enough of him left to make a positive identification,
and for the pathologist to come up with an approximate date
of death. He reckoned he'd been lying out there for over a
month.'

'It's possible, then, that the time of death was just before
Beth Horton arrived in England on the seventeenth of last
month.' I said. 'Was the pathologist able to suggest a cause
of death, Steve?'

'You're going to love this, Harry. His expert medical opinion
was that Horton was murdered with a humane killer.'

'Which is what killed Bruce Metcalfe. It's all beginning to
fall into place, Steve,' I said, hoping that I was not reaching
an unjustified conclusion. 'If I remember correctly, you said
that Greg and Beth Horton disappeared from Blair during the
early part of July. That tends to tie up with the time of Greg's
murder, and Beth Horton arrived in the UK a short while
later.'

'There's something else that might interest you,' said
Granger. 'The Northern Territory CIB are investigating the
murder, of course, and after Greg Horton's body was found
they did a thorough search of his bar premises in Blair. Among
the items they discovered was a seven-year-old letter postmarked London, England. It contained a note from Diana
Barton, written from Tavona Street, Chelsea, and a copy of
her will. The note explained that she had got married again,
to a James Barton, a director of a hotel company, who was
twenty-seven years older than she was. It went on to explain
that in the event of her death, and she made the assumption
that it would be after that of her new husband, her entire estate
would be left to Greg. Diana Barton also assured her son that,
in that event, he would be worth several million pounds.'

'And that, Steve, has all the hallmarks of a grade-A motive
for murder,' I said. 'What are the latest developments in
Australia?'

'The NT Police also found a humane killer on the premises that yielded a DNA trace matching that of Greg Horton.
There were fingerprints on it, too, and they produced a match

with some of the prints found in the bar. They're probably Beth's, but they can't be sure because she doesn't have a record. Yet! However, that didn't stop the NT CIB obtaining a warrant for Beth Horton's arrest, and at their request the Federal Police in Canberra have issued an Interpol red-corner circular. So you can now arrest her, and my government will apply for a fugitive offender's warrant for her return to Aussie. The boys at Federal Police HQ promise they'll fax me all the necessary paperwork as soon as they can.'

'I'm not surrendering her to you if I can prove she murdered Bruce Metcalfe, Steve. If that's the case, and I get a conviction, you can have her back in about twenty years' time. And that's assuming the judge is lenient.'

'We couldn't care less either way, Harry,' said Steve, 'so long as someone succeeds in getting her sent down. But all you've got to do now is find the bitch.'

'If she's still in the UK,' I said.

'I doubt she'll have gone back home,' said Steve. 'She must know that Greg's body would be found sooner or later. Unless she'd hoped the dingoes would consume it completely.'

'It looks as though she found Diana Barton's will,' I mused aloud, 'and decided that with Diana and Diana's husband out of the way, she'd benefit from the will. Provided Greg was out of the way, too.'

'So where does your man Metcalfe fit into it, Harry?'

'You told me that she and Metcalfe had had a relationship when he worked on her grandparents' farm. And that it possibly continued after she married Greg Horton.'

'That's the information I got from our man in Darwin.'

'Well, I reckon she must've discussed Diana Barton's letter with Metcalfe, and that they hatched a plot to dispose of the Bartons and Greg. She probably agreed to split the proceeds with Metcalfe. The next thing that happened was that Metcalfe came over here and murdered Diana and James Barton. But I suspect that the greedy Beth then decided to top Metcalfe so that she'd have all the loot to herself. But I'll bet she never reckoned on it amounting to as much as eighteen million quid. And I daresay she was banking on the two murders in England never being tied up with the one in Australia.'

'I'll leave you to it, then, Harry,' said Granger. 'As I said, the AFP in Canberra will forward the paperwork to me, and I'll get the High Commissioner to endorse it and send it across to your authorities. The rest is down to you.'

When Dave and I arrived at Curtis Green, I called Kate into the office and told her the latest information that I'd received from Australia. 'All we've got to do now is find Beth Horton,' I said.

'D'you reckon she'll eventually show up at the Hortons' place at Pinner, guv?' asked Kate.

'Possibly.'

'I was thinking in terms of an obo,' suggested Kate.

'An observation would take up a lot of manpower.' As I said it, I was grateful that Kate wasn't one of those feminists who insisted on adding 'and womanpower'.

'What about an intercept on the Hortons' telephone, guv?' said Dave.

I considered both proposals. 'I doubt that Beth Horton will go anywhere near her father-in-law's place,' I said eventually. 'I'm sure she only said that she'd be staying with Maurice Horton as an excuse to get past the immigration people, and she's lucky he said yes. If she's on the run from the Australian police she'd know that Maurice Horton would be the first person we'd contact. I think we'll let the idea of an obo or an intercept sweat for the time being.' As it turned out, an intercept on the Hortons' telephone might have saved us a little time, but in the end it didn't matter. 'In the meantime, Dave, get Colin Wilberforce to add to her details on the PNC and in the *Police Gazette* that she's now wanted on a fugitive offender's warrant for murder in Australia. Add the usual caveat: not to be questioned.'

'What about the shares, guv?' asked Kate.

'What shares?' I have to admit that this investigation was getting more than a bit complicated, and I wondered, briefly, what Kate was talking about.

'The shares that Diana Barton held in Maurice Horton's company. Presumably, now that Beth Horton's inherited them, she'll want to put them into her name, otherwise she won't get the dividends.'

'D'you think she'll bother? She's just become eighteen million pounds richer. Not that she'll ever lay hands on the money if she's convicted of Greg's murder. But she probably doesn't think it'll come to that, and wouldn't know the law anyway.'

'In my experience, guv, people with a lot of money always want more,' said Kate philosophically.

'See if you can get alongside the people at Companies House, then, Kate. If she re-registers the shares, she'll have to provide an address.'

Dave scoffed. 'And it might even be a genuine one,' he said.

'Should we let Maurice Horton know about the death of his son, guv?' Kate asked.

'We should do, I suppose,' I said thoughtfully, 'but I'd rather see what you find out first. Only Inspector Granger, and the three of us know that Steve told us of Greg's death today. I'm still not happy about the Hortons, and before we visit them again I'd like a little more ammunition.'

'Got it in mind to shoot them, then, guv?' asked Dave.

It was midday the following day by the time that Kate Ebdon came up with the goods. At least, that was my first impression, but the information she'd obtained only served to create further problems.

'Believe it or not, guv, Beth Horton has registered herself at Companies House as the new owner of the shares,' she said, as she and Dave came into my office.

'You're joking,' I said.

'No, she sent them an email, and before you ask, she sent it from an Internet cafe in the West End. The address she gave them is a bank in Earls Court,' said Kate, handing me the details.

'What a surprise.'

'But Companies House are obliged by law to stay the implementation of the change of ownership until probate is issued.'

Dave emitted a cynical laugh. 'That'll slow it down,' he said. 'With shares in England and probate in Australia it could take forever.'

'Nevertheless, we do have the bank's details,' said Kate.

I glanced at Dave, my expert on the Police and Criminal Evidence Act. 'Well, Dave, what's the form?'

'We could just ask whoever is in charge of the bank, guv, but I'm in no doubt that he'll refuse unless we've got the

appropriate piece of paper. Bank documents are called "special
procedure material" under PACE, and we'll need to obtain an
order from a circuit judge.'

That's what I meant about complicating the issue. And it
was a bloody nuisance.

The Central Criminal Court at Old Bailey was where the nearest
circuit judges were to be found, and having prepared my 'information', I set out to try to persuade one of them to issue the
appropriate order.

I was in luck. Having mentioned the Fugitive Offenders
Act, my need to trace a person wanted for murder in Australia,
and possibly another murder here, I obtained my order. But
only after a bit of verbal jousting with His Honour.

Dave and I went straight from the Bailey to the bank that
Beth Horton had nominated as her address.

In the face of an order from a Crown Court judge, and that
the subject of that order was wanted for murder, the manager
in charge of the bank at Earls Court sent for the relevant documents without demur.

'Here we are, Chief Inspector,' he said, opening a slender
file containing a computer printout. 'Mrs Elizabeth Horton
opened an account here on Wednesday the thirty-first of July,
and produced an Australian passport to confirm her identity.
At that time, she deposited the sum of one hundred pounds.
When I asked for her address she furnished it as care of Maurice
Horton at En Passant, Roget Road, Pinner, Middlesex.'

'The saucy bitch,' muttered Dave.

The manager looked up in some alarm. 'Is there something
wrong with that address? Is it false?'

'There's nothing wrong with the address,' I said. 'In fact,
Sergeant Poole and I have been there. It's the address of Mrs
Horton's father-in-law, but she's never been there, and isn't
expected. In fact, we've no idea where she is.'

'It's just as well that I refused to activate the account until
such time as confirmation of the address was produced, then,'
said the manager. 'I've written Mr Horton a letter, but have
received no answer so far. Perhaps I should telephone him,
and see what he has to say.'

'I'd rather you didn't,' I said. 'In the unlikely event that
Mrs Elizabeth Horton does contact Mr Maurice Horton, I don't

want her alerted to the fact that we're looking for her. As I explained, she's wanted for a murder in Australia.'

'But this leaves the account in a rather unsatisfactory state of limbo.' The manager gave the impression of being unduly concerned about loose ends and bits of paper. He'd get on well with my commander.

'I shouldn't worry too much about that,' I said, and related, as briefly as possible, details of the eighteen million pounds that Elizabeth Horton was set to inherit once probate had been granted. 'But I doubt that she will,' I added. 'If Mrs Horton's convicted of her husband's murder the law prohibits her profiting from it. But in your trade you probably know that.'

'Eighteen million?' The manager's eyes lit up, albeit briefly. But then he shrugged as he realized that any chance of making interest on that amount of money had just slipped through his fingers.

Dave and I returned to Curtis Green. We'd gone to all the trouble of obtaining an order from a circuit judge, but it had been to no avail. But neither of us was surprised.

FIFTEEN

The telephone call came at just gone midday on the day after my visit to the bank.

'Chief Inspector, it's Bernie Graves. D'you remember you came to see me at Golders Green about the party at Diana's place?'

'I do indeed, Mr Graves. How can I help you?'

'It's more a case of how I can help you,' said Graves. There was a note of triumph in his voice. 'I spotted Samantha this morning. That's to say, the woman you said was Beth Horton. The girl who was at the party.'

It was ironic, but somehow predictable, that a journalist should eventually be the one to point us in the right direction.

When I'd handed Bernie Graves my card, I'd thought no more about it. I always gave my card to witnesses with a request that should anything more occur to them they should let me know. It rarely did, but now Bernie Graves proved that there could always be an exception.

'Where was this, Mr Graves?'

'She was shopping in Knightsbridge.'

'What were you doing in Knightsbridge?'

'Shopping, of course.' The tone of Graves's response indicated that he thought it a pointless question.

'What time was this, that you saw her?'

There was a pause. 'First off, at about eleven o'clock, I suppose.'

'Did you speak to her?'

'No, but I followed her. We journalists can be quite good at that sort of thing.'

'Where did she go?' I asked. God preserve me from amateur sleuths.

'She went on quite a tour of the shops in that area, and seemed to be spending a lot of money,' said Graves, and went on to list the establishments that Beth Horton had visited. 'It was pretty bloody obvious that she was on one hell of a spending spree.'

'Did you happen to notice how she paid for her purchases?' I asked, hoping that, in addition to his surveillance skills, Graves also possessed a journalist's eye for detail.

'With a credit card, but I wasn't going to get close enough to see the details. Not without her sussing me out. She might've remembered me from Diana's party, you see.'

'And where did she go after she'd finished shopping?'

'She hailed a taxi and took off.' Graves paused in his narrative. 'I'm afraid I lost her. There wasn't another cab in sight. But there never is when you want one. Bit like coppers really.'

'Well, thanks for your help, Mr Graves. That's all been extremely helpful.' And I meant it. Assuming that it was Beth Horton that he had seen, there was a chance that we could trace her through her credit card. Providing that she'd used her own name to acquire it, and that we could link it to the shops Graves said she'd patronized. And if it happened to be an Australian credit card, that would simplify the enquiry, but life was never that easy.

I got hold of Charlie Flynn, an ex-Fraud Squad sergeant who knew his way around credit card companies, repeated what Graves had told me, and asked him to make a check on the shops that he'd told me our suspect had visited. 'See if you can get details of the plastic she was using, Charlie,' I said, and gave him a list of the shops and the approximate times she had entered each one.

It was not until three o'clock on the following afternoon, Friday, that Charlie Flynn was able to produce an answer of sorts.

'I visited all the shops that were on the list that Graves gave you, guv. Based on the times he said Beth Horton went into each one, I was able to get details of the credit card that was used on each of those occasions. It's in the name of Samantha Crisp. I then went to the company that issued the card, but the bad news is that the address they have for her is En Passant, Roget Road, Pinner. I think that's the address of her in-laws.'

'Yes, it is, Charlie, and I'm not surprised. But how the hell did she get a card that she was able to use so quickly? They seem to chuck these things around like they're going out of fashion. Did the company do a credit rating check?'

'Yes, guv, but not the usual one. The credit manager told me that this Samantha Crisp referred her to a Mrs Faye Horton, and Mrs Horton vouched for the girl. Apparently Mrs Horton, Mrs Faye Horton, that is, has a card with the same company and agreed to stand as guarantor. I took a statement from the woman who made the phone call.'

'I think we're getting somewhere at last, Charlie,' I said.

Flynn looked surprised. 'Is that good news, then, guv? It looked to me like it was a dead end.'

'On the contrary, Charlie, it's great. I've had my suspicions about Faye Horton from the word go. Ask Miss Ebdon to come in.'

'Charlie Flynn said you were pleased about something, guv,' said Kate, appearing in my office moments later.

She already knew what Graves had told me, and now I brought her up to speed on the result of Flynn's enquiries. 'I reckon that Faye Horton has a lot of questions to answer, Kate, and the sooner we start asking them, the sooner we might track down her step-daughter-in-law.'

It was just on six o'clock by the time that Kate and I arrived at the Horton residence at Pinner. I'd decided against bringing Dave; three was a somewhat oppressive crowd in the circumstances, and the presence of Kate would be useful. Particularly if it got to the point of arresting Faye Horton, a course of action that was beginning to look more and more likely. And with that in mind, I'd arranged for a car with a driver.

The Mercedes and the Lexus were outside, together with a Rolls Royce and a Jaguar. There was also a maroon Bentley parked there.

'Crikey!' exclaimed Kate, pointing at the Bentley. 'I hope that's not the Queen paying a visit. If it is, I don't suppose they'll be having a barbie in the backyard.' As those of us working in the capital knew, many of the royal fleet of cars had maroon livery.

'I doubt it,' I said. 'That Bentley's got a number plate, and the Queen's hasn't.'

Katya Kaczynski opened the door. This evening she was dressed formally in a black dress, albeit with a very short skirt, black tights and shoes, and a white frilly apron. It looked as though we were about to interrupt a dinner party. 'Ah! The police persons. You wish the Mr Horton, is it?'

'We wish indeed, Katya,' said Kate.

The reaction of the Hortons was predictable.

'My God, this is intolerable!' exclaimed Maurice Horton, staring at us malevolently. In a group around him stood an elderly grey-haired man smoking a cigarette, a younger man with a moustache, and an olive-skinned fellow with a neatly trimmed goatee beard. They were all wearing dinner jackets and holding crystal tumblers. Faye Horton and another woman, a rather overweight blonde of about forty, were seated in armchairs, sipping champagne. Two other women were seated side by side on a wide sofa. All four were elegantly attired in full-length evening gowns that must have cost a small fortune. Kate told me later that Faye Horton was wearing silk sandals by Jimmy Choo. It meant nothing to me, but doubtless would have impressed my girlfriend.

'I'm sorry to disturb you, Mr Horton,' I said, 'but it's important that I speak to you, preferably alone.'

'Won't this wait?' demanded Faye Horton. 'It can't have escaped your notice that we're entertaining guests. And we're proposing to sit down to dinner very shortly.'

'This gentleman is my solicitor.' Maurice Horton indicated the grey-haired man, but didn't mention his name.

I hoped that Kate wouldn't make some smart remark about guilty conscience, but fortunately she remained silent. Nevertheless, it was interesting that Horton saw fit to mention the occupation of only one of his guests.

'It won't take long, Mr Horton.'

Horton glanced at his solicitor friend. 'I'm sorry about this, Geoffrey, but the police have been plaguing the life out of us recently. It's all to do with Diana's death.' He turned to face me. 'You'd better come into my study.' Still holding his glass, he led the way.

The study, on the far side of the spacious hall, was a snug thickly carpeted room. In addition to a custom-built workstation on which were a hi-tech computer and all the gismos that went with it, the room had a number of leather club armchairs. I suspected that they had been selected for their appearance rather than their comfort. However, we were not immediately given the opportunity to test my theory. At one end of the room stood a faux antique desk with an inlaid leather top; a captain's chair was positioned behind it.

'Well?' Maurice Horton stood near the desk beneath a tasteful full-length life-size painting of a naked woman. She was standing side-on to the artist, but she was looking directly at him. I recognized the subject of the portrait as Faye Horton.

'Well?' snapped Horton again. His feet were apart, his stance implying extreme annoyance, animosity, and a general lack of willingness to co-operate.

'I'm sorry to have to tell you that your son has been found dead, Mr Horton.' There was no easy way to break news of this kind, and I'd found over the years that a straight, bald statement was the best way of doing it.

'Oh God, no!' Horton's jaw dropped and, swaying slightly, he reached out to the desk for support before sitting down in the chair behind it. 'How did he die?' he asked. All his initial hostility had vanished.

'I'm afraid he was murdered, Mr Horton.'

'Murdered!' Horton suddenly realized that we were still standing. 'Please sit down.' He glanced at Kate. 'I'm sorry, my dear,' he said, 'I'm forgetting my manners, but this has come as a terrible shock.' Slowly lifting a whisky decanter from his desk, he poured a substantial measure into his glass with a shaking hand. 'Are you in a position to give me any of the details, Chief Inspector?' He paused, confused. 'Oh, er, would you like a drink?'

'No thanks.' I emphasized my refusal by making a staying motion with my hand. 'Your son's body was discovered on the fifteenth of this month, but we've only just been advised of it by the Australian authorities,' I said, bending the truth only a little. 'He was found in the outback near a place called Tamorah in the Northern Territory. It's not far from the City of Darwin.'

'Do you know who was responsible for his death?'

This was the part that I knew would distress Horton even more. 'The Northern Territory Police have obtained a warrant for the arrest of your daughter-in-law Elizabeth Horton. We'll be receiving papers seeking her return to Australia under the provisions of the Fugitive Offenders Act.'

'His wife murdered him? But why? This is the most terrible news.' Horton shook his head like a boxer who'd just received a debilitating blow to the solar plexus.

'And I have certain evidence that causes me to believe she might also have been responsible for the murder of Bruce Metcalfe. He, of course, was the man who, scientific evidence seems to indicate, was guilty of the murders of Diana Barton and her husband James.'

'Have you any idea where Elizabeth is?' Horton spoke haltingly, as though all this information was too much for him to take in at one time.

'Not at the moment, Mr Horton, although we have reason to think that she's still in this country. Enquiries have been put in hand to trace her. However, we believe that your wife might be able to assist us in that regard.'

'Oh really? How can you possibly think that Faye might have anything to do with it?' Some of Horton's hostility returned with that question.

I explained about the credit card, and that we had a statement from the credit manager at the Visa company that issued it, testifying that Faye Horton had stood as guarantor for Beth Horton.

'I don't believe it,' said Horton, although his expression indicated that he was merely making a token denial.

'When your wife was telephoned by the credit manager, it was explained to her that a woman named Samantha Crisp was applying for a credit card, and claimed to be living at this address. Your wife confirmed that that was the case, and offered to guarantee her repayments. We believe Samantha Crisp and Elizabeth Horton to be one and the same.'

It was opportune that, at that moment, Faye Horton entered the study. 'Are you going to be much longer?' she demanded haughtily. Although she looked at her husband, the question was meant for me. 'We're waiting to sit down to dinner.' Paradoxically, her very hauteur made her more attractive. Her emerald-green silk gown was strapless, and displayed her elegant shoulders to advantage, their tan suggesting hours spent on a sun bed. A single string of pearls and matching stud earrings completed the picture of a stylish, rich and pampered woman.

'Sit down,' said Horton curtly.

'I *beg* your pardon, Maurice!' Faye's very pose emanated fury, but at once revealed an animal magnetism that had not been apparent before.

'I said sit down. The chief inspector has some questions to ask you.' Horton's brusque tone of voice brooked no refusal.

Without another word, Faye Horton took a seat in the only vacant club chair. She crossed her legs, linked her hands in her lap, and gazed imperiously at me. 'Well?'

But I let Kate kick off.

'You undertook to stand as guarantor for a woman called Samantha Crisp when she applied for a credit card, Mrs Horton.' said Kate. 'You were told that that woman claimed to reside at this address, and you confirmed it. We have a statement to this effect from the credit manager.'

'I don't know what you're talking about,' said Faye, but her sudden breaking of eye contact with Kate belied her denial.

'How long have you known Samantha Crisp?'

Faye looked at her husband. 'D'you think I need Geoffrey up here, Maurice.'

'Why should you need a solicitor?' asked Horton coldly. 'Have you done something wrong?'

'These people are trying to confuse me.'

'Really? Then you must be easily confused. It all seems perfectly straightforward to me. Did you get such a telephone call, Faye?'

I decided to intervene. 'Perhaps you'd let Inspector Ebdon establish what happened, Mr Horton.' If Horton carried on with his questioning it could well have an adverse effect on the outcome of any charges we might bring against Faye Horton. And right now that was becoming more of a likelihood.

'Yes, I did,' said Faye quietly. Her confidence had completely vanished in the face of Kate Ebdon's relentless accusations.

'And you knew that Samantha Crisp was, in fact, Elizabeth Horton,' continued Kate. 'Gregory Horton's wife.'

'Yes.'

Kate glanced at me. I knew what that look was asking, and I nodded.

'Faye Horton,' said Kate, turning back to Horton's wife, 'you are not obliged to say anything, but it may harm your defence if you do not mention when further questioned something you later rely on in court. Anything you do say will be given in evidence.' And to emphasize what she had just said, Kate took her pocketbook from her handbag, opened it on her knee and made a note.

'You've known all along where that damned woman is, haven't you, Faye?' said Horton. 'Well, you might be interested to know what Mr Brock has just told me. Gregory's dead, and the police in Australia have a warrant for Elizabeth's arrest for his murder.'

'They have?' Faye's two-word response managed to convey shock at what her husband had just told her.

'Where is Elizabeth?' asked Kate.

'I don't know,' said Faye. 'But I have a phone number for her.' She opened her silk ruched clutch bag and took out a small diary. Finding the relevant page, she handed the book to Kate. 'That's it there, Inspector.' She pointed to a scribbled entry.

'I'm seizing this diary as evidence,' said Kate, placing the book in her own handbag. 'I'll give you a receipt for it later.'

'I take it you knew that the police wanted Elizabeth Horton,' said Kate.

'Yes, but I didn't know exactly why. She said that you suspected her of a murder in London, but that she hadn't murdered anyone. The way she said it convinced me that you had got it all wrong, and that there'd been some terrible mistake.' Even then, as we later discovered, Faye Horton was not telling the whole truth.

But that was good enough for me. 'Faye Horton, I'm arresting you for assisting an offender, namely Elizabeth Horton. I would remind you that you're still under caution. I'm also obliged to tell you that other charges may follow.'

Faye looked at her husband, a pathetic, sympathy-seeking expression on her face. 'Can they do this, Maurice?' she implored.

'Yes, they can. That woman murdered my son.' Horton seemed to have no doubt that the Northern Territory Police had got it right, and had promptly abandoned his wife to her fate. It was only later we learned the reason. 'Why, for God's sake? You had everything. What possible excuse could you have had for helping that fucking woman? You've betrayed me.'

Faye Horton looked a little stunned at her husband's outburst, but otherwise took no exception to his obscene language. Perhaps she'd heard it too often, and it made me think, yet again, that the Hortons' marriage was more than a bit rocky.

'That'll do, Mr Horton,' I cautioned. I turned to Faye. 'You might wish to change into something more suitable, Mrs Horton. Inspector Ebdon will come with you.'

Kate escorted Faye from the room, watched by Maurice Horton, a look of utter contempt on his face.

'What will happen now, Chief Inspector?' Horton asked.

'Mrs Horton will be taken to Charing Cross police station for further enquiries to be made,' I said. 'Depending upon what we learn, she may well be charged.'

'Does she need a solicitor?'

'That's a matter for her,' I said. 'But if your friend decides to act, you can tell him where she's being taken.'

'I doubt that he'd be of any help,' said Horton dismissively. 'Geoffrey's speciality is property deals and drawing up wills for the rich and famous.'

Fifteen minutes later, Faye and Kate returned to the study. Maurice Horton's wife was now attired in a sober grey trouser suit and high-heeled shoes, and she'd applied fresh make-up. An expensive shoulder bag hung from her left shoulder.

'I'm ready,' she said.

What I didn't know at the time, however, was that the Hortons' entire performance that evening had been a charade. And I could only admire their dramatic skills when eventually I learned the truth.

Before we escorted Faye Horton from the house, I stepped outside, called Dave on my mobile, and gave him the telephone number from Faye Horton's little book.

Ten minutes later Dave rang back with the answer. 'The number goes out to a flat in Clarges Street, guv,' he reported.

'I want you to get round there with a couple of female officers and arrest Beth Horton, Dave,' I said, 'but I don't want you to arrive there only to find that she's out.'

'I'd thought of that, guv. I've already sent Nicola Chance and Sheila Armitage round there to see what they could find out. Discreetly, of course.'

I was happy with that. The two DCs Dave had picked for the job were extremely good detectives.

We took Faye Horton out to our car, and set off for London.

Just before we reached Charing Cross police station, Dave rang again.

'Sheila spoke to the resident janitor, guv. It's an expensive apartment, previously occupied by an up-market call girl who catered for very rich men. The janitor said that Beth Horton does live there, but she's out at the moment. Or at least, the woman who occupies the flat is out. However, the janitor reckons she is an Australian, but he doesn't know her name, so he said.' Dave had no high opinion of janitors, and gauged their worth as informants against the value of the Christmas gifts they received from grateful residents.

'I just hope it is the Horton woman,' I said. 'Where are Sheila and Nicola now?'

'In the vicinity in case Beth Horton returns,' said Dave.

'I'll leave you to it, then, Dave. DI Ebdon and I will take Faye Horton to Charing Cross nick and start questioning her. I'll see you later when, and if, you've got Beth Horton in custody.'

'I will have, guv,' said Dave confidently. 'Sooner or later.'

But Beth Horton did not return that night. And that caused two other officers a great deal of annoyance and loss of sleep.

SIXTEEN

Once the custody sergeant had logged Faye Horton's arrival, Kate and I took her into the interview room at Charing Cross police station. Kate set up the recorder, and announced who was present.

'I would remind you, Mrs Horton, that you're still under caution.' I glanced at Kate and she repeated it, just so that Faye Horton, or more to the point her counsel, would have no cause for complaint. I'd worked out that, given the lifestyle Faye Horton and her husband appeared to enjoy, some of the best brains at the bar would be marshalled in her defence. 'You are entitled to have a solicitor present. If you do not nominate one, you may have the services of a duty solicitor who we will call for you.'

'What on earth do I need a solicitor for?' demanded Faye Horton, her hauteur having now returned. I imagine that she was sufficiently convinced of her innocence not to require legal advice.

'We have evidence that satisfies me that you actively assisted Elizabeth Horton to evade arrest,' I began. 'I am also satisfied that, at the time, you were aware that she was wanted by the Australian police for the crime of murder.'

'I didn't know any such thing,' protested Faye. But the colour rose in her cheeks.

'I have no further questions to put to you, Mrs Horton. Is there anything you wish to say before you are charged?'

There was a long pause during which time Faye Horton stared pensively at the table. Eventually she looked up.

'I'm not in this alone, you know,' she said.

'Would you care to elaborate on that?' I asked.

'Maurice knew all about it,' said Faye. 'You might think we've got a lot of money, but we're damned near bankrupt. Oh, yes, it's a fine house, but it's mortgaged up to the hilt. We've got two expensive cars that we can hardly afford to run. In fact, Mr Brock, the whole edifice is on the point of collapsing like a house of cards. Being a venture capitalist is somewhat akin to being a professional gambler. You speculate and sometimes you win, but just as often you lose. And I'm afraid that Maurice has had a run of bad luck over the past couple of years.'

'You say that your husband knew all about it, Mrs Horton,' said Kate. 'Do you want to tell us what you mean by that?'

Faye Horton gave a scornful laugh. 'The shares that his ex-wife held are as worthless as the rest of his business. They're completely valueless, and of no use to Maurice. But when we learned what Diana was worth, and realized that it would all go to his son Gregory, and then to that little bitch that he'd married, it made our blood boil. I don't know about Maurice, but I guessed that Elizabeth had murdered Gregory. And when she suddenly arrived at Heathrow by herself it seemed to confirm it. Anyway, Maurice and I decided that we'd speak to her, and persuade her that some of that money was rightfully Maurice's. Oh yes, Mr Brock, Maurice knew all right. Elizabeth had telephoned us asking for help because the police were after her, but that it was all a terrible mistake. And so I arranged to meet her in London. The rest you know.'

'Are you prepared to make a statement implicating your husband, Mrs Horton?' I asked.

'No, I'm not,' said Faye spiritedly. 'I've no intention of doing your dirty work for you.'

And that, I'm afraid, was that. The verbal statement of one accused against another is of little use if it's likely that they'd conspired. And even if it were, there are all manner of checks and enquiries to be undertaken before it can successfully be adduced at a trial.

Faye Horton had made it clear that she was going to take the full blame. I hoped her husband would appreciate it. But perhaps Faye thought she'd get away with a slap on the wrist.

Once Faye Horton had been charged with assisting an offender, I rang Dave's mobile.

'What's happening, Dave?' I asked.

'Nothing, guv.' Dave sounded fed up. 'There's no sign of her. What d'you want me to do?'

'You'll have to hang on until I can get a relief sent up there, Dave. I'll get it organized as soon as possible.'

I rang Gavin Creasey in the incident room, and asked him

to get hold of DI Len Driscoll. Driscoll was another of my inspectors, but one who was not involved in my current enquiry.

After a short pause, Driscoll came on the line.

'What's the problem, guv?' he asked.

I explained, as succinctly as I could, the story so far. 'Get a couple of DCs up there, Len, to keep obo on Beth Horton's apartment. If she returns, I want to hear about it immediately. If she doesn't show, I'll have your two relieved first thing in the morning.'

'Right, guv,' said Driscoll. 'That'll make a couple of my blokes very happy.'

But Beth Horton didn't return to her apartment that night. Len Driscoll's two DCs spent an unpleasant twelve hours sitting in a car in Clarges Street trying not to look too obvious.

At eight o'clock the next morning, Saturday, Dave telephoned me to say that he and DCs Chance and Armitage had taken over from Driscoll's officers, and resumed the observation.

'But she still hasn't shown up, guv,' he said.

A quarter of an hour later, Dave rang again.

'She's just arrived, guv. There's no doubt it's her. She's definitely the bird in the photograph that Mr Granger got for us; the one that was in Greg's Bar in Blair. She got out of a taxi about ten minutes ago, looking as though she'd spent the night on the tiles.'

'Don't do anything until I get there, Dave. I want to be in at the kill.' I got hold of John Appleby and told him to organize a car.

My car drew up some distance from the flat where Beth Horton lived. Dave Poole and Sheila Armitage appeared as if from nowhere.

'She's still in there, guv,' said Dave.

'And you're sure it's Beth Horton.'

'No doubt about it in my mind, guv.'

'OK, here we go,' I said to Dave. 'You come too, Sheila.'

I told Sheila to knock on the door while Dave, Nicola Chance and I stayed out of sight.

The door to the flat opened, and Sheila said, 'Good morning, Mrs Horton. May I come in?'

Before Beth had time to refuse, or even to reply, Dave, Nicola and I were in the flat together with Sheila.

'Who the hell are you, and what's this all about?' protested Beth in a strong Australian accent.

'We are police officers,' I said. 'Are you Elizabeth Horton?'

'No, I'm Samantha Crisp,' said the girl.

'And you're Australian.'

'Is that against the law, then?' she asked sarcastically.

'In that case, I need to see your passport.'

'Why?'

'To satisfy myself that you're not in the country illegally,' I said.

'I've lost it.'

'No she hasn't,' said Sheila Armitage, who had already begun a cursory search of the apartment. She handed me the document.

'It says here that you are Elizabeth Horton, née McDonald. And the photograph is undoubtedly of you.'

'What if I am?' demanded Beth Horton churlishly.

'Elizabeth Horton, I'm arresting you under the provisions of the Fugitive Offenders Act pending the arrival of a warrant issued at Darwin in the Northern Territory,' I said. 'If you are returned to Australia, you will be charged with the murder of your husband Gregory Horton sometime prior to the fifteenth of this month.' And I cautioned her.

'I don't know what you're talking about,' said Beth Horton. 'My husband was alive when I left Australia.'

'We've arrested Faye Horton,' I said quietly, but got no reaction from Beth Horton.

Sheila tapped me on the arm. 'We've found a credit card in the name of Samantha Crisp, sir, and quite a lot of corres.'

'Thanks, Sheila. You know the drill.'

Sheila started to bag and label the seizures while Dave spoke to Beth Horton.

'You heard what Mr Brock said about our having arrested Faye Norton,' Dave said, 'and she told him how she assisted you to get a credit card.'

'Did she tell you what she was going to get out of it?'

'What was that?'

'Money, mate. What else?'

'We'll take Mrs Horton to Charing Cross, Sheila,' I said.

'But I want you to stay here pending the arrival of Linda
Mitchell and her team.'

'Right, sir.' Sheila pointed to an object in a drawer she'd
just opened. 'Is this what we're looking for, sir?' she asked,
indicating a humane killer.

'Probably,' I said cautiously. I studied the device without
touching it. It was almost certainly the murder weapon. 'Leave
it in situ and point it out to Linda as soon as she gets here.'

Rather than convey Beth Horton to the police station in his
car, Dave had summoned a custody van to take her to Charing
Cross police station.

Once at the nick, I told Dave and Nicola Chance to go back
to Curtis Green, and to send Kate Ebdon here.

Given that Kate was also an Australian, she was the obvious
choice to join me in the interview room, and we started at
half past nine.

Kate moved a little closer to Beth. 'That's a Jo Malone
perfume you're wearing, isn't it?'

'Yes.' Beth looked as though she wondered why Kate had
posed that question, but Kate knew it was one of the Jo Malone
range of perfumes that Linda Mitchell had detected when
Bruce Metcalfe's room at Talleyrand Street was searched.

I decided not to risk questioning Beth Horton about Bruce
Metcalfe's murder, even though I was confident that his DNA
would be on the humane killer that Sheila had found at the
Clarges Street flat. But I was in no doubt that Beth's fingerprints would be on it.

Although our prisoner was still under caution, I got Kate
to repeat it once the tape recorder was switched on. You can't
be too careful. Beth refused the services of a solicitor, but
perhaps, like Faye Horton, she too was confident enough to
believe she didn't need one.

'When you were told that Faye Horton had been arrested,
you said that she wanted money. What did you mean by that?'

'After I arrived here in the UK, I telephoned the Hortons'
house at Pinner, and spoke to some foreign woman. I already
had the phone number, you see. Greg often phoned his father.'

That was news; Horton had said that he'd had nothing to
do with his son since he went to Australia. But there seemed
to be no reason for his having said that.

'Yes, go on.'

'She was called Katya, I think. Anyway, she put Faye on the line. I explained that I was over here to sort out Greg's will.'

That didn't ring true. Probate for Greg's last will and testament would be dealt with in Australia, but then only if Diana's will had been proved in this country. I sensed that we were about to hear a fanciful tale.

'You knew that Greg was dead, then.'

'Yes. He died of a heart attack last month.'

'You mean July?'

'Yes. That was last month, wasn't it?' replied Beth caustically.

That certainly accorded with what Steve Granger had told me, except that the heart attack had been brought about by a humane killer. But Beth had omitted to mention that, even though Kate had told her that she was being arrested for his murder.

'Where is he buried?' I asked.

'He was cremated, and his ashes were spread in Tamorah. It's a place not far from Darwin,' said Beth, continuing with the fiction.

At least that tallied, in a manner of speaking, but she'd probably hoped that the dingoes had left no trace of him. 'And what did Faye Horton have to say when you phoned her?'

'She asked why Greg's father hadn't been told about his death, and I said that I thought he had. Anyway, she asked to meet me in London to discuss the matter. So, a couple of days later, we met at the Ritz in Piccadilly for afternoon tea. Very bloody genteel, that was. Well, I hadn't even started my first cup of Earl Grey when she accused me of murdering Greg for his money. Of course, I denied it, but she said that she'd got friends in high places – that was her exact phrase – and that one phone call would tell her whether I was telling the truth.'

'What did you say to that?'

'I sussed out straight away what she was after, so I asked her how much she wanted.'

'And what was her reply to that?' I asked.

'She said that she'd say nothing if I split the inheritance with her, straight down the middle.'

'And you agreed?'

'What option did I have? Then she asked how much was at stake, and when I told her that it was about thirty million dollars Australian, her bloody eyes lit up, I can tell you. I reckon she could see the dollar signs coming up in her personal bank account already.'

'I imagine so,' said Kate quietly. 'Enough to make anyone's eyes water. So, what was to be her part of the bargain, mate?'

Beth Horton stared at Kate for some seconds before replying. Kate was very good at disguising her Australian accent, and it was only at that point that Beth realized that Kate was a fellow countrywoman. It seemed to disconcert her. 'She said she'd help me as much as she could to get away. But she said that as soon as I'd handed over the cash, I was to get straight on the next bloody flight back to Aussie, and that she didn't want to hear from me ever again. She promised she'd keep shtum, she said, but if I didn't pay up, she'd inform the authorities.'

There was little point in questioning Beth Horton any further. She'd as good as confessed to the murder of her husband, despite her pathetic denials. That Faye Horton had challenged her about it, and threatened to expose her to the police was sufficient. It was blatantly obvious to me that Beth wouldn't have agreed to pay up unless she'd been guilty of Greg's murder. I hoped that an Australian jury would see it in the same way. If they ever got the chance. But that would depend on the result of her trial for Metcalfe's murder, provided we got that far. The truth of the matter was that if she were innocent of Greg's murder she'd've gone to the police and alleged that Faye was attempting to blackmail her.

But there was one other thing that I hadn't thought of, but Kate Ebdon did. She produced the letter that she'd seized from Makepeace, and placed it on the table.

Beth picked it up, glanced at it and smiled. 'I wrote that,' she said.

'But it's all fiction,' said Kate.

'Not quite. All right, most of it's made up, but the important bit was in the PS about Marlene giving birth to a twelve pound seven ounce boy.'

'What's significant about that? This Marlene woman doesn't exist. The Northern Territory police checked it out for us.'

'Of course she didn't.' Beth laughed at Kate's apparent naiveté.

'It was code. The weight of the baby was actually a date: the twelfth of July. That was to let Bruce know when Greg had died.'

'There was only one problem,' said Kate. 'Bruce didn't get it. I did.'

I was amazed by Beth Horton's candour. She obviously didn't realize that the Australian court that would eventually try her for Greg's murder was a court of record. As such, it had the power to demand my attendance to give evidence of the damning admissions she'd made during the course of this interview. Not that that would please the commander, unless he could persuade the Australian authorities to foot the bill for my travel and hotel expenses.

But we'd finished with Beth Horton for the time being. As far as Metcalfe's murder was concerned, we'd have to await the result of the examination of the humane killer that had been found in Beth's apartment. It didn't matter, though; she wasn't going anywhere.

On Monday morning, Beth Horton appeared before the City of Westminster magistrates. It was the first step in the tortuous process that would lead to her eventual extradition as a fugitive offender.

In a loud outburst from the dock, Elizabeth Horton protested her innocence. But the paperwork had arrived from the Australian High Commission over the weekend, and it was a matter of routine for the senior district judge to order the Australian woman's remand in custody pending any appeal she might wish to make.

I applied to have her detained at Charing Cross police station in order that we could interview her regarding another serious matter. The district judge gave us twenty-four hours, with the proviso that we could apply for an extension should we require it.

Fortunately, the report regarding the humane killer was waiting for me at Curtis Green when I got back from court. The DNA found on the weapon was that of Bruce Metcalfe, and Beth's fingerprints had been found on it, and at Talleyrand Street. Gotcha! Kate and I went straight to Charing Cross police station.

*   *   *

I wasted no time in putting the evidence before Beth Horton, having once more cautioned her.

'Mrs Horton, I have here a report from the Metropolitan Forensic Science Laboratory. They have examined the humane killer found in your apartment. It had your fingerprints on it, and it carried the DNA of Bruce Metcalfe who was found murdered in his bed-sitting room at fifty-four Talleyrand Street, Earls Court on the fourteenth of this month.'

'I don't know a Bruce Metcalfe.'

It was a pitiful and expected denial, but I doubted that she could think of anything else to say.

'Your perfume, one of Jo Malone's, was detected at Talleyrand Street, which is where he was murdered,' said Kate.

'So what? I'm not the only woman to use it.'

'You were living with him for a while, though, weren't you?'

'Could've been anyone,' said Beth, still attempting to distance herself from the murder.

'Perhaps so,' I said, 'but your fingerprints were found there. I shall, therefore, charge you with Bruce Metcalfe's murder.' I waited until Kate had cautioned her yet again.

Beth Horton shrugged. 'Well, that's it, I suppose,' she said. 'At least that bitch Faye won't get any of the money now.'

I forbore from saying that I didn't think Beth would either, but there was no point in unnecessarily antagonising the woman, not until I'd got the full facts.

'Is there anything else you want to tell me? I have to remind you again that you're entitled to the services of a solicitor.'

'What good would that do? No thanks. It's all gone bloody wrong.'

'Would you care to tell me why?'

'Diana sent Greg a copy of her will, and I found it. But Greg was a no-hoper, a bludger, and he never fitted into the Australian way of life. He opened a bar in Blair after we were married, but it went bottoms up in no time at all. The locals didn't take to him, and Greg drank most of what little profit there was. He always seemed to get into punch-ups with the customers, and that was no bloody good for trade, I can tell you. So, when I saw that he was likely to inherit a load of money it just made me sick. I knew what he'd do with it: he'd just have pissed it up against the wall, and I wouldn't have got a look in.'

'And Bruce Metcalfe?'

'I knew Bruce before I was married; he was a jackaroo on my grandparents' station near Tamorah. I told him about the will, and he said he could make sure that I got the money provided I split it down the middle with him. But first we had to get rid of Greg, so I topped him and dumped his body in the outback near Tamorah.'

And so Elizabeth Horton finally admitted to the murder of her husband.

'Yes, go on,' I said.

'Well, to cut a long story short, Bruce came over here and did in Diana and her old man.'

Beth spoke in a matter-of-fact way, as though the whole conspiracy was a business arrangement, and an opportunity that was too good to miss. Unfortunately for her, neither she nor Bruce Metcalfe was bright enough to see that the plan had no chance of succeeding, mainly because neither of them was conversant with the law of testacy.

'And you went to a party at Diana Barton's house the night she was murdered.'

'Yes. It wasn't a bad bash either. Bruce had it away with some bird called Liz, and I got laid by some journo called Bernie.'

That was an interesting revelation. Despite Liz Edwards's disdainful dismissal of the party as 'not her sort of thing', she'd obviously been lying. As for Bernard Graves, well, he *was* a journalist, and they do have problems with the truth. And that lack of honesty doubtless accounted for Graves's statement that he'd hardly spoken to Beth Horton, or Samantha as she'd called herself.

The enigma was that Graves had later telephoned me to report a sighting of Beth Horton in the West End, a sighting that led eventually to her arrest. I could only speculate on what sort of vengeance had prompted that. Or maybe it was his nose for a story that took priority over any other feelings or thoughts he might have had. He'd struck me as the sort of man to whom a one-night stand was meaningless.

But despite all that, I still found it hard to believe that a woman, even this woman, could be so hard-hearted and calculating as to kill her husband and be complicit in the murders of Diana and James Barton.

'Have either of you got a cigarette?' Beth asked.

One of the more ridiculous pieces of legislation to emanate from Westminster prohibited smoking even in police station interview rooms, but what the hell?

I produced my packet of Marlboro, and offered her my cigarette lighter.

Beth lit her cigarette, returned my lighter with a lingering smile of thanks, and blew a plume of smoke into the air. 'But after that greedy bastard Bruce had done the job, he demanded three-quarters of the inheritance instead of the half we'd agreed, and said that if I didn't come across he'd dob me in to the police. Well, that was bloody stupid because I could've done the same for him, but I realized that he was a bloody drongo, and that made him a danger, so I had to get rid of him. If he'd had his way, we'd both have finished up doing time.' She stubbed out her half smoked cigarette. 'But now it looks as though I will anyway,' she added in matter-of-fact tones.

And that was it: a full confession, and the single incredible motive behind each of the four murders.

Our next task – and an onerous one that took us a whole week – was to prepare the report and submit it to the Crown Prosecution Service.

Another week went by before we met the lawyer who was handling the case.

'A pretty kettle of fish, Mr Brock.' The lawyer leaned back in his chair, steepled his fingers and stared thoughtfully at the ceiling. 'Clearly a charge of murdering Bruce Metcalfe in the case of Elizabeth Horton. And as far as Faye Horton is concerned, I think we've a more than fifty per cent chance of getting a conviction for assisting an offender. From the statements she and Elizabeth Horton made, it is patently obvious that she was aware that Elizabeth Horton was wanted by the police. I think we'd be safe in giving it a run.' He paused, and leaned forward again. 'Elizabeth Horton will obviously have to be put up first though. Once we get a conviction there, we'll have a better chance of getting Faye Horton sent down. But if Elizabeth Horton's acquitted, the case against Faye Horton falls apart. Such is life, Mr Brock.' He sighed, and placed the weighty file on top of a pile of similar dockets. 'All done and dusted, then.'

'What about the fugitive offenders warrant?' I asked, determined to throw a verbal spanner into this urbane lawyer's works, if only slightly. 'Elizabeth Horton's wanted by the Australian authorities for murder in Darwin.'

'Ah, yes, so she is.' The lawyer shot forward in his chair, and linked his hands on his desk. 'Frankly, Mr Brock, that's a bit of a pain in the arse. Probably the best idea is to get the Metcalfe murder dealt with, and leave it to the judge to decide what to do about the Australian question, eh what?'

'You're the lawyer,' I said. *And a clever one at that*, I thought.

SEVENTEEN

The first of the three trials was held in late September at Kingston Crown Court.

Thomas Hendry was indicted on one count of arson at 27 Tavona Street, Chelsea on Sunday the twenty-eighth of July, and pleaded not guilty. As Jock Ferguson had predicted, the Crown Prosecution Service had decided not to proceed with the dangerous driving charge for the time being. Consequently, it had been left on file pending the outcome of the arson trial.

I gave evidence of my interview with Hendry, and produced a copy of his signed confession.

Following a brief conversation with Hendry, his barrister, a young white-wig, rose and changed Hendry's plea to one of guilty.

'It's a pity he didn't plead guilty in the first place,' said the judge. 'That would have saved the time and expense of empanelling a jury.' And with that acid comment, he sentenced Hendry to ten years' imprisonment.

'The nearest our ex-steward will get to any seafaring for a while, guv,' said Dave as we left the court, 'is a trip across the Solent to Parkhurst prison on the Isle of Wight.'

The trial of Elizabeth Horton began in court thirteen at the Central Criminal Court a month later. The Australian Government had made a few token noises about the warrant for her arrest and return, but they realized that it would not be acted upon until Beth's trial for the murder of Bruce Metcalfe had been dealt with. And if she were convicted of that murder, the Australians accepted that a very long time would elapse before they would have the opportunity of trying her for her husband's murder.

Probate of the Bartons' wills was being handled in London, while that of Gregory Horton's will would be dealt with in Australia in due course. I understood from Steve Granger that the authorities there had wisely put it on hold pending her return.

As Granger had told them, it could well be some time before they were able to interview her.

Nevertheless, despite being apparently penniless, Elizabeth Horton had still managed to acquire an expensive barrister to defend her. Dave cynically pointed out that the British taxpayer was probably footing the bill.

Elizabeth Horton was arraigned and pleaded not guilty. Counsel for the Crown, an eminent silk, immediately rose to his feet. As was customary, he first introduced himself and counsel for the defence.

'However, My Lord,' he continued, 'there is a matter that should be raised before the jury is sworn. My Lord, I am in some difficulty here. As Your Lordship is aware, an Australian warrant is in existence for the arrest of the accused on a charge of a murder unrelated to the case before this court. However, it will be necessary for me to make reference to it in the course of this trial. Nevertheless, I shall attempt to limit such reference in an attempt not to prejudice the jury.'

The judge glanced at defence counsel. 'Do you wish to make an application?'

'No, My Lord. I quite understand my learned friend's difficulties.'

'Very well,' said the judge. 'The jury may be brought in.'

After the jury had been accepted by both leading counsel and sworn-in, and all the other panoply and flummery of getting the proceedings under way had been completed, the trial began in earnest.

Prosecuting counsel's opening address began with a description of Diana Barton's 'kitchen' party, finished with Beth Horton's arrest at her Clarges Street apartment, and her virtual admission of guilt following the discovery of the humane killer.

'I shall prove, My Lord and members of the jury, that Elizabeth Horton's murder of Bruce Metcalfe was premeditated and prompted by avarice. Her perpetration of this foul crime was motivated by greed and greed alone. It was a murder that she imagined would make her richer by some eighteen million pounds.'

There were a few gasps from the jury at the enormity of the sum involved.

I was the first witness. I started my evidence by repeating

what Crown counsel had said about the party at Diana Barton's house. But that was as far as I got.

Although it had been mentioned in prosecuting counsel's opening address, by convention not challenged, defence counsel immediately objected on the grounds that details of the party were irrelevant and prejudicial. But he was overruled by the judge who said that what had occurred at Tavona Street was an integral part of the chain that culminated in Metcalfe's murder.

I was allowed to continue uninterrupted to the point where I gave evidence of Elizabeth Horton's arrest at her Clarges Street apartment, and produced a transcript of her recorded interrogation.

Once I had finished, the other police officers involved followed. After a break for lunch, Henry Mortlock, Linda Mitchell and two forensic scientists, trooped into the witness box to give their damning evidence.

Once the prosecution's case had been concluded, Elizabeth Horton's counsel, an eminent QC, attempted in his opening address to justify his client's actions by claiming that she was strongly under the influence of Bruce Metcalfe, and he likened their relationship to that of Svengali and Trilby. But judging from the blank expressions on the faces of the jurors, it appeared that they were unfamiliar with the plot of George du Maurier's novel about an artist's model and a musician.

Elizabeth Horton's counsel had wisely decided not to call his client to give evidence in her own defence. The only witness he produced was a forensic scientist who unsuccessfully attempted to dispute the evidence regarding the humane killer. It was to no avail; the telling scientific details of Beth's fingerprints and Metcalfe's DNA found on the humane killer were overwhelming. After that, the case was as good as over, and her counsel found that there was little he could do to prevent the inevitable outcome.

After retiring for just two hours, the jury found Beth Horton guilty. With an expression of cynicism, the stony-faced judge listened to the eloquent plea in mitigation by her counsel, but there was little that the latter could do in the face of the armoury of evidence that had been adduced, and to which no real defence could have been mounted. There was little doubt in my mind that the account of the lewd goings-on at the

Barton house on the night of Diana's murder, even though they had played no part in proving the murder of Metcalfe, had swayed the jury in favour of a guilty verdict. Yes, it is unfair, but that's the way the English trial system works.

Years ago it was the practice that sentence was imposed at the close of a trial, but these days we have to wait several weeks to learn the penalty that follows a conviction. All manner of reports have to be prepared regarding the convicted person's state of mind, her social standing and income, and her family background. Believe me, there aren't many cases that come before the courts nowadays without some contribution from psychiatrists, the social services and the probation service. Most of it, I have to say, of little value.

Six weeks later, we returned to the Old Bailey to hear the sentence. After dismissing the psychiatric and other reports, and delivering a lengthy little homily about avarice and immorality, His Lordship sentenced Elizabeth Horton to life imprisonment. After a short pause, during which he appeared to be considering the matter, he imposed a tariff of twenty years before she could apply for parole. I thought that was a tad on the lenient side.

'You were right, Harry,' said Steve Granger, who had been sitting in on the sentencing hearing at his high commissioner's behest. 'It looks as though we'll have to wait to get her back.'

'Don't hold your breath, sir,' said Dave to Granger. 'O what a tangled web we weave, when first we practise to deceive!' he added.

'Who said that?' I asked.

'I did, guv,' said Dave.

'But Sir Walter Scott wrote it,' said Granger.

'Two of you,' I muttered. 'That's all I need.'

Shortly after Beth Horton had been sentenced, an arrangement was arrived at between the British and Australian governments to allow Beth Horton to serve the balance of her sentence in her own country. On arrival, she was tried for the murder of her husband, and found guilty. She was sentenced to twenty-five years, to run concurrent with the sentence imposed at the Old Bailey.

But she never laid hands on the eighteen million pounds.

The law, both here and down under, does not allow a murderess to profit by her crimes.

'I reckon it'll be forfeit to the Australian government, Harry,' said Steve Granger, when we met for a drink a few days later. 'All thirty million dollars of it.'

'That'll make the Hortons' day for them,' commented Dave.

A week later we were back at the Old Bailey for the trial of Faye Horton. By some bizarre coincidence it was in the same court thirteen that had seen Beth Horton tried, and before the same judge.

Faye had surrendered to bail earlier that morning, and appeared in the dock soberly dressed in a navy blue jacket and skirt. She wore a plain white, high-necked blouse, but had decided against wearing any jewellery. I found it significant that her husband was not in court.

Faye pleaded not guilty to the single indictment of assisting an offender, and the trial began.

Prosecuting counsel led me through my evidence in great detail, and inevitably Faye's barrister decided that he would cross-examine me.

'Mr Brock,' said the silk, rising to his feet with a contrived expression of perplexity on his face. 'Do you not think that my client should have been offered the services of a solicitor during your interrogation of her?' It was a blatant attempt to render my evidence inadmissible.

But before I had a chance to reply, the judge interrupted. 'I'm sure that in your brief you have a transcript of the recording made during that interrogation,' he said to Faye's counsel. 'Unless it differs from mine, it is apparent that Detective Chief Inspector Brock told Mrs Horton that she was entitled to the services of a legal advisor, but she refused.'

'Ah, quite so, My Lord,' said counsel. 'I do apologize. I'd confused that with another interview.' *Like hell, he had*. He turned back to me. 'Let me now turn to the interview you conducted with Mrs Horton in her husband's study on the evening of Friday the twenty-third of August, Inspector. Do I have the date right?'

'Yes, sir,' I said. 'You have the date right, but you have my rank wrong. I'm a *chief* inspector.'

'Ah, quite so. My apologies.' That momentarily derailed

counsel, and he consulted his brief again. 'Yes, Chief Inspector, I understand that a solicitor friend of the Hortons – Mr Maurice Horton's own solicitor, in fact – was in the house at the time. Is that so?'

'Yes, sir.'

'Do you not think that she should have been given the opportunity of consulting him before you began questioning her?'

'No, sir, I don't.'

'Oh? And why not?' Counsel shot an appealing glance at the jury.

'Mrs Horton was not under arrest at that time, and I didn't make the decision to arrest her until later. I was not, therefore, obliged to offer her the services of a solicitor. However, had she sought to have her husband's solicitor present, I would have raised no objection.'

'Ah, quite so.' Faye's counsel had tried to muddy the waters, but had failed. 'I have no further questions, My Lord.'

'Good,' said the judge.

Defence counsel then went on to make an impassioned closing address larded with appeals for clemency. 'Despite the fact that Elizabeth Horton was but a step-daughter-in-law,' he said, 'the assistance that Mrs Horton afforded to her, although unlawful, was nonetheless prompted by a misplaced family loyalty, and led her to take a course of action which she now bitterly regrets.'

It was to no avail. After the judge's summing-up, the jury took less than an hour to find her guilty.

Weeks later, we were back at the Old Bailey yet again, this time to hear the sentence. The fact that she had assisted Elizabeth Horton to evade arrest for profit decided the judge that the appropriate sentence would be five years' imprisonment.

'Of course, we now know why she did it,' said Kate Ebdon when we were on the way back to Curtis Green. 'The Hortons hadn't got any money after all.' She laughed. 'Amazing, isn't it? When you looked at the house she shared with her husband, and the cars, including the Lexus,' she added with a hint of envy, 'you'd've thought they were rolling in it.'

'It was all show, Kate,' I said. 'They were in debt up to the hilt.'

'Incidentally, guv,' continued Kate, 'I ran a check on the cars that were parked outside on the night we nicked Faye. One of them went out to a Russian millionaire. I reckon that Maurice Horton was trying to tap him for an investment in one of his shaky enterprises.'

'Yes, but Russian millionaires are like all millionaires, Kate,' I said. 'When they've got it, they know how to hang on to it. But it's a pity that the CPS didn't bring a charge against Maurice Horton for assisting an offender. And I thought that Faye was the hard one of the two. But when it came to it, he just let her go without a backward glance.'

'I wonder what he's going to do now that his wife's banged up.'

'He'll divorce her, Kate,' I said, 'and go in search of a rich widow who'll bail him out, I expect.'

But it was Dave who had the last word. 'And to think that on the night of Diana Barton's murder, PC Watson put "All quiet on arrival" in the logbook,' he said. 'Funny old world, isn't it?'

N Ha HH MH